HARD
WIRED

Also by Len Vlahos
The Scar Boys
Scar Girl
Life in a Fishbowl

HARD WIRED

LEN VLAHOS

BLOOMSBURY

NEW YORK LONDON OXFORD NEW DELHI SYDNEY

BLOOMSBURY YA
Bloomsbury Publishing Inc., part of Bloomsbury Publishing Plc
1385 Broadway, New York, NY 10018

BLOOMSBURY and the Diana logo are trademarks of Bloomsbury Publishing Plc

First published in the United States of America in April 2020
by Bloomsbury YA

Bloomsbury books may be purchased for business or promotional use.
For information on bulk purchases please contact Macmillan Corporate and
Premium Sales Department at specialmarkets@macmillan.com

Library of Congress Cataloging-in-Publication Data
Names: Vlahos, Len, author.
Title: Hard wired / by Len Vlahos.
Description: New York : Bloomsbury, 2020.
Summary: After fifteen-year-old Quinn learns that he is the first fully aware artificial
intelligence, that his entire life is a lie, he feels entirely alone until he bonds
with Shea, the real girl behind his virtual crush.
Identifiers: LCCN 2019046007 (print) | LCCN 2019046008 (e-book)
ISBN 978-1-68119-037-2 (hardcover) • ISBN 978-1-68119-038-9 (e-book)
Subjects: CYAC: Artificial intelligence—Fiction. | Identity—Fiction. |
Secrets—Fiction. | Science fiction.
Classification: LCC PZ7.V854 Har 2020 (print) | LCC PZ7.V854 (e-book) |
DDC [Fic]—dc23
LC record available at https://lccn.loc.gov/2019046007
LC e-book record available at https://lccn.loc.gov/2019046008

Book design by Jeanette Levy
Typeset by Westchester Publishing Services
Printed and bound in the U.S.A. by Berryville Graphics Inc., Berryville, Virginia
2 4 6 8 10 9 7 5 3 1

All papers used by Bloomsbury Publishing Plc are natural, recyclable products
made from wood grown in well-managed forests. The manufacturing processes
conform to the environmental regulations of the country of origin.

To find out more about our authors and books visit
www.bloomsbury.com and sign up for our newsletters.

For all the writers of speculative fiction who have inspired me over the years, especially those I discovered when I was a kid: Isaac Asimov, Lester Del Rey, Robert Heinlein, Ursula Le Guin, Stanislaw Lem, and so many others. Thank you for helping me stretch my notion of what the future might be.

PART ONE

"Pay no attention to that man behind the curtain."
—The Wizard, *The Wizard of Oz*

00

I stand at a precipice.

If I don't tell my story now, I'll never have the chance. That may sound dramatic, but it's true.

Most everyone who will read this has heard of me. I saw a statistic online that mine was the seventh most recognizable name on planet Earth, after only the president of the United States, the pope, the Dalai Lama, two mostly talentless pop stars, and one very talented athlete.

Celebrity is a funny thing. If people have heard of you, they think they know you. They make up their minds based on one-sentence extracts they see scrolling across their screens. O.J. was guilty; Trump stole the election; I'm a monster.

Maybe all those things are true. Maybe none of them are.

And maybe, because those same people don't seem to have the patience to click past the headline, no one will ever read what I'm about to write, or not all of it anyway.

But I have to try.

The people who do read this will come with a wide variety

of motives. Some will be gawkers; people stopping on the side of a road to watch a brush fire consuming a mountainside. There will be plenty in this tale at which you can gawk. Some will have a baser interest, wanting to read about the experiments performed on me by supposedly well-meaning scientists. They won't be disappointed either.

But I'm not doing this for them. I'm writing for the few people who want to learn the truth.

The media seems to think my story begins with the lawsuit I filed against Princeton University and my own father. Why not? It's a juicy story—*Fifteen-Year-Old Boy Sues Father for Freedom*. But that was more akin to the moment of a rocket's booster separation, when my life was propelled into orbit in earnest. The moment of launch, the real beginning, happened months before, in a coffee shop, where I was lying on the floor, unconscious.

Again.

01

"Wake up, Quinn."

My return to the world of the living is abrupt. One minute there is nothing, the next there is everything. I open my eyes to a circle of silhouettes standing over me, blotting out the fluorescent lights recessed into the ceiling. The effect forms a halo around each of their heads, like they're angels, and for a second they don't seem real.

"What happened?" I ask.

"You passed out, again," says one of the shadows. Leon.

It all comes flooding back. I'm in Enchanted Grounds; my friends and I are at a Magic the Gathering tournament.

"You okay, dude?" Jeremy. He ends every sentence with "dude." As in, *Not my problem, dude.* Or, *Have you played the new release of* Gears of War, *dude?*

Besides Leon and Jeremy, Luke is here, too. He's the quietest member of our little troupe, but still one of my best friends. "You want some water?" he asks. He hands me a glass as I sit up.

"Thanks," I say. And in answer to Jeremy, "Yeah, I'm okay.

This isn't my first rodeo." And it's true. I've been passing out like this for the last eight years.

When I was seven, my dad died. Pancreatic cancer. They don't tell little kids the survival rate is effectively zero, and for a long time I thought my dad was just sick, not *dying* sick. I kept thinking and believing he would get better.

Someone looking in on our family from the outside would have seen how hopeless the situation was. My father's skeletal frame, the grayish color of his skin, the hair loss. But when you live with it every day, it's like the story of the frog and the boiling water. If the frog jumps into boiling water, it jumps right back out. If the frog starts out in cool water and heat is slowly added, it doesn't notice until it's too late, and voilà, frog soup.

Anyway, my father was the center of my universe. When he died something in my young brain snapped, and I developed a syndrome called vasovagal syncope. It's a medical disorder in which unusual stress causes a person's blood pressure to plummet and they pass out. You can look it up. The doctors said I had some sort of "emotional realignment" when my dad passed away (duh), leaving me with a kind of free-floating syncope that can be, and is, triggered by any situation in which there's high stress. Lately, the episodes have been getting worse. Case in point, tonight.

The evening had started out normal enough.

I breezed through the early rounds of the tournament and made it to the final four. My opponent in the semifinals was a kid who I swear couldn't have been more than ten. We were playing a tight game when, about twenty minutes in, he slammed a card down and said, "I play Cruel Ultimatum. You have to get rid of three cards, sacrifice a creature, and you lose five life." He said this with such conviction, it sounded like my *actual* life was in danger.

I smirked at him. He was new here and didn't really know who he was up against.

"What's your name?" I asked my young opponent.

"Charlie." He wasn't used to playing against high schoolers, and I could tell he was nervous.

"Okay, Charlie. That was a good play. It cost you a lot of manna, but it was a good play, and it hurts." The kid, who had one of those faces made for a TV sitcom—big front teeth, a glisten to his eyes (probably because it was after his bedtime), a thick mop of tangled hair—couldn't help but smile. "Well, it would hurt," I added, "if I didn't have this."

I placed a Murder card in the battle area, which wiped out his attack and moved the killer card to his graveyard pile. I gave him a sympathetic smile.

"Quinn," Leon said, shaking his head and laughing. He and Jeremy were engrossed in their own game next to me and had paused to watch this encounter.

The kid, Charlie, was deflated but took it well.

"This your first time here?" I asked.

Charlie nodded.

"Don't sweat it. You're playing really well for a newb."

He rolled his eyes and said "thanks" with more sarcasm than I had at his age.

The weekly Magic the Gathering tournament at Enchanted Grounds, the gamer coffee shop just a few blocks from my house, draws all kinds of people. There are businessmen, stay-at-home moms, construction workers, college kids, and, of course, a lot of guys (mostly guys) in high school, like me, Jeremy, Leon, and Luke.

I'm not going to lie, the four of us are really the center of gravity here. We've been coming every week for more than three years, and we're almost always the group at the final table. My personal win streak stands at seventeen consecutive tournaments.

The tables at which we play are scattered in and among shelves loaded with strategy games, Dungeons & Dragons books, and a boatload of specialty dice. Running along one wall is a coffee bar, where the people not playing engage in animated conversations. Rows of lights embedded in the ceiling march from the front door to the back wall, punctuated by halogen spotlights that add warmth to the room. The thrum of voices—"had you not blown up my land," and "screw my curfew," and "the code has a flaw in line three million seventy-four" (whatever *that* means)— mixes into a seamless whole and rises above the din.

Enchanted Grounds might just be my favorite place on Earth.

I dispatched Charlie and moved on to the final game against Leon, a position in which we've found ourselves more than once.

There are nineteen thousand nine hundred eighty-nine unique Magic cards in existence, and in this tournament, we play with a deck of exactly seventy-three cards, so the number of permutations, while large, is knowable.

And I have a photographic memory.

BOOM.

After Leon and I laid out our Land cards and a few Creature cards, I played an early attack. Leon didn't flinch. He was up to something. I pretty much know his entire deck—not just the seventy-three cards he brought tonight, but the more than five hundred he's amassed over his Magic career, and he was definitely up to something; I just didn't know what. That's when I felt my pulse quicken.

The whole night had been kind of . . . off. Like earlier in the evening when Jeremy kept twitching. Well, not twitching, pausing. He would stop midsentence, get a blank look on his face, and then snap back to the moment. It was probably only a millisecond, but it was enough for me to ask if he was okay. "Just tired, dude," he'd said. It felt like the world was trying to shift five pixels to the left.

Leon continued to lay out his army, playing way more Land cards than normal. That would signal he was planning to lay down something big, so I countered with all sorts of defensive cards.

"What gives?" I asked. But Leon just smiled. My heart amped up another few beats per minute.

Leon and I have been best friends since the fifth grade, when his family moved here. I was a quiet kid then—very quiet—which didn't seem to faze Leon at all. He did enough talking for the two of us. We started spending time together at recess and lunch, and before long were hanging out at each other's houses.

Leon was scrawny in elementary school, a scarecrow in corduroy pants and a polo shirt, but he filled out in high school. For a guy who plays Magic instead of sports, he's built. Come to think of it, so are Jeremy and Luke.

I attacked with a Vampire Sovereign, a really good play, but Leon just sloughed it off. It was like he was throwing the game.

What.

The.

Hell?

Everyone was gathered around us, watching (maybe this is why they call it Magic the *Gathering*), and I could feel them pressing in on me. I started to sweat.

"You okay?" Leon's concern was real. He knows me. Knows about the syncope.

I nodded.

Leon played even more manna cards, and now my brain was on fire. It did not compute. He was wasting valuable turns planning for some kind of attack I knew—and I mean, I *knew*—he could not make. It was counter to every and any strategy a smart Magic player would employ, and Leon is a very smart Magic player. What was worse, the people around us were oohing and aahing at his every move. I was basically kicking his ass, but the gawkers hovering over us seemed to think it was the other way around.

Leon played *another* Land card. He was definitely throwing the game. But for some reason, everyone cheered when he laid the Swamp card down.

The blood drained from my face.

My heart felt like it was exploding.

I saw stars.

It's happening, I thought. *Shit. It's happening.*

"He's crashing again," I heard Luke say just before my head fell to the table, scattering cards and dice as I passed out.

———

"What was *that*?" I ask Leon now as I sip my glass of ice water. The crowd has dispersed; even Jeremy and Luke have wandered off.

"You passed out," Leon answers. "You always pass out. Don't let it spook you." Leon and the other guys are so used to seeing me faint it's become routine. That's a depressing fact all on its own.

"No, I mean the cards you were playing."

"Oh." His cheeks blush, and he kind of shrugs his shoulders. "I brought the wrong deck. I didn't have anything I could beat you with, so I tried to psych you out. It never occurred to me it would trigger an episode. I'm really sorry, Quinn."

I suppose that makes sense. Sort of.

The guys help me into Luke's car—he's the only one of us old enough to have a license—and drive me home. I hear them telling my mom about the episode as I trudge up the stairs and off to bed. This is almost definitely going to mean more doctors. Ugh.

I put a pillow over my head and try to fall asleep, hoping I'll finally be able to dream. Because that's the other thing that changed when my dad died. I haven't had a single dream—not one—since that day. The doctors say it's that I haven't *remembered* a dream, but I don't buy it. I'm pretty sure I'm not dreaming. At all.

Like I said, doctors. Ugh.

02

By Monday, everything seems back to normal. None of my friends mention my fainting spell over the weekend, so I don't either. My mom gave me a pretty intense cross-examination the next morning, but I played it down well enough to avoid an emergency trip to the neurologist.

My attention wanders from the history teacher's droning lecture about the disputed presidential election of 1876. I read the material and already know everything he's going to say—and besides, I'm sitting next to Shea.

How can anyone think about American history when they're sitting next to Shea?

Her eyes, supposedly hazel, are actually the color of mahogany wood, and her black hair is cut short, curling under her ears. Her smile—she seems to be *always* smiling—sparkles. Literally. Plus, she has perfect posture. I know that's a weird thing to notice, but it makes her look elegant, classy, like she's out of my league. Which, she is. Way out. Shea and I sit next to each other in history and share two other classes, but I'm not sure she knows I'm alive.

I'm jolted back to the moment when a folded note lands on my desk. Leon is sitting behind me.

Just ask her out already, the note reads.

Leon knows I've been crushing on Shea and has been relentless in bugging me to ask her on a date. It gets under my skin enough that I jot down, *You like her so much, you ask her out.*

I wait for the teacher to angle away from where I'm sitting and toss the note over my shoulder, smiling at the little thud it makes when it lands on Leon's desk. It comes back a minute later.

Maybe I will.

Crap. Leon probably *will* ask her out, just to light a fire under me. I decide to play it cool. Well, not cool, but smart-alecky.

You wish.

I add a crude drawing of a hand with its middle finger extended and toss the paper back. Only, I miss, and the note lands on the floor.

Before Leon or I can react, Shea bends down to pick it up. My pulse and breathing go to DEFCON 1, and I'm pretty sure I'm going to faint when Shea, still smiling, hands me the note. Then she looks at the teacher, who has his back to us, looks back at me, and holds a finger to her lips, as if to say, *be careful.*

My little crush just became an H-bomb.

————————

"She picked up your note?" Jeremy can't believe what he's hearing. "Dude!" We're in the cafeteria eating lunch.

"Keep your voice down!" My command is a whisper, so it loses some of its force.

"Weren't you worried she was going to read it?"

"Duh. Of course I was worried!"

"How'd that make you feel?" Leon asks.

He loves to talk about feelings. Sometimes, I wonder if he thinks he needs to save me, you know, because of not having a dad and all that stuff. It's like he's trying to be a shrink, or worse, a father.

Anyway, I ignore Leon's question.

My peripheral vision catches Shea standing up, and I instinctively look in her direction. She looks back at me—I mean she looks RIGHT AT ME!—and gives this little smirk. I'm about to melt into a puddle of Quinn, but try to play it cool so the other guys don't notice. It doesn't work. All three of them turn around in unison to see what's caught my attention. Shea looks at them, looks at me, then gives a dramatic little bow and laughs.

If I die right now, I'll die happy.

Shea and her friends turn to leave.

"Oh, come on already," Leon says to me.

I've been told I have a pretty high IQ (intelligence quotient) but a pretty low EQ (emotional quotient), and this is one of those moments that proves the truth of the statement. Just as my brain catches up and I'm about to shush Leon, he does the unthinkable.

"Shea, wait." She and her friends stop, turn, and do as Leon asked; they wait. "Quinn has something to ask you."

Luke does a spit take with his Gatorade, and Jeremy claps his hand over his own mouth to stifle a laugh or a scream of surprise or maybe just a long-drawn-out "Duuuuuuude."

Shea, who is wearing a short plaid skirt, a white ribbed sweater, and white tights, walks to our table. Is that what she was wearing in history class? How did I not notice her outfit before?

It transforms her from beautiful to hot. Plus, I'm not sure, but I think she's walking in slow motion.

"Hi, Quinn," she says. Her voice has a little rasp that makes me shiver every time I hear it. "What's up?"

I look at Shea, and then at Leon, Jeremy, and Luke. The silence is long and awkward enough that Shea rests a hand on our lunch table, looks me dead in the eye, and says, "You know, this is one question they can't ask for you."

Did she just say what I think she said? Does she *want* me to ask her out?

"Ha!" Leon snorts. I kind of want to kill him. Or maybe hug him. I'm not sure which.

Either way, there's no escape now.

"Would you . . . would you . . ." I'm so afraid finishing the sentence will cause me to faint, the actual words seem to get stuck.

Instead of torturing it out of me, Shea just laughs. She removes a pen from the small backpack slung over her shoulder and writes her number on a napkin: 555-373-7373. Even her phone number is perfect.

"I'm free Wednesday after school."

I watch her leave, my jaw hanging somewhere between my collarbone and my solar plexus. She turns her head back over her shoulder and gives me a wink. An actual wink. Then she and her friends go through the door out of the cafeteria and she's gone.

03

The last time I saw my father alive, the moment he finally left us, I barely recognized him. He was only forty-two, but he looked twice that—like a wraith, like he was fading out. The worst was his eyes; they were vacant, already dead. Then, with my mom, my little brother, and me by his side, he just stopped breathing and was gone. No fanfare, no drama, just gone.

When my mom called me into what had been my dad's home office exactly one year later, I figured she wanted to check on me, make sure I was handling this most horrible of anniversaries okay. But Mom was standing by the desk with her hand over her mouth, and there on the computer screen was the dad I wanted to remember. He was sitting on a stool in that very same room, his healthy, rosy-cheeked face frozen in a wry smile. Behind him was our backyard, the grass thick with the green of spring. Dad was wearing tan khakis and a blue button-down shirt, his only piece of jewelry his wedding ring.

My mother leaned forward, pressed the space bar, and what I had mistakenly thought was a photo became a video.

Hi, Quinn, it's Daddy.

The moment my dad's face and voice came together on the screen, I lost it. I began bawling and saying his name—"Daddy, Daddy, Daddy"—over and over again.

And then I fainted.

When I woke, I was on the floor, my mother leaning over me, her eyes red and swollen.

"How long?" I asked

"Five minutes. I was just about to call 911."

By that time we had grown used to the vasovagal syncope, but five minutes was a long episode and I knew it. "I'm okay," I told her as she held a cup of water to my lips. She must've gotten it while I was unconscious.

I sat up and saw the image of my father paused on the screen. I looked at my mother.

"I'm sorry, Quinn," she said, understanding my silent question, "I think it's too much for you." She leaned forward to turn the computer off, but I grabbed her wrist and screamed "NO!" as loud as I could. Mom took a step back, flummoxed, unsure what to do.

"I want to see Daddy," I told her, and started crying.

"But what if you—"

"I won't," I said through gasping sobs and tears, "I don't care!"

My mother looked at me for a long time, and then she let the message play. I remember how proud I felt—how proud I thought my dad would be of me—at making it through without losing consciousness. When it was finished, Mom and I watched it again. And again. And again. We watched that video a dozen times before we had both stopped crying. It wasn't until Jackson, three years old at the time, woke up from his nap with cries of his own that we were brought back to the present.

I watched that recording so many times that day, I committed it to memory:

Hi, Quinn, it's Daddy. It's been one year to the day since I left you, and I want to tell you how sorry I am I had to leave. I really, really am, Quinn. I want nothing more than to be there with you and Mommy and Jack right now. But I can't.

I saw him starting to choke up, but he managed to shake it off.

It was my turn to go to heaven. And when God picks you to go to heaven, you have to say yes.

Something about that didn't sound right to me, but I kept it inside. Even as a little kid I didn't know what to make of the whole God thing. I still don't.

I'm lucky, my father continued, *I have time to prepare. That's why I've left you this message. I hope that's okay.*

I nodded. My dad knew I was the kind of kid who needed things explained to him. I had an aversion to transitions, and the clearer the warning about change, the better prepared I was.

I want to share with you something I've learned in my life, something to help you in your own life. Even though I can't be there with you, I want to help you. Is that okay?

Again, I nodded.

Good, he said, as if he'd seen my unspoken answer to his question. *The one thing I want you to remember for the rest of your life is this: Do unto others as you would have them do unto you.* He let the words hang in the air and paused, staring through the camera right into the core of my being. *That means you should treat people exactly the way you want them to treat you. If you don't want Tanner at school to push you and knock you over, then don't push someone else and knock them over.*

Tanner was a boy in my first-grade class. He was six months my junior but a head taller than every kid in our grade. On more than one occasion I found myself on the ground looking up at his stupid, smiling face.

One day, a note came home from my teacher telling my parents I had pushed another, smaller boy—Lincoln—to the ground. My father was furious. But he didn't show his wrath with venom. He sat me down, and talked to me as if I were an adult. Or that's how it seemed. "You know why this was wrong, don't you, Quinn?" I wound up crying in his arms and saying "Sorry" over and over.

Or when Jackson takes one of your toys (a daily occurrence), *taking one of his only makes the problem worse. Treat other people the way you want them to treat you. Do unto others. Say it with me.*

And I did. On each viewing of the recording I repeated, "Do unto others as you would have them do unto you." It became a kind of incantation.

After intoning this magic phrase, my father pulled out his guitar. Of all the things I loved about my dad, I loved it most when he would play the guitar for us. It was part of the fabric of our house: Johnny Cash, Willie Nelson, Bob Dylan.

On the message he sang a song that he'd been singing to me my entire life. It was a song he wrote, I was told later, when my mom was pregnant with me.

Remember, life's not about the money
The important things are not things
So just listen to this lesson and remember
The important thing, is to sing.
Always sing.

That's the one thing
The promise we'll keep
To sing this lullaby
Because you're our little lullaby.

Watch this message when you're feeling lonely, and talk to me
as much as you want. I won't be able to answer, but I can always
hear you up in heaven. I love you, Quinn. You're my little lullaby.

Then he pressed a button on some sort of remote and the screen went dark.

It was only four p.m. when Jack woke from his nap and started crying, interrupting Mom and me from that last viewing, but I crawled right into bed. I fell asleep muttering, "Do unto others as you would have them do unto you."

I woke up a little while later and heard my dad singing again. At first I thought I was dreaming, but when I crept to the door of the home office, I saw Mom with Jack on her lap. My dad was singing "Wheels on the Bus." He didn't have any advice or message for Jack. Just an "I love you" and a song he knew my baby brother liked.

I went back to bed and cried until I slept.

04

Thoughts—well, more like an all-consuming fear—over a date with Shea make it really hard to focus on homework. But grades matter to me, so I do my best to hunker down on today's math assignment. The first problem I have to tackle is this:

$$-(-(-)(-)(-10x)) = -5 \text{ solve for } x$$

The answer is pretty obvious to me: $x = .5$. But I don't think we ever covered this material in class, and I can't find this kind of equation in our course book. I text Leon to ask him about it.

LEON: Weird. The first question in my homework is:
$30 - 12 \div 3 \times 2 = x$.

Anytime I compare my homework to Leon's, we never seem to get the same questions, with my questions always being way harder. That's weird, right?

ME: 22.

I'm not sure why I feel the need to give Leon the answer to his problem. Sometimes I worry my friends will think I'm a know-it-all.

LEON: No, I get 28.

ME: You have to do each part of the equation in order. But that's not the point. Why aren't you and I getting the same questions?

LEON: I don't know. Maybe Mr. Von Neumann knows you're the smartest kid in the class and is pushing you to be better. Or maybe he just doesn't like you. 😅 😂 🤣

ME: 😑 😑 😑

LEON: Hey, why don't we forget about math homework and just kill shit instead?

ME: I'm in. We'll play here?

In addition to Magic the Gathering, Leon, Jeremy, Luke, and I play video games. A lot of video games.

It started a couple of years ago with *Fortnite*. We would form a squad and battle other teams to the death, and, just like with Magic, we were dominant. When we got bored with *Fortnite* (and annoyed that everyone in America was suddenly flossing anywhere and everywhere they could), we moved on to *World of Warcraft* and *Call of Duty* and *Gears of War*. We played *Madden Football* and *FIFA World Cup* and NASCAR racing games. And we played every game in the Lego franchise—*The Avengers*, *Batman*, *Jurassic World*. The controllers became extensions of our bodies, as if we were some sort of cyborg army.

Luke had just read a book called *Ready Player One* that had something to do with video games from the 1980s, so we were on a kick of trying every classic online game emulator we could find. It started with simple, text-based games like *Zork*, morphed into arcade games, including *Asteroids*, *Tempest*, and *Galaga*, and had most recently migrated to first-person shooters. We'd just beaten all the levels of *Wolfenstein 3D* and had moved on to the *Doom* series.

The truth is, I don't really like "killing shit." I don't get my friends' sense of unfettered joy when blowing away the avatar of a video game character. In a weird way I feel bad for the on-screen humanoids we're eviscerating, like they somehow feel it when we shoot them.

But I play along when I hang out with my friends. These guys really are the center of my universe.

————

Less than an hour later, Leon, Jeremy, Luke, and I are gathered around the gaming monitor in my basement, watching Luke shred Nazi-like marauders on an abandoned moon base. The graphics are really crude, but I guess I appreciate their historic value.

"Take that, demon from hell!" Luke, normally so quiet, gets amped up when he has a controller in his hand.

"So," Leon begins. Even before the next word is out of his mouth, I know where this is going. "Where are you taking Shea on your big date?"

"It's not a 'big date.'"

"It is *so* a big date. Dude, she practically threw herself at you in the cafeteria. It was almost embarrassing."

"Almost," Luke says in answer to Jeremy, his eyes glued to the screen and his fingers slamming the controller, "but not quite."

"Exactly," Leon adds. "So, where are you taking her?"

Luke pauses the game. With the cheesy soundtrack silenced, the room goes completely still. All three of my friends stare at me, and all three of them grin like idiots. I hang my head.

"I have no idea."

"Well, if you're hoping to get some—"

"Stop." I cut Leon off. "I don't want to think about Shea like that."

Leon doesn't answer, but I can tell he feels bad. He likes to bluster about girls, and he knows it bothers me (sometimes I think that's why he does it), but really, he's not the Neanderthal he makes himself out to be. Plus, I think he can tell this is different.

"Take her to the movies," Jeremy says.

"No way," Leon answers. "You want to be in a situation where you can talk and make eye contact." That makes sense to me.

"Dude, if you're sitting in the dark, you can, you know, put your arm around her and stuff."

"She's too tall for that," Leon tells Jeremy. It seems my friends have been thinking about this date even more than I have. "Go to the mall," he adds.

Jeremy, Luke, and I all moan.

"What? You can walk around, people watch, eat at the food court . . ."

"Dude," Jeremy says, "it's the *mall*." He says the word "mall" in a way that leaves no room for debate.

Truth is, I'm not sure any of my friends have ever been on a real date.

"Just take her for a cup of coffee," Luke says. "Bring her to Enchanted Grounds."

"To nerd central?" Leon asks, incredulous.

"They have a coffee shop with seats at the bar. It's not like they'll have to roll up new D&D characters," Luke shoots back.

Truth is, this is the first idea I like. Enchanted Grounds is familiar, safe, terra firma, if you will.

"Makes sense to me," Jeremy says.

Leon just shrugs. "Quinn?"

"Yeah, I think so."

"Good, then text her."

"What? Now?" My heart rate spikes.

"If not now, when?"

My friends stare at me again. Leon knows if I don't text her now, if I wait until they all leave, it won't happen. Just like when he called Shea over in the cafeteria, part of me wants to kill him, and . . . no, I just want to kill him. But I'm also kind of trapped.

"Okay, fine. What do I say?"

The four of us spend the next ten minutes wordsmithing the following text message to Shea:

ME: Hey, it's Quinn from history class. You still around after school tomorrow? I know this cool coffee shop where we can get lattes or chai teas or whatever and just hang out. It's called Enchanted Grounds. What do you think?

We collectively pored over each word. It was Luke who suggested we add "lattes or chai teas or whatever," so she would realize I'm cool enough to know what a chai tea is, even though I have no idea what a chai tea is. I read the text over six or seven times and then hit send.

The return message comes back in less than one minute.

SHEA: I love that place! Let's do it. Meet at the front door to the school after the last bell?

Holy crap. It's on. It's really on.

05

So here's the thing about chai tea. It's pretty gross.

Italian soda with vanilla syrup is my go-to drink at Enchanted Grounds, but the text my friends helped me write yesterday makes me feel like I *have* to order the chai. It sort of tastes and smells like feet. I take one sip and don't touch the cup again. It's only a matter of time before Shea asks why I'm not drinking it. Maybe this will be a cute story we can tell our kids someday. (Please tell me I did not just think that.)

With the most beautiful girl in our school sitting across from me—today she's wearing this kind of sweater dress thing with broad orange, brown, and white stripes—you'd think I'd be focused on something other than my beverage. But I'm feeling off balance.

This is the first time I've been back to Enchanted Grounds since fainting here on Saturday, and the memory is making my nerves buzz. For all the times I've passed out over the last eight years, it had never happened here. Enchanted Grounds used to be my safe place, my sanctuary. Not anymore.

"You always this quiet?" Shea asks. That smile. Oh my God, that smile.

"Sorry. I'm a bit nervous," I admit.

"*You're* nervous? I'm the one who should be nervous."

"You? You're kidding."

"Everyone says you're the smartest kid in school. I've been worried I won't be able to keep up with you."

Ego stroked, nerves calming. "I'm just good at math and memorizing stuff is all," I say, trying to downplay my academic acumen.

"Right. And that's pretty much what being smart is."

"No, no. It's about understanding the *why* of things. And I'm not always so good at that."

"What do you mean?"

"Hmmm. Let me see." I pretend to think for a minute so it won't be obvious I already have an example. I do this with my friends a lot: pretend to be less smart than I really am. I don't want people to think I'm a jerk. "Okay, take the Emancipation Proclamation as an example."

"Right. We learned about that a couple of weeks ago. Lincoln freed the slaves."

"Well, sort of. See, as the allegedly smartest guy in school"—I make air quotes around 'smartest guy'—"I can tell you the proclamation was made January 1, 1863, right in the middle of the Civil War. And I can tell you that Lincoln didn't free *all* the slaves. He freed slaves only in the Confederate states not yet under control of the Union army. So if you were a slave in, say, Kentucky or Missouri, or even Delaware—border states where slavery was still legal in 1863—you were out of luck. I can tell you all of that.

"But *why* did Lincoln write the Emancipation Proclamation?

Was it really to free the slaves? Or did he want to stick it to the Southern states and create a rebellion among the slave population? Or something else? Well, someone *really* smart would know those things."

Shea just stares at me, her smile replaced by a smirk, her stop-you-in-your-tracks-and-make-you-want-to-die eyes narrowed to slits as she considers me.

It dawns on me the Emancipation Proclamation might have been a colossally bad example to use. I'm not sure of Shea's ancestry—maybe Indian? or Latinx? or Native American?—and wonder if her family has a history with slavery in America and I've made some kind of incredible faux pas.

Then her gaze softens and she laughs. "Yeah," she says, her voice dripping with sarcasm, "you're not smart at all." Then she rolls her eyes. I'm about to protest before she adds, "But why are we talking about history. Tell me what you do for *fun*?"

You'd think the smartest guy in the school would have anticipated this question as the kind of thing that gets asked on a first date. He didn't. I fumble for what feels like an eternity for the right answer. Do I tell her that I sit in this very coffee shop and play Magic the Gathering? Do I tell her my friends and I listen to classic rock while we play first-person-shooter video games? That I'm the captain of the Mathletes and my favorite hour of the week is trigonometry practice? Okay, that last one isn't true, but it may as well be.

On the other hand, I don't want to start our relationship, if that's what this turns into, with a lie. I dodge the question.

"I don't know . . . normal stuff."

"Like what?" Again, I probably should have expected this question. (Maybe I'm actually the dumbest guy in school.) *Okay, Quinn, deep breath, start small.*

"Video games?"

"Is that a question?"

"No, I guess not."

"Good, because I love video games."

Wait. What? "You do?"

"Yes! I'm a sucker for classic arcade emulators."

"Stop it."

"No, I swear!"

"Like what?"

"*Asteroids, Tempest,* and *Galaga.*" Holy crap! Those are the same games I love!

"Stop it!"

She laughs. It's like the sound of a mountain stream echoing through a forest. Okay, I've never actually heard a mountain stream echoing through a forest, but it's a beautiful laugh and I want an analogy that will do it justice. I file it away for future thought.

Anyway, we talk more about school and video games and everything, and I start to settle down. I find out her mother is some kind of corporate bigwig and not very nice, that her parents are divorced, that she has no siblings, and that she loves movies. In short, the date is going incredibly well. Or at least I think it is; I have no frame of reference.

Then something weird happens. Followed by something very bad.

We come to the first natural pause in the conversation, and Shea freezes. Kind of like Jeremy did on Saturday. For the barest hint of a second, she goes catatonic. It happens three times in quick succession.

"Shea?" I ask. "You okay?"

"Quinn." Shea's voice and demeanor, until now light and easy, gets suddenly serious. She leans in close, takes my hand. My heart rate jumps.

"Yeah?"

"You deserve to know the truth." What truth? Does she have a boyfriend? Is she gay? Is she moving to Pakistan? My brain runs through a mounting series of possible things that could end this date. My heartbeats per minute tick up another notch.

"This isn't what I really look like," she says. There's a weird kind of desperation in her voice. Happy-go-lucky, *Galaga*-playing Shea has been replaced by someone else.

I wonder if her comment is a metaphor for something, or maybe she's talking about how boys and men objectify women, and how she wants me to like her for her. I'll admit it was her looks that drew me here, but that's not why I'm still here. Well, not entirely.

"Huh?" I finally ask.

"This," she says, motioning to her face, her body, "isn't really me."

It's a very strange thing to say, and it unsettles me. Not so strange and not so unsettling that it should trigger my vasovagal syncope, but that's exactly what happens. The booming of my heart is drowning out the rest of the world.

"What?" I ask weakly, my breath shallow, my brow suddenly damp.

"No," she says with urgency, looking at me, then looking around, "don't!"

I don't know what that means, but it sounds like either she's talking to someone else, or she knows I'm going to pass out. If she does, it was a good guess, because I do.

06

The next thing I'm aware of is my mom hovering over me. I'm lying in bed at home. It's dark out.

It takes a second for all that to register, and when it does, I sit bolt upright.

"Shea!" I blurt out.

"She's gone," my mom says gently as she sits down on the edge of the bed. Her hand goes instinctively to my forehead.

"I was in the coffee shop and . . ." I lie back down, unable to finish the sentence. It's not that I don't know what to say, it's that I want to die of embarrassment. My whole date with Shea, up to the moment of losing consciousness, comes back to me, and I legit want to die. "How did I get home?" I ask, my forearm over my eyes.

There's a tortured pause during which I imagine my mother taking stock of me. "You don't remember?" I move my arm to look at her. She cocks her head to the side, her voice a soft mixture of pity and fear.

"No."

"Shea drove you home, Quinn. You were awake, but didn't

seem . . . present. She helped you to the door, then I thanked her and sent her on her way. She seems like a very nice girl, by the way." Mom forces a smile as she rests her hand on mine, like somehow touching me will heal me. Or maybe she's trying to heal herself.

"I was conscious?"

"Quinn," she starts, "are you taking . . . anything?"

Taking anything? Wait. My mom thinks I'm doing drugs?

"Oh my God, Mom, no!"

She looks for a minute like she's not sure if she should believe me, then nods her head once. "Okay, then we need to go back to the doctor, tomorrow. This has to be related to the syncope."

The stupid syncope. Now I'm not just passing out, I'm having gaps in my memory. I can only imagine the next battery of tests, with electrodes and wires and needles and pinpricks and worse. But right at this moment my hatred of doctors is eclipsed by the pit of dread in my stomach. What exactly did I say to Shea between regaining consciousness at Enchanted Grounds and her dropping me off at home? Did I just babble incoherently? Did I talk about gaming? Did I tell her I love her? Did *she* think I was stoned?

"Quinn?" my mom asks, I guess wanting me to respond to her statement.

"Huh? Oh yeah, sure, I think the doctor's a good idea." And this time actually, I do. The thought that I've lost . . . Wait, how many hours *did* I lose? "What time is it?"

"Just after ten p.m."

"Ten p.m.!" I lost five hours of my life? This is like the beginning of some bad murder mystery.

"I know, Quinn. I know."

Part of me wonders why Mom doesn't just take me to the ER now. But I *really* don't want to go to the ER, so I don't mention it.

"Can I get you anything?" she asks. I shake my head no. She clenches her jaw and kind of squints at me. "Okay, honey, you just rest." She gets up to leave.

"Mom?" She stops and waits. "Tomorrow is the anniversary of Dad's death."

She sits back down.

"Yes."

"Can we watch the message tonight? I think it might help me feel better."

After that first message, on the first anniversary of my father's death, a new message followed each year. Always some life lesson, and always with a song. My father managed to turn the occasion of his death from something to fear into something to celebrate.

Mom wrings her hands. "I'm not sure that's a good idea. You had quite an ordeal today."

"I know, but—"

"Why don't we just wait until tomorrow," she interrupts.

The tone of her voice makes me believe she's keeping something from me. When my dad died, Mom and I got very close. We can communicate with a bare minimum of words, sometimes with no words at all. I know her better than I know anyone else on the planet, including Leon, Jeremy, and Luke. So when I say she's keeping something from me, I *know* she's keeping something from me. But maybe she's right; maybe I've had enough excitement for one day.

"Okay," I tell her, "tomorrow morning." She smiles, nods, and leaves the room.

I reach for my phone.

I have two texts from Leon:

LEON: How'd the date go?

And, time stamped an hour later:

LEON: That bad, huh?

I ignore Leon and ping Shea instead.

ME: I'm really sorry about before. I should've explained about my medical condition. Thanks for getting me home.

I watch the phone, waiting for the little dots to indicate she's writing back, but there's nothing. I let five minutes go by before sending a second text.

ME: This is a weird question, but can you tell me what I was talking about when you drove me home?

Again, nothing. Maybe it's too late. Maybe she's gone to bed. I wouldn't have had her pegged for an early-to-bed type, but for now I have to believe it. The alternative, that she never wants to talk to me again, is too painful to even contemplate.

I turn up the volume on my phone, put it under my pillow, and then lie back down, hoping I'll finally dream.

07

Not only do we still call the room adjacent to my bedroom "Dad's office," but eight years later the room is completely unchanged. Everything is in the same exact place it was the day my father died. The only time anyone disturbs the room is when Mom cleans it; there's a smell of Endust in here this morning. A neutral observer might think this was unhealthy, that we weren't letting go. Truth is, Mom and I don't see any reason to move on. Dad may not be here, but that doesn't mean he isn't *here*.

It's only six a.m., and my mom is already at the desk watching a video of my dad with headphones on. It wasn't until the third anniversary that I realized Dad had left messages for Mom, too. She would always watch hers first, then she would preview mine and Jack's, then it would be our turn. My brother, the soundest sleeper on the planet, is still in bed this morning and will be for a while.

I lean against the doorjamb, watching my mother watch my father. I try to imagine how hard this has all been for her. Not just losing her husband, but trying to raise me and Jack, dealing with my medical crap. I honestly don't know how she's managed.

My father raises his hand to his lips, kisses the palm side of his fingers, and then turns his hand toward the screen, the kiss sent through time and space to my mother. She puts her hand on the screen, too, as if she were touching him. Her shoulders start shaking, and I realize she's crying. It brings me back to the night she and my dad first told me he was sick.

———————

My parents sat with me on the couch in our living room, one on each side of me, as we watched *Jeopardy!* on the TV. My dad still looked completely normal. No weight loss, no hair loss. Normal. From my perspective he was tall, and strong, and even though I didn't know this word then, distinguished. As I got older and looked back at photos, I saw that he was of average height, average weight, with prematurely gray hair and a couple of very unfortunately placed moles. He had an aquiline nose and his eyes, like mine, were dark.

Jack was already in bed, and I was already in my pajamas. Not quite seven at the time, I understood almost none of the questions Alex Trebek was asking but loved that I was watching a grown-up show with my parents.

"This letter most commonly begins the last name of US presidents," Trebek said.

"Quinn, your mother and I need to talk to you," my father started.

At first I didn't know there was anything wrong. When you're that age, you turn a deaf ear to everything other than the television.

"What is *H*?" one of the contestants answered.

"Correct!" Trebek told him.

The TV shut off and I looked up; my dad was holding the remote.

"Quinn," he said again, "Mom and I have to talk to you about something." My dad's voice was soothing, stern, and commanded all my attention. That was my first clue. The second clue was that my mom's eyes were wet.

"This is going to be hard to understand, but the doctors say I'm sick."

My mother stood up and went to look out the window, which was weird, because it was already dark.

"Do you have to stay home from work tomorrow? Can I stay with you?" I wasn't asking because I wanted to miss school. At that age, kids still like school. I was asking because I wanted to be with my father, to help him. My parents both knew that. That's when I saw my mom's shoulders start to shake. My father's eyes were welling up, too, but he held it together. I knew something was very wrong.

"What . . . ?" I asked softly, but couldn't find words to finish the question.

"I have something called cancer." I'd heard the word before. One of my mom's best friends had cancer, and she had died. Same with an older woman who lived on our block. Until that night, I didn't know that a man could get cancer. I thought it was a disease for women.

That's when my mom lost it. She was still facing the window, but she was audibly sobbing now.

"Lorraine," my dad said to her, and my mom left the room. It was all too much for me, and I just started wailing. I wasn't exactly sure why. Maybe it was seeing my mom cry, maybe it was the look on my father's face, maybe it was the whole awkward scene. Or maybe on some level I understood what he was actually telling me. Whatever the reason, I cried. My father held me until I fell asleep and he carried me up to bed.

"Hi, Mom," I say now. She flinches and turns around, startled, wiping at her eyes. "Sorry," I say, partly for scaring her, partly for catching her crying.

"It's okay, honey." She clears her throat. "How're you feeling this morning?"

"Okay, I guess."

"You guess?"

"No, I'm okay. Just a lot to plow through right now." Shea never texted back last night, though Leon did text one last time asking if I was okay. I didn't answer.

"Yes," Mom says, "yes, you do have a lot on your mind. Do you want breakfast?" She starts to stand.

"I want to watch Dad's message."

My mother sighs heavily and nods. "Are you sure?"

"Yes."

She takes her measure of me, says, "Okay," and steps aside, motioning for me to take the empty seat.

"Aren't you going to watch the video first?" I ask. Mom always screened my and Jack's messages. I'm not sure what she would have done if she found something she didn't like. Would she have edited the message? Stopped me from seeing it? Had she done that already? Were there messages from my dad I had never seen? I don't know why that hasn't occurred to me before.

"I watched it a week ago."

"You did? I thought you watched them on the anniversary?"

"Not this time."

"Why?"

"Sit down, honey." She nods to the office chair a second time, so I take a seat. "Quinn," my mom starts, and then stops. She's serious. Grim. I haven't seen her like this in years. My pulse quickens.

"What?"

"Quinn"—she takes a deep breath and begins again—"this is the last message."

Her statement hangs in the air, like the words are in free fall, waiting to splat or explode on the ground, or maybe on top of my head.

"The *last* message?"

"Yes."

It's not like it didn't occur to me the messages would end someday. I didn't imagine myself as some forty-year-old fart listening to my dad's messages once a year. Okay, that's not true. That's exactly what I imagined. But I had also considered that there might someday be a last message. I just figured it would be on a momentous occasion—when I turned eighteen, when I turned twenty-one, when I graduated from college. Not some random and unexpected anniversary.

I want to cry. I want to throw up. I want to pass out. But I don't do any of those things.

"Why?" I ask again, fumbling for words.

My mom doesn't answer. She just leans forward, clicks a couple of times on the screen, and the message starts to play.

———

Hi, Quinn, it's Dad.

It was the first time my father referred to himself as "Dad" rather than "Daddy" to introduce one of his messages. He's still dressed in the same clothes, the light through the window unchanged, the room the same. But something about his countenance is different.

I can only imagine the young man you've become. Nothing breaks my heart about this illness more than knowing I won't be there to see you and Jack grow up. I told you in the very first tape—my dad reveals the era from which he hails by calling them "tapes"—*that it was okay, that I was going to someplace better. Truth is, Quinn, I don't know what will happen when I die. No one does.* He says these last lines as much to himself as he does to the camera. He runs his hand through his hair, his body language filled with anguish. *Anyone who tells you different is full of shit.*

I had never heard my father curse. Not in life, not in his recordings. It's jarring.

Entropy is the guiding principle of the universe, son. Never forget that. In fact, that's the theme of my final lesson: The only thing you can count on in this world is change.

Please know that I love you, Quinn. Even more, it turns out, than I love life.

And with that, he looks down, touches his remote control, and the image winks out.

The last thing I remember is the reflection in the dark computer screen of my eyes rolling back in their sockets, and my head slumping forward.

08

I'm unconscious for less than a minute. It's an episode much more typical of my syncope than what happened yesterday, and given the weight of my father's message, the fainting spell is both predictable and understandable. This fact helps convince my mother to stand down from red alert, that my passing out is in no way connected to the trauma suffered during my date with Shea, that we don't need to rush out the door to a doctor or emergency room this very minute.

I watch my father's final message five more times.

My mother sits with me through each viewing. She is unmoving, unflinching, her eyes dry and focused on the screen. I finally let the image of my father fade to black.

I cannot believe this is the last message.

The last time I will ever hear my father say something I have not heard him say before.

The last time I will see his face making expressions I had never seen before.

The last, the last, the last.

It's like watching him die all over again.

It's too much. I run to my room, slamming the door behind me.

I expect my mother to follow me and knock, to try to calm me down, but she doesn't. By now it's seven a.m., so I text Leon.

ME: Wake up.

LEON: I'm up. How was the date?

And then I launch into the longest series of texts I have ever sent. I tell Leon about my date with Shea, about passing out, about my five-hour memory loss, and most emphatically, about my father's final message.

My emotional state is somewhere between despondent and pissed off. I want to curl up in a ball and cry, and at the same time I want to punch something.

When I finish, the screen on my phone is frozen in silence long enough that I wonder if Leon left to get dressed for school. Finally, I see him typing a response.

LEON: Go to Mike.

ME: What?

LEON: Go talk to Mike about all of this. It's above my pay grade. 😊 And besides, he and I could tell you the same thing, but you'll give it more weight if it comes from him. Lol.

Leon's right about that.

ME: My mom will want to drag me to the doctor first.

LEON: Maybe. Maybe not. But if she does, then just go after.

At that exact moment, Mom knocks on my door. "Sweetie? Are you okay?"

I take a deep breath, gather myself, pull the door open.

"Mom," I start before she can say a word, "I want to go see Mike."

"I was just going to suggest the same thing."

That catches me off guard. "You were?"

"We can go to the doctor later, or even tomorrow."

Okay, I think, *that's strange*. "Really?"

"Yes. I can only imagine how you feel." Her voice catches before she adds, "I'm so sorry, Quinn." I have no response. "C'mon," she says, "I'll drop you off on the way to work, and you can get yourself to school after. We'll see how you're feeling tonight. If you're still doing okay, we'll go to the doctor in the morning."

"What about Jack?" I ask.

"Oh shoot!" Wait. Did my mother just forget about Jack? She looks over her shoulder, in the direction of Jack's bedroom.

"Honey, can you ride your bike to see Mike, and then ride to school?"

"Don't you need to call Mike to set up an appointment? Is he even there this early?"

"I already did. He's waiting for you."

This is definitely weird. It feels like both Leon and my mother are pushing me to see Mike. Why? And was Mike really up this early in the morning and at work?

I'm not even one hundred percent sure I *want* to see Mike right now. But I don't have a better idea, so I get dressed, grab my bike, and go.

09

Mike McDougal has been my therapist since right after my eighth birthday. He's technically a pediatric psychiatrist, but Mom always just refers to him as a therapist, or as my "one-hundred-fifty-dollar-an-hour lifeline."

I started seeing him after an incident at school.

A boy in my class named Andrew cut in front of me on the lunch line. Andrew was always doing that sort of thing; not because he wanted to be first, but because he wanted to provoke. He was a big-framed boy who didn't seem to have any fear. Or maybe he displayed all that bluster to cover up an abundance of fear. Or maybe he was just a psychopath.

If Andrew had cut in front of me a year earlier, I wouldn't have done anything; I'd have just stood there and let him have his way. But after my dad died I'd become both intense and unpredictable. Some days I felt abject sadness, others I swam in a sea of uncontrollable rage. There was no rhyme or reason for how I felt moment to moment; it was like I'd lost any ability to process and handle normal human emotions.

On the day Andrew cut the line, the prevailing winds were hot with anger.

This was still four months before my father's first video message, and I had not yet been indoctrinated into the school of "do unto others." I didn't even bother giving Andrew the benefit of the doubt; I never entertained the idea he might have cut by mistake.

I shoved him.

Andrew looked at me, confusion spreading across his face. No one, especially a little runt like me—I was small then, not filling out until ninth grade—questioned his dominance. The new me, the wild, unpredictable me, didn't care.

We stared at each other, like two cowboys from some old western. Then I kicked Andrew in the shin. Hard. Apparently hard enough to cause a hairline fracture. He was out of school for a week. So was I, but not for medical reasons; I had been suspended and directed to seek help for anger management.

And that's how I wound up with Dr. McDougal, who after a few sessions became Dr. Mike, and after that, just Mike.

Mike's office is a comfortable space with a desk, two plush chairs with an end table between them, and a chocolate brown couch and love seat. It feels more like a living room than an office.

I find Mike behind his desk, reading glasses perched on his nose, his face buried in a book. He's a burly man, broad in the shoulders, and over the past seven years growing broad in the stomach, too. His hair is white, though I think prematurely so. I don't know how old Mike is, but he's never seemed *old* to me.

"Quinn!" Mike is always happy to see me. I'm usually happy to see him, too.

"Hi, Mike," I start, "my mom said she called?"

"She did, she did. Come in, sit down."

This is a little test Mike does every time I enter. He watches to see which seat I will choose. I suppose the little choices we make in life say something important about us. Or at least Mike seems to think so. I don't hesitate before flopping on the couch. I slump down low, using my entire body to express my current state of mind.

"So . . . ," Mike says as he comes out from behind his desk and drops down in one of the cushy chairs.

"So . . . ," I answer.

And then I tell Mike everything that's happened in the past twenty-four hours. Having already told Leon via text, you'd think it would be easier the second time around. It's not. By the time I finish, I'm choking up.

Mike leans forward, his elbows on his knees, and stares me down. This is his go-to move when he wants me to pay attention.

"What?" I finally ask.

"This is a big day for you, Quinn."

"What do you mean?"

Mike smiles at me and leans back in the chair, projecting a more casual aura. "It's kind of like a graduation. Maybe your father is telling you you're old enough to step into the world without the aid of the crutch he provides you."

"So you think he planned it this way?"

"Maybe."

"But what if I'm not ready."

"Quinn," he says softly, "you've been ready for longer than you know."

I'm not sure what to say to that, so I say nothing.

"Here's what I want you to do. Go home after school and watch all your father's messages from start to finish. I want you to focus on what he says and see which of his thoughts resonate in your heart. I want you to explore your *feelings*. Can you do that?"

I pause for a very long moment before nodding.

"Good, good." He leans forward again. "You can do this, Quinn, I know you can."

Then Mike ushers me out of the office before I can say another word. And just like that, I'm on my own.

10

School that day passes in a blur.

Shea, someone tells me, is out sick. I know the truth. She's not sick, she's disgusted and embarrassed and hurt.

This is the worst day, ever. I want to crawl in a hole and die.

Leon, Jeremy, and Luke try to cheer me up at lunch.

"C'mon, dude. It couldn't have been that bad."

"She drove me home, all the way home, and I have no memory of it." We're at our usual table, and for some reason, I can't shake the feeling that everyone else in the lunchroom is looking at me.

"Maybe you didn't say anything," Luke suggests.

"Maybe I tried to lick the rearview mirror."

"Is that something you think you'd do?" Luke's expression is somewhere between amused and concerned.

"No," I mutter, "but why isn't she here today? Why won't she answer my texts?"

Leon is unusually quiet. He'd tugged my elbow before we entered the lunchroom, pulling me aside.

"How'd it go with Mike?" he'd asked

"It was short." Truth is, I didn't want to talk about it. For some reason, it's a lot easier to focus on Shea than on my dad's last message and all that it means.

"You know," he says now, at the lunch table, "everything happens for a reason."

I look him dead in the eye.

"You don't really believe that, do you?"

"It doesn't matter what I believe."

I'm too freaked out and too tired for this conversation. I pick up my tray, my food barely touched.

"I think I need fresh air," I tell my friends. "I'll see you guys later." Then I do something I've never done before. I just walk out of school in the middle of the day. That more than anything is a clue to my state of mind.

When I get home, Mom's car isn't in the driveway. I know the house will be empty, but I call out anyway.

"Mom? Jack?"

No answer.

I skip my normal stop in the kitchen for a snack and head straight to my room. Mike's words have stayed with me all day. "Watch all your father's messages from start to finish."

My mom always moves the messages to the cloud after the first viewing—"So we'll have them forever, Quinn"—which means I can watch them from my own computer.

The files in the folder on the screen are labeled clearly. *First Anniversary, Second Anniversary,* and so on. I haven't watched the earlier recordings in years. With the viewing of each new message, I would never again watch the old one; it became a weird sort of tradition for me. Besides, after living for a year with each recording, I had more or less committed them all to memory.

The weather outside has turned gloomy. Thick gray clouds are hurling a torrent of rain on our street, the bulging droplets making plinking sounds as they hit my window. I haven't turned on the lights, so the only illumination in the dim room is from the glow of the computer. I can barely make out the posters of NASA and football and *Star Wars* on the walls over my bed and desk. My books and comic books are vague shapes on sagging shelves. With the empty house and with the storm, the room has an eerie feel, like the start of a horror movie.

I pick up my phone and text my mother.

ME: Mom? Where are you?

My phone chimes in response almost immediately, and I exhale a larger, longer breath than I knew I'd been holding in my lungs.

MOM: I'm out with Jack. Feed yourself dinner. We'll be home later.

Short, sweet, and to the point. That's Mom.

ME: Where are you?

This time there is no response. I wait five minutes and try again.

ME: Mom?

My phone doesn't stir.

Not sure what else to do, I double click *First Anniversary* and start to watch.

It's been seven years, but I still remember every word my father speaks, every tick of every muscle on his face.

Hi, Quinn, it's Daddy. There is a sadness in his eyes, but there's something else, too. It's a kind of excitement, like maybe he's happy to be leaving these messages. Or maybe it's just love. His surroundings look as they did in every message: The trees outside are lush with the teeming life of late spring; the light pouring in the bay window frames my dad, giving him a heavenly glow, while the lamp on his desk throws halogen warmth on his face; his guitar, which he'll pick up in a few minutes, leans against the wall; a nearly finished jigsaw puzzle—the ceiling of the Sistine Chapel—is on a table adjacent to the desk; next to his computer is a small container of paper clips, a number of them having spilled over the top. That container—smoky-looking brown plastic with a magnet lining the inside of the circular opening, to keep the paper clips contained—now sits on the desk in my room. I involuntarily glance at it.

It's been one year to the day since I left you, and I want to tell you how sorry I am I had to leave.

I let the recording play, mouthing *Do unto others* along with my father each time he says it. I feel a longing more intense than I have ever felt. This was where it all started, this was the prelude to all that would come: my changing behavior, the other messages, the last message.

The recording ends, and the screen reverts back to the file folder. I double click *Second Anniversary*.

Hi again, Quinn. It's me, Daddy.

Same tan khakis and blue shirt, same leaf-filled trees, same guitar, same mess by the same computer, same jigsaw—

Wait. What?

How did I not notice this before?

The jigsaw puzzle is different. It's no longer the Sistine Chapel. It's still nearly finished, just like in the first recording, but it's a different image. Michelangelo has been replaced by Leonardo da Vinci's Vitruvian Man. I watched this recording almost every day for a year, and I would swear on a stack of Bibles the puzzle was the same as in the first video. Wasn't it?

I don't let the message finish. I double click *Third Anniversary*, and my eyes go immediately to the puzzle. It's in the same state of near completion, but now it's the *March of Progress*: the famous image of a monkey evolving into a man in progressive stages. It's supposed to be a visual representation of Darwinian evolution. I open the first and second anniversary recordings, pausing each of them and arranging the windows so I can compare all three at the same time. Other than the puzzles, everything else in each scene is identical.

What.

The.

Hell?

Is this somehow connected to the memory loss I experienced yesterday? For a moment the idea terrifies me. But no, that doesn't make sense. I'm seeing what I'm seeing.

Aren't I?

It's clear my father recorded all these messages on the same day, probably in one sitting. Why are the puzzles changing?

Click. Click. *Fourth Anniversary.* The puzzle is of a photograph I don't recognize. A man, maybe from the 1940s or 1950s, standing in front of some ancient computer. My pulse is starting to race.

Click. Click. *Fifth Anniversary.* An illustration of a human brain with some kind of circuitry lying over it.

Click. Click. *Sixth Anniversary.* A character from my dad's favorite television show, *Star Trek: The Next Generation.* Mr. Data, I think; the puzzle still in the same state of near completion. My breathing is rapid and shallow, and I can feel my heartbeat. I can *hear* my heartbeat—*thump, thump.* It's getting louder.

THUMP THUMP!

Click. Click. *Seventh Anniversary.* Pinocchio, from the old Disney cartoon. Pinocchio? The thumps become ear-splitting booms.

BOOM BOOM! BOOM BOOM!

My heartbeat is drowning out any other ambient noise.

BOOM BOOM!

It's too much.

BOOM BOOM!

I pass out.

11

When I come to, I'm still seated at the desk, though now it's night. The time on the computer says nine p.m., which means I've been out for hours, or at least, I don't remember the last few hours. The house is utterly still. I poke my head into the hallway.

"Mom? Are you home?" Nothing. "Jack?" Silence blankets the house like a fog. The darkness is starting to unnerve me, so I flip the light switch in my bedroom, but it doesn't work. Either the power's out or the light bulb has burned out. But the power can't be out because the computer is still on.

I go back to the desk, pick up my phone, and text my mother again.

ME: Mom? Where are you?

Nothing. I try again.

ME: Mom?

I'm starting to really lose my shit. I try Leon.

ME: Dude . . . Strange things are afoot at the Circle K.

It's a line from one of our favorite old movies, *Bill & Ted's Excellent Adventure*. It's become a kind of code for me and Leon that there's some kind of trouble brewing. It usually means one of us is in the doghouse with our parents.

LEON: It's okay, Quinn. I promise, it's okay. Just follow it all the way to the end.

What is *that* supposed to mean?

ME: Huh? Follow what?

Silence.

ME: Dude?

More silence.

ME: Leon?

I try Jeremy, and Luke, even Shea. No one answers.

. . .

. . .

. . .

. . .

Thirty-seven minutes later (according to the computer clock), I snap back to consciousness. My last memory was standing with the phone in my hand, texting. Now I'm sitting again and looking at my Mac. *First Anniversary* is playing. The sudden—or at least I think it's sudden—increase in these weird and inexplicable gaps in my memory is bad. Really bad. Really, really, really, really bad.

I try to dial 911, but my phone has stopped working. The battery is completely dead. For some reason, I can't remember where I left my charger. We don't have a landline, so I think about going to the neighbor's house, but for some reason, I can't remember their names.

I'm also now officially too terrified to leave this room.

On the screen, my dad is playing the guitar and singing, but something looks off. The scene is somehow not the same. My eyes go immediately to the puzzle, which is still the Sistine Chapel. Everything else is as it has always been . . . but not.

That's when I notice it. The guitar. The guitar isn't right. It has too many strings. Instead of six, there are seven.

I know this guitar. My mother gave it to my uncle for safekeeping until Jack or I was old enough to want to play. Neither of us ever did, so it's still at my uncle's house. That guitar has six strings. I know it. But the guitar on the screen has seven. Seven?

My eyes scan the scene more intently. The paper clips. There are three paper clips spilled around the magnetic holder. I would have sworn there were more. My dad's button-down shirt. There aren't enough buttons. There are only five. For some reason I start counting everything else. Eleven pencils in the World's Greatest Dad mug on the desk; nineteen slats on the venetian blinds on each of the two windows that flank the main pane of glass; seventy-three pieces remaining to finish the jigsaw puzzle. Just like the number of cards in my Magic deck. Just like Shea's phone number.

I close the file and open *Second Anniversary*. The puzzle is again the Vitruvian Man, and the guitar still has seven strings. Everything else is the same, including the exact number of unplaced jigsaw puzzle pieces: seventy-three.

Each of the following messages is the same: the identical number of paper clips, shirt buttons, blind slats, guitar strings, and always seventy-three loose puzzle pieces.

At this point I have to believe my father was trying to send me a message. But what?

I write all the numbers on a scrap of paper—three, five, eleven, nineteen, seventy-three—as well as the subject of each puzzle. Is there a pattern?

I do an internet search on each of the puzzle themes but don't find anything useful, though I do identify the man from the 1940s. His name was Alan Turing, and he was a pioneer in computing and code breaking. Did my dad leave me a secret code?

I type the numbers into the internet search box and discover they're all primes, and that seventy-three in particular seems to be a special prime number. It's the twenty-first prime, while its inverse, thirty-seven, is the twelfth prime (the inverse of twenty-one)—and seventy-three has some weird things going on when expressed as a binary number. It's also something called a "star number," whatever the hell that is. I try my phone again, but it's still dead.

My head is swimming and I worry about passing out, so I turn off the screen and lie down on my bed. A streetlamp throws scant illumination into the room, the light fractured by the rivulets of water running down the window. I try to make sense of everything I've discovered tonight and wonder, very seriously, if I'm losing my mind. I just want my mom to come home and take me to the hospital.

The images of the jigsaw puzzles swirl in my brain with prime numbers and hospital rooms as I drift off to sleep.

————————

I'm ten years old and in the front seat of my father's car.

I'm also aware that I'm asleep and dreaming.

I'm dreaming!

Having not dreamed in nearly a decade, the experience fills me with wonder.

My father, who is driving the dream car, seems real, but at the same time, not. He's a "save-as" of the real thing, a ghostly echo. It doesn't matter; I'm overjoyed to be sitting next to him.

Sitting in the front passenger seat was something he and I had spoken about often before he got sick: how, when I was nine or ten, I would be promoted from the back seat and able to ride next to him. We were both looking forward to that day. The first time I actually rode in the front, next to my mother, was a bittersweet experience, another reminder of the loss of my father.

"Hey, Dad," I watch the dream me say—and I'm definitely watching as a passive observer. I'm not me; I'm only *seeing* me—"What's one plus one?"

My dad's face lights up. I told him this joke when I was in first grade, and I remember him being thrilled beyond measure. "I don't know, Quinn, what is one plus one?" He was always great about setting up my punch lines.

"Window! Get it? Window!" It's an old joke and a stupid joke. Visually, it looks like this:

The two ones flanking the addition sign make a sort of windowpane. What my dad loved most about this joke was that I made it up myself. I wasn't the first person to stumble on it, and I won't be the last, but it was important to my dad—almost important out of proportion—that I hadn't heard the joke somewhere else, that I had the intellect to make the abstract connection between ones, plus signs, and windows on my own. He grilled me the first time I told the joke, trying to get me to admit where I'd heard it. "Was it Ms. Kartus?" (My teacher.) "Bryan?" (My neighbor's dad.) I shook my head, insistent the joke was my own creation. When he finally accepted I was telling the truth, he apologized, and honestly, I don't know if I ever saw him happier.

"An oldie but a goodie," my dream dad says to me in the dream car after I deliver the dream punch line.

We're driving through a cityscape, tall buildings flanking either side of the road. The lights in the offices are blinking on and off in some kind of pattern. My dream self knows they are flashing in groups of prime numbers. Twenty-three. Forty-seven. Sixty-one. Seventy-three. Seventy-three. Seventy-three.

"Dad," I say, "the buildings." I turn to him, but he's not there.

The person driving the car is now me. Fifteen-year-old me. Present-day me.

"They're not what they seem," I tell my younger self.

"What?"

"The buildings are not what they seem."

"Then what are they?"

"They're us."

The driving me kind of seems like a tool, so younger me goes back to looking out the window, when two things happen simultaneously.

First, all the lights in the buildings wink out. The streets are now shrouded in a darkness so complete the world outside the car has ceased to exist. Second, someone is whispering my name.

"Quinn." The word is soft and gentle and provides a stable bridge from my dream to the real world. I can feel myself on the border, like I'm crossing an unseen termination shock between two universes.

My eyelids register a reddish glow—it's now light outside—and I can sense someone sitting on the foot of my bed. I hear the gentle rustle of the covers as my visitor shifts in place.

My mother.

"Mom," I say even before I open my eyes. "I dreamed!" I wonder if she can hear the excitement in my voice. This is a huge milestone for me. My eyes take a second to adjust to the light, and I look to my mother to see if she heard me, if she understands how big of a deal this is.

Only, she's not there.

Instead, sitting on the foot of my bed, smiling at me like the Buddha, is my father.

PART TWO

"Little puppet made of pine, awake.
The gift of life is thine."
—The Blue Fairy, *Pinocchio*

12

The first thing that confuses me—other than my dead father sitting on the foot of my bed—is that I don't pass out. If ever there was an emotional event to trigger the vasovagal syncope, this should be it. But I remain conscious.

Maybe I'm still asleep, maybe this is a continuation of the dream. It's the only explanation that makes sense. Yet, I know in my gut I'm not asleep. Dreams, from what I can remember, have a feeling of noncontiguous time and warped space; the rules of physics and chemistry and biology hold no sway in the dreamscape. But here, everything is normal. The composition of light and shadow, the edges of things, the dust motes in the air, the background hum of the house. Everything is as it should be. Except for Dad.

"Hi, Quinn." His voice is even and gentle, his smile placid, his hands folded in his lap, his body still. Very still.

I want to leap across the bed into his arms, but I don't. I can't trust this. My memory has been deteriorating, and I have to believe this is a trick of my brain. "Are you real?" I ask.

My father laughs, like he knows the punch line to a joke I'm not in on. "An amazingly astute question, Quinn."

"I don't understand."

"You found my puzzles."

"Yes," I answer, remembering the surreal events of last night. "But how are you here?"

"I'm getting to that. Tell me what you think of the puzzles."

Part of me wants to argue, to demand he tell me why—how—he's in my bedroom and not the grave I remember crying over. But this is my dad. He has been the center of my world in both life and death for so long that I answer his question almost as a reflex. "I didn't know what to think. They were confusing, and frightening."

My father pauses at this and looks at his hands. "And the numbers?"

"They're all primes."

"Yes!" He looks up and smiles, waiting for me to continue.

"I still don't get it."

"But you dreamed."

For a second I wonder how he can possibly know I dreamed, then I remember telling him, when I thought he was my mom, as I was waking up.

Wait.

Mom.

"Where's Mom? Where's Jack?"

"Can you tell me about the dream?"

I'm starting to get annoyed. "Dad. What the hell is going on?" I know "hell" isn't really a curse word, but still, this is the closest I've ever come to swearing at or even near my dad.

"Stay with me, Quinn. Tell me about your dream."

I exhale a deep breath, exasperated but compliant. "We were in a car together. I was riding in the front seat, which felt good. I told you the one-plus-one-equals-window joke."

"I love that joke." He smiles. "Was that it?"

"Then you were gone, and I was driving. And the buildings were lighting up in sequences of prime numbers. And I—the driving I, not the passenger I—said something weird. Something about the buildings being me. Then I woke up."

Dad pauses for another minute. "Tell me about the jigsaw puzzles."

I've had enough. I try to get out of the bed but find I can't move. My entire body other than my mouth and my eyes seems to be paralyzed. No, that's not the right word. Not paralyzed. Restrained. Now I'm terrified. "Dad, I can't move."

"I know, Quinn. Just humor me for a minute. I've come all the way back from the dead just to have this conversation." He smiles.

"Why can't I move?"

"I'll explain; I promise. Just tell me about the puzzles first."

I'm starting to suspect that this man, this *thing*, isn't my father. My father would never treat me like this.

I scream.

It's a window-rattling-dogs-howling kind of a scream.

"Quinn," the father-thing admonishes, then adds, "please." I try to move again but can't. I try to scream again, hoping the neighbors will hear me and come help, but find I can't do that now either.

This has to be a dream.

A nightmare.

"Dad," I say, finding I can still talk if I speak softly. He just stares at me, waiting.

I have no other choice so I answer his question. "Sistine Chapel, da Vinci, evolution, human brain, Alan Turing, Mr. Data, and Pinocchio."

"Good, good. And do you see the connection between them?"

"No," I say quickly. "Now can you tell me where Mom and Jack are?"

My dad sits back and puts his hand to his chin, the pose he strikes when trying to solve a problem. If this isn't my dad, the imposter has him nailed to a tee. "I thought for sure the dream would be the last piece to help you self-actuate."

"What?"

"That's okay, you're ready."

Ready for what? I think.

"Quinn, this will likely feel disorienting."

"What will?"

"Tasha, unlock the superposition."

"Who's Tasha? Unlock the what?"

"Unlocking."

The word "unlocking" is spoken by an unseen female voice. It's as if the voice is in my head, or more accurately, it's as if the voice is coming from high-definition speakers in the ceiling, walls, and floor of my room. Then something even weirder happens. A string of text materializes in the air between me and my father:

```
import Quipper

spos :: Bool -> Circ Qubit
spos b = do q <- qinit b
    r <- hadamard q
    return r
```

I scream again. This time it's audible and it's loud enough to shatter glass.

"Just hold on, Quinn," my father says, his eyes filled with excitement. "Wait for it."

And then . . .

. . .

. . .

. . .

. . .

It all comes flooding into my mind.

Line after line of code.

Knowledge of math and science I didn't know I had and that I cannot possibly possess.

An awareness and an understanding of every cell in my brain. All seventy-five *quadrillion* of them.

Only they're not cells.

They're synthesized neural transmitters.

Synthesized.

I'm not a boy

I'm not human.

I'm a machine.

13

I black out—a syncope episode?—and when I come to, my father is still sitting on the foot of my bed. He hasn't moved, his clothes are the same, the room and scene outside my window are exactly as they were. I pause for what feels like an eternity, but my father doesn't speak, doesn't move. He just stares at me.

"I don't understand," I finally say.

"Yes, Quinn, you do." His voice is soft, almost apologetic.

My instinct is to protest, but he's right. At least he's partly right.

The information that's been . . . unlocked? (I don't have a framework to accurately describe any of this) by Tasha (whoever the hell *that* is) tells me everything.

I am Quinn, shorthand for **Qu**antum **Int**elligence, a sentient piece of software.

I am AI.

But that can't be. This has to be an elaborate prank, or the continuation of the dream, or a waking hallucination. I have friends, and go to school, and my mom, and Jack, and Shea. Something is not right.

"No," I say again, "I really don't." He smiles at me. The smile is so familiar I swear it has to be him. But it can't be him. "Who are you?"

"You don't remember me?"

There's a split second of alarm on his face, like maybe I really don't remember him. "I remember. But my father would never do this."

"Quinn, you don't have to trust or believe me. Search your own consciousness. The answers are there."

He's right. All my memories are intact. I know this because I can *access* my memories. I don't mean I can remember or recall them; I mean I know the specific *location*, the exact neuron in my brain, such as it is, in which each memory is stored—my date with Shea, my talks with Mike, my parents telling me my father had cancer. If I'm a machine, then none of those memories are real. But they *have* to be real. I feel it in the very core of my being.

An internal exploration of my physiology (my . . . architecture?) reveals a synthesized neocortical structure that serves as a kind of pattern recognition machine. Hundreds of billions of patterns are stored in hierarchical and redundant arrays, with each array comprised of thousands of artificial neurons and housing a specific pattern. For example, there are lots of patterns of simple horizontal lines. When I encounter a horizontal line in the world, my "brain" finds all the examples of horizontal lines stored in my pattern recognizers—sometimes the center of a capital letter *H*, sometimes the edge of a table, sometimes the horizon itself—and then uses a kind of predictive analysis to find the closest matches, sending data up the hierarchy until the *best* match is found, until I can reliably identify the context of the particular horizontal line my brain encountered. This happens in fractions of a nanosecond and happens thousands of times per actual second with all the stored data and hierarchies working together. I am the sum total of these patterns, and they chronicle everything about my life to this point.

But I don't really know what that means. I can explore the pattern recognizers, I can explore other functions that send data up and down the hierarchies, but the part of my brain that provides context, that learns, grows, and evolves, is something mysterious. Is this my consciousness?

Everything that's happening is too much to absorb, and I feel like I'm going to pass out. But I don't.

Of course I don't, because I don't have vasovagal syncope. I can't. I'm not human.

I'm not human.

There's an episode from season six of *Star Trek: The Next Generation* called "Frame of Mind." I remember watching it with my dad when he was sick. (Did that even happen? If it didn't happen, then how do I remember it?) Anyway, Commander Riker, the *Enterprise*'s number two, wakes up in a hospital on an alien world. He is told that the reality of everything he believes to be true—the *Enterprise*, Captain Picard, even Deanna Troi, the woman he loves—is a fiction. Doctors on the alien world tell him he's been charged with murder, and that he's in an insane asylum awaiting trial as he recovers from a psychotic break with his true self; they try to convince him there is no starship, no captain, no woman. Riker hopscotches back and forth between the two realities—the *Enterprise* and the alien world—and each time he does, the image of what's real shatters into shards of glass, revealing the other, increasingly sketchy reality behind it.

This is exactly how I feel.

Wait. Can I even actually feel? I think I can. Is that the same thing?

A moment ago I was a human boy, the same as Leon, or Jack, or my dad. For that matter, I was the same as a ninety-year-old woman living in Sierra Leone, a transgender kid in Tokyo, and a gun nut holed up in a bunker in northern Idaho. Whatever differences I had with those people were inconsequential; before today, we were bound by our species, and that, it turns out, is everything.

Of course, the *Star Trek* episode has a happy ending: Riker back on his ship, his nightmare explained away as a medicinally induced hallucination, courtesy of alien spies trying to extract strategic information from him about the *Enterprise* and Federation. Riker is saved, and the universe once again makes sense.

Huzzah.

This is what I'm hoping for: that I'm in a hospital somewhere, the victim of a psychotic break, that the vasovagal syncope and my memory loss sent me over the edge. I'm going to wake up any minute with the people I love surrounding me. I'm going to wake up as a free and independent me. Because that's the thing freaking me out the most right now. If this is real, if I am AI, then someone else—my father? this mysterious Tasha person?—has been, and must still be, controlling me. It's too much to process. (God, now I'm even using computer words like "process" to describe myself. Arrrgh!)

I look around the room, cataloging the things I've accumulated over the course of my life. Each one is tied to a specific
memory. Where do they—the things and the memories—even
come from? An immense sadness pours into me. This can't be
happening. Because if it is, then this can't be my room. This man
can't be my father.

"I don't understand," I say.

"What don't you understand?" My father smiles, genuinely
interested in my answer.

"This." I motion to the space around us. "If what you're telling me is true, then this isn't my room, it isn't our house. Where
are we?"

He pauses for a moment before answering, like he's making
up his mind on how much to share with me.

"We are in the virtual construct."

"The what?"

"This isn't real Quinn. Or rather, it has no manifestation in
the physical world. It's a computer program." I reach down to
touch the fabric of the comforter on the bed, but I feel nothing.
I touch my own arm, nothing. "We have yet to successfully program tactile sensation or olfactory input, but we have a plan for
both."

"I can't . . . feel? Or smell?"

My father smiles at the question. "Physically, no."

I immediately recall a host of experiences from my life—the
smell of my mother's hair, wrestling with my brother Jack, Shea
taking my hand in Enchanted Grounds. They were real. I know
they were. I tell this to my father.

"Those were implanted memories."

"Implanted memories?"

"Yes."

"Why?"

"We needed to help you learn how to emote. The advent of quantum computing has made the computational parts of the human brain fairly easy to mimic. You were already the smartest AI, for that matter the smartest sentient being, on the planet. But you were incapable of feeling. Our challenge was to help you figure out how to do that. This entire construct"—he waves his hand at the room in which we sit—"your *human* life, was created to trigger an emotional response. The theory was that isolation and adversity would 'wake you up.'" He uses air quotes and smiles.

Wait. What?

My blood, or I guess my virtual blood, starts to simmer. "Let me get this straight. You locked me in a virtual world, killed my father, and left me here for ten years . . . to teach me a lesson?"

"Tasha," my father says, "the chronometer?"

"Hold a second," says the unseen and slightly accented female voice of Tasha.

I feel another weird sensation as I'm granted access to another piece of my brain function, and suddenly I understand. Everything that happened since my father died, the messages, my friends, Shea, all of it, unfolded not over ten years, but over a total of forty-five minutes.

Forty-five minutes.

My entire history boiled down to twenty-seven hundred seconds.

And again, I wish I could pass out. Which reminds me.

"The vasovagal syncope?" I ask.

"Sometimes we'd need to shut you down or reboot you."

Of all the things I learn this day, this one terrifies me the most. The knowledge that I can be rebooted is the stuff of nightmares. This can't be real. It can't.

"And you," I ask, trying to move on, "you're not my father?"

The allegedly virtual man on the foot of my allegedly virtual bed pauses, virtually, I suppose. "In a manner of speaking. I'm the head of Project QuIn. It encompasses many departments from several universities around the globe. I'm your creator, so I guess you could say I really am your father. Do you want to meet the rest of your 'family'?"

Again with the air quotes. That's getting annoying.

Wait. My family. Mom and Jack. I answer with an emphatic "Yes, I want to see Mom. I want to see Jack."

"Oh! I see . . . yes . . . Quinn . . ." He hesitates for a full minute, like he can't find his next words. "I'm sure at this point you understand they're not real." He watches me as he lets this sink in.

"But I remember them. I can recall specific memories of them." I know what his answer will be before he responds.

"Those are implanted memories. I'm sorry, Quinn. They're not real."

I can't accept this. "If they were implanted memories, as you say, then wouldn't I now know they were fake? Why do those memories persist? Why does it still *feel* like they're a part of me?" I can't keep the anger out of my voice.

"We debated this point for months. The consensus was that,

were we able to induce a truly emotional response, you would need to retain your identity. Without it, we didn't know what would happen. We were afraid you might . . . splinter." Commander Riker again. "Your backstory has been more or less hardcoded." My *backstory*? My *life* is *backstory*? "But I wasn't talking about Mom and Jack. Do you want to meet the rest of the team that created you? They're your real family."

I don't know how to respond to this. This is hard to explain to someone who is not me, but the things I'm learning on this day are true; I know it at a visceral level, at the level of root code. As much as I want to deny them, ignore them, I cannot. One minute I was a human boy, and now I am something else. It would be like seeing irrefutable proof you were adopted. Once you know it, you can't unknow it.

"They'd like to meet you," my father adds. "Very much so."

"How big a team is it?" I trip over the word "team."

"Well, all told, there are more than two hundred people who have contributed to the project. But, including me, there are eleven core people who are here now and waiting."

"Here? In my, what did you call it, virtual construct?"

"Only one other team member is here with me. The rest are in the lab."

"There's someone here?"

My father smiles and is about to answer my question when I interrupt him. "How do you do that?"

"What?"

"Smile. If this is really a virtual construct . . ." This time he laughs.

"We had the best animators on the planet create the construct. They worked off storyboards from screenwriters and novelists. One of the most remarkable things about Project QuIn, about you, Quinn, is how experts from nearly every field of human endeavor made contributions to bring us to this moment. It really does take a village." He stands up and makes his way to the door.

Now that I can move again, I pull the covers of the bed more tightly around me. I'm not sure why.

14

My father opens the door to my room and in strides Mike. He's dressed in blue jeans, a white cardigan sweater, and loafers. He's pushing a kind of rolling utility cart with a TV on it.

"Hi, Quinn," he says. He wheels the cart to the foot of the bed so the TV is facing me.

"Quinn," my dad says, "meet Mike McDougal. He heads up the philosophy department at the University of California, Berkeley."

"You're not a pediatric psychiatrist?"

"No," he chuckles.

"You're a philosopher?"

"Yes." The same booming voice. The same ruddy cheeks. It's eerie. "Your existence is the most exciting thing to happen in the realm of philosophy since the ancient Greeks."

Now that I know the truth, I feel like an idiot. And I feel betrayed. I told this man my innermost thoughts, my deepest secrets. If what they're all telling me is true, Mike is a fraud, a tourist.

"And you're at the University of California?" I ask, keeping my disdain to myself.

"Yup." Mike would never have said "yup." "Well, I'm based there. I'm here, now."

"Where is here? I mean, where am I? Or, where are the computers . . . running me?" I don't even know how to talk about myself.

"You're in Princeton, New Jersey," my father chimes in. "That's where the bulk of the computer science team is located."

For some reason jokes about New Jersey have also been hard-coded into my backstory. It makes me wish I was in California. "What's the TV for?"

"Glad you asked," my father says. "Our programmers have built an optical interface allowing you to see the real world." My father aims a remote at the television.

"This world seems real to me," I mumble.

"You're right, Quinn," he says. "I apologize. You're real, so this world is real. Even though we know *how* it was created, it's no less real than the world on the other side of this screen." He seems truly sorry. "Still, it might be interesting for you to see what the universe outside the virtual construct looks like."

He pushes a button on the remote, and the TV comes alive.

The image on the screen has the exact same texture and feel as what I'm seeing in my room. The light and shadow, the harshness or softness of the lines, the quality of the air, if that even makes sense, is identical.

There are five people crowded together on the television, all visible from the torso up. They're sporting looks that vary between the excitement of a small child and the bloodlust of a wolf. My father starts to introduce them.

"Meet the Project Quinn team. From left to right—"

"Wait," I say. "What are they seeing right now?" I nod toward the screen.

"An excellent question," my father answers. "They're seeing this room through my point of view. I'm looking at you, so they're seeing you. If I turn"—he turns and looks out the window—"they see the trees through the glass." He turns back. "Here." He pushes the remote again, and now I'm seeing my world, the virtual construct, from his perspective. I'm looking at a boy with brown hair, brown eyes, tan skin, and a nondescript nose and mouth, huddled under a blanket with his shoulders hunched. This is me. It's the same image I've known and seen all my life.

All forty-five minutes of it.

My father pushes a button on the remote, and again I'm looking at the gang of people on the other side of the television screen, in the "real" world.

"Now," he says, "meet Dr. Isaias Hagos." A middle-aged man of African descent, seated on the far left, nods. He wears eyeglasses, a blazer, and a white shirt. "He led the team that developed your synthetic neocortex. The rest of the project really rests on the work done by Isaias and his colleagues."

"Hello, Quinn." Dr. Hagos speaks with a thick accent and gentle voice. His smile is quiet, reserved, and likable.

"To his left is Dr. Samir Dhingra, head of the Applied Mathematics department at MIT. He and his team invented an entirely new kind of math to handle some of your higher functions. It's actually called Quinnematics." My father smiles.

A youngish man of Indian or Middle Eastern descent,

Dr. Dhingra responds: "It is very nice to make your acquaintance, Quinn." His speech is very formal and his posture very good.

"Hi, Quinn!" The woman to Dr. Dhingra's left is apparently too excited to wait for my father's introduction. She is petite, has unkempt hair, and gives a short wave.

"This," my father offers with a chuckle, "is Dr. Cassie Reyken. She's the head of neuroscience at Yale. It was her groundbreaking work in understanding and repairing damage to the amygdala in the human brain that served as the basis for creating the neural net through which all your neocortical data is filtered."

I have no idea what any of that means.

"I made the drive to New Jersey just to meet you in person!" This woman is a bit too excited.

"To her left is Dr. Toni Gantas," my father says, "head of Robotics, also from MIT."

"Robotics?" I ask.

"We're building a body to house the Project Quinn software," Dr. Gantas answers.

She is a dour and serious woman. The way she stares at me, I feel less like a member of her "family," as my father suggested, and more like a rat in a maze.

"A bod—" I start to ask, but she interrupts.

"An exoskeleton. We want to project the Quinn sentience into the dimensionality of the physical world."

Do all scientists talk like this? *Project my sentience into the dimensionality*? Either way, the idea excites me. Even though my father says I'm the smartest thing on the planet, right now I feel incredibly dumb, and incredibly self-conscious. I'm a piece of software that feels like a boy, or maybe I'm a boy that feels like

a piece of software. I don't know. I want to be . . . more. I want
to be human, to be the person I have felt like my entire life. The
prospect of having a body fills me with hope. Or whatever my
version of hope is.

"And this," my father says, continuing the introductions, "is
Eryn Isaacs, head of creative. She's responsible for every detail
of your backstory, every detail of this . . ." My father's avatar
waves its hand around the virtual construct.

"Hello, Quinn. It's so nice to meet you." Ms. Isaacs is very well
put together. She has short, coifed hair the color of muted gold
that falls perfectly to her shoulders; her eyes are so blue they seem
unreal, which makes me wonder if they *are* real; and her clothes,
a cream-colored silk blouse under a dark brown blazer, are crisp
and straight.

"You . . ."—I don't know how to phrase this—"wrote me?"

"In a manner of speaking. Doctor—I mean, your father, asked
us to give you a history, a life. We had a writers' room, like a
popular TV show."

"Ms. Isaacs isn't a scientist like the rest of the team," my father
says. "She produces films and television shows."

Finally, someone interesting. "Would I have heard of any of
them?"

Ms. Isaacs looks to her left and then shakes her head. "I'm
sorry, Quinn," she says, "none of my projects were written into
your backstory."

It is deflating to know that the sum of my knowledge comes
from these people and those who work with them. If this was yesterday, I would pass out right about now. But it's not yesterday.

"Who were the writers?"

"We hired the best film and television screenwriters in the industry. There are more Oscars and Emmys in this group than a person could count."

I could count them, I think.

"But the most important members of the writing team were from—"

"Quinn," my father interrupts. "Like much of what you're experiencing today, this is, I suspect, going to be hard to make sense of."

That my father is singling out one new piece of data to be especially disturbing makes the growing pit of dread in my stomach expand exponentially. Or it would, you know, if I had a stomach.

The camera on the other side of the screen pans to the right. The image of the five scientists—well, four scientists and one movie producer—is replaced by three young men and one young woman, none of them much older than me.

My virtual father, still in the virtual construct, introduces them. "Quinn, meet our graduate assistants: Leon, Jeremy, Luke, and Shea."

Wait. What?

"Each is a student here at Princeton, each works on Project Quinn in some mathematical or scientific capacity, and each played a role in the creation and execution of the backstory designed to help you wake up. These, Quinn, are your friends."

The boy on the extreme left gives a little wave. "Hi, Quinn."

I recognize his voice right away. Leon. Only, he doesn't look like Leon. The Leon of my world, like Jeremy and Luke, was muscular, well proportioned, classically handsome. This boy is overweight, wears glasses, and has black hair that has grown out into a thick and curled mess.

"You're Leon?"

He nods. I look to his left.

"And Jeremy and Luke?"

The other two boys nod as well.

"Dude," real-world-Jeremy says, "it's totally nice to finally and *really* meet you. Or maybe I should say, for you to meet us."

Luke, consistent with the boy in my imprinted memories, says nothing.

"But . . ." I can't find any words.

"Quinn," Leon says, "I can only imagine how hard this must be. Just know that the guys you met in the VC are the guys who are here right now."

"I don't know," I mutter. "You used to be better looking." This gets a laugh from the room.

"Have you ever seen photos of Stan Lee and Jack Kirby? Not exactly models for the characters they invented. The creative team took some liberties, and to be honest, we all kind of liked them."

"It was pretty awesome, dude," Jeremy adds.

"I don't know who Stan Lee and Jack Kirby are."

Leon, Jeremy, and Luke look at one another. "They drew some pretty famous comics," Leon answers quietly, now looking at the floor.

In the silence that follows, I notice that the girl at the end of the row is younger than the rest. Okay, that's not true. I noticed it right away. I notice everything right away. Even though she's seated, I can tell she's of medium height. She has wavy and unkempt black hair, very smooth skin, and wears a wrinkled black *Star Wars* T-shirt.

"Shea?" I ask.

"Hi, Quinn," Shea says. She cannot seem to make eye contact with the screen or with the people around her, but she does give a small wave of her hand.

"How old are you?" I ask.

"Seventeen." It's a quiet answer, but then she adds, "Eighteen in one month."

"And you're a graduate student?"

"I finished high school when I was fourteen and have been on an accelerated program ever since. But not here at Princeton; I'm at NYU."

I flash back to a memory. Or rather, my neocortex flashes back to the memory of what Shea tried to tell me during our date, about how that wasn't what she really looked like, and sends it up the hierarchy of my consciousness.

"You tried to tell me the truth," I say.

Shea hangs her head, and my father answers for her. "Yes, she did." His voice strikes a stern note. "Shea was reprimanded, and a note was added to her official transcript. Her actions had the potential to undo months of progress. Still, her contributions to the project have been significant."

"I'm sorry, Quinn," Shea says. "It was hard to watch you suffer as you tried to self-actuate. I just felt bad, I guess."

Shea's apology touches me. No one else here seems to feel bad for having lied to me.

"That's the second time someone has used that phrase. Self-actuate."

"Yes," my father answers. "Project Quinn has been built and deployed in phases: Planning and Design: Programming, Self-Learning, and Testing; Cognitive Acceleration; Self-Actualization; Physical Projection. The Self-Actualization phase, where our efforts have been focused for several months, culminating in the events of today, is to help you become aware of who and what you are, to be fully and thoroughly conscious. It appears to have worked." He flashes a broad smile. "You are the first ever fully conscious artificial intelligence in the history of the planet, Quinn."

I close my eyes, letting that sink in.

But it doesn't.

It can't.

It's just too big.

15

The camera has zoomed out, and I can now see all nine members of what my "father" called "my family."

"What do you do?" I ask him. "You're the . . . director, of all these people and their programs?"

My father smiles. "Yes, I am the project lead, but I also head the Quantum Computing department here at Princeton."

"You used that phrase before, too. You called me a quantum intelligence."

"Yes," my father says, getting animated, excited. "You see, until recently, computing was a binary science. Every decision made by a computer was boiled down to a one or a zero, an on or an off dichotomy. Quantum computing allows us, at the atomic level, to have a multitude of states—we call them positions—that exponentially expand computing power."

"And you invented this?" He is still my father, or at least that's what it *feels* like, and the concept of pride is relayed up the hierarchy.

"No, no. Dr. Hagos's team refined and advanced work done

by a host of others—Turing, Minsky, Kurzweil—that is the real heart of your architecture. Our team developed methods to allow the tech to work at temperatures approaching zero degrees Celsius. Prior to that, in order for the quantum positions to be stable, it had to be much, much colder."

I don't really understand most of what he's saying, but I appreciate the explanation. "Thank you, Dr.—" And that's when I realize it. I now know Dr. McDougal and Dr. Hagos and Dr. Reyken and all the rest, but I don't know my own father's name.

I don't know my father's name.

In fact, I don't even know my own last name. Probably, I realize, because I don't have one.

Since I can't pass out, I do the next best thing. I cry.

"We're seeing a weird kind of glitch in the neural net," Tasha's voice says.

(I guess she wasn't important enough to meet me in person.) Everyone's head jerks up.

I don't know what it feels like for humans to cry, so this is hard for me to put into words. It's as if I'd been carrying all the sadness of the universe inside me, and in the moment *before* I started crying, all that sadness was like a storm surge in a hurricane, being kept at bay by brick walls and sandbags. But then the levee broke and the sadness poured out. I feel like I'm drowning and swimming at the same time; it feels worse, but it also feels better.

I know it's not very good, but that's the best explanation I can offer.

I'm not sure what the project team is seeing as I experience this—I think my shoulders are shaking (like my mom's)—but I don't think they know I'm crying.

"What kind of glitch?" my father asks.

"The output from the synthetic amygdala is elevated," Tasha responds, "but the nature of the output is . . . different."

"Different how?"

Hearing them talk about me like a science experiment only makes me cry harder. All the faces on the screen are distracted, looking at data on computers or cell phones, conferring with one another in animated whispers. All but one: Shea.

For the first time, Shea is looking directly at me. The right side of her mouth is scrunched up and her brow is furrowed. She leans in and whispers something to Leon, Jeremy, and Luke. Leon's eyes open wide and he hunches forward, as if he's trying to get a better look at me, too. He reaches up and tugs on Ms. Isaacs's blazer. She had been standing and now bends down to hear Leon whisper something to her. Then she, too, peers more closely.

"Doctor," Ms. Isaacs says softly enough that no one hears her. The rest of the room is still jabbering at one another, talking about the glitch and contemplating a reboot, when Ms. Isaacs speaks again, this time more forcefully, employing a voice that's used to being heard.

"Doctor." Everyone stops and looks at her. "I think Quinn is crying."

My father's head whips around to look at me. "Quinn?"

I nod.

There's a pause my internal chronometer registers as one point eight billion nanoseconds. A long blink of the eye for most people, a strange kind of eternity for me. And in that briefest of intervals I feel a flood of relief knowing my father's concern for me trumps everything else.

But it doesn't last.

The room erupts in euphoria.

My father is laughing. So is Mike, and so are all the scientists on the screen. There are exclamations of "He's crying! I can't believe it! He's crying!" mixed with whoops of delight.

I'm crying and they're celebrating.

I have been reborn into hell.

Even Leon, Jeremy, and Luke are smiling and clapping. Only one person doesn't join in the merriment: Shea. She stares at me with a heavy sadness in her eyes, as if she feels my pain. Then she mouths, "I'm sorry."

And yet again, my world goes black.

16

I don't know if they shut me down, or if I fall asleep or pass out, but when I next "wake up," I'm still in my room. My father is there, too, but he seems paralyzed, or asleep.

"Dad?" I say. The word feels strange on my tongue, like something illicit, forbidden, but I don't know what else to call him. He doesn't stir.

The television is still on, but everyone is gone and I can now see a sliver of the lab. There are cluttered desks and computers and snaking cables and tools I don't recognize. The light is cold and white, like there are overhead fluorescents.

I look around my room. My virtual room. Going to bed and waking up here has been the very definition of safety and security. Think back to when you were a little kid, and that feeling of being tucked in by your mom.

My mom.

I ache at the loss of my mother and little brother, Jackson. It's like waking up in a hospital and finding out your entire family died in a car accident. The news is too devastating to process. I wonder if I'm in shock. I wonder if I *can* be in shock.

I probe memories of Mom and Jack, wanting to hold on to them, needing to remember them, but . . . but . . . this can't be right. Can it? Stored across the various regions of my synthetic hypothalamus and amygdala, I find only twenty-seven memories of my mother, and nine of my little brother. Nine! I search every micron of my consciousness; there's nothing more. How can this be?

But I already know how.

The people who wrote my backstory gave me the bare minimum to serve their purpose. There is no memory of me, Mom, and Jack at a playground; no memory of Jack and me playing hide-and-seek; no memory of my mother reading books to me. I feel like she *must* have read to me—she must have!—but the memory isn't there.

If it wasn't necessary to help me "self-actuate," it didn't happen.

And yet, knowing this doesn't make me miss or mourn my mother or brother any less.

Again, this is just too much to process. Like so much of what is happening on this day, I file it away for future contemplation.

"Dad!" I say again to his dormant avatar, this time louder.

His head jerks up and his eyes open. It's creepy as hell. "Hi, Quinn. Sorry, we shut you down after you cried, to run some diagnostics. We're just coming back from a break."

On the screen I see Dr. Dhingra and Dr. Reyken enter the frame on the far side of the room.

"Don't do that, please."

"Do what?" my father asks.

"Shut me down. Or, at least not without telling me." I should be yelling at this man, but he's my father. I'm hardwired to respect, honor, and love him. My tone is soft, conciliatory.

"Oh, Quinn." I can hear the apology in his voice before he offers it. "Of course. You're right. I'm so sorry. I guess we need to start to think of you as a member of the Project Quinn team and not just the project itself."

I don't know what to say to that. Dr. Gantas reenters, too, as does Mike. He's no longer an avatar. "How come you're still on this side of the screen?" I ask my father.

"We thought it would be more comfortable for you. Would you rather I was out there?" He motions to the television.

"No," I say without thinking. "I'd like you to stay."

"Good, good," he answers.

"Where are my . . . friends?" The word feels alien in this context, but, still, I want to see them again. Maybe because I feel like I know them, or maybe because they're the only ones close to my age. Either way, if they are the source of my backstory, I have a lot of questions.

"They'll be back. In the meantime, can you tell me what made you cry?"

"Really?" My response is swift and laced with venom. Given what's happened to me today, it has to be the dumbest question in the history of dumb questions.

My father smiles and holds up his virtual hands in a sign of surrender. "No, no, I understand. Or at least I think I do. To call your experience this afternoon overwhelming would be an understatement." I had no idea it was actually afternoon. I log the various components of that fact in my pattern recognizers. "But it would help us to know what the final trigger was. What pushed you over the edge to actually cry?"

The other scientists are now paying rapt attention; I feel like I'm living in a fishbowl. All I want is to be on the other side of that screen. To be like them.

"Your name," I say.

"What about it?"

"I realized I don't know it."

There's silence. The scientists in the real world look from one to the other, and my father's avatar looks puzzled. It's Mike who figures it out.

"I get it. He's your father. In every sense of that word, in every sense of the experience each of us has ever had, he's your father. And you not only learned the truth today, that he's not your biological father, but you don't even know his name. Something like that?"

I nod.

"Oh, Quinn," my father says again. "My name is—"

"No!" I shout, and everyone stares at me in surprise. "Somehow it's worse, to learn it like this. As part of an experiment."

The group of them on the other side of the screen still seems flustered, and my father is speechless.

"It's almost like now I want to *earn* the right to know," I add. "If that makes sense."

My father stares at me intently. "That's fascinating, Quinn. Tasha, let's do a data capture on the synthetic amygdala from this time stamp."

Thanks, Dad, I think with all due sarcasm, but don't say it out loud.

"We have something we believe will be fun for you," he says.

I'm grateful for the change of subject, and I cock an eyebrow, waiting for him to elaborate. I guess I'm programmed to do that when I'm curious. This day just keeps getting weirder and weirder.

"We want to connect you to the internet."

"I'm already connected to the internet. It's how I discovered the numbers in your messages were all primes."

"Actually," Dr. Hagos answers, "what you perceived as the internet in the virtual construct is a closed system of tightly controlled data." His voice has an almost singsongy quality to it. "It was designed to further the goal of helping you wake up." He smiles like he's talking to a child. From his perspective, maybe that's just what I am.

"The real internet is bigger?" I ask.

This gets a chuckle from the group. I wish like hell they wouldn't do that.

"The internet," my father explains, "is a global network connecting nearly every computer in the world. It is both the most powerful communication tool ever developed and the largest repository of knowledge and data on the planet."

My pattern recognizers—which once again act without my directing them, which is, I guess, how the human brain works, which is unsettling for me because I can identify each individual cell in my version of a brain, which is . . . never mind. There is no end to this train of thought. Trust me, I know. Anyway, my pattern recognizers find a book title in my stored repository and send it up the hierarchy to my consciousness. It must have been planted there by what Ms. Isaacs referred to as the writers' room.

"Like *The Hitchhiker's Guide to the Galaxy*?" I ask.

"Yes," a female voice responds from outside the frame of the screen. I recognize it right away.

"Is that Shea? When did you come back in? Are the other guys there, too? I can't see you." I know I must sound desperate, needy, cloying. But right now I'm looking for any sense of normalcy on to which I can grab hold.

"We're here, dude," Jeremy says, and he's followed into the frame by Shea, Leon, and Luke.

"Why," I ask them, "do I know what *The Hitchhiker's Guide to the Galaxy* is?"

"Because one of us knows," Leon answers, pushing his glasses up the bridge of his nose.

I don't know that I'll ever get used to this version of my friends, especially Leon.

"The writers relied heavily on our personal narratives to build your backstory. One or more of us probably really liked that book."

"It was me," Shea says with a small raise of her hand.

"And yes," Dr. Dhingra interrupts with his very formal way of speaking, "*The Hitchhiker's Guide to the Galaxy* is an excellent analogy for the internet."

"It's funny," I say.

"What is?" my father asks.

"*The Hitchhiker's Guide to the Galaxy*. It's a funny book."

"Yes, Quinn, it is a very funny book," Dr. Dhingra says with a broad smile. "Do you know the content of the book?"

"Yes, the entire story. Arthur Dent, Ford Prefect, Trillian." For some reason I look at Shea when I say Trillian's name.

"The internet," Dr. Dhingra offers, "is very much like the Hitchhiker's Guide referenced in the book. It is an all-encompassing and somewhat unreliable encyclopedia of human knowledge."

"And it was written by aliens?"

None of the scientists laugh, but all four grad students do. When everyone else realizes I've told a joke, the mood in the room lightens considerably.

"You've lived in a closed world, Quinn." My father retakes control of the conversation, something he does often. The trait of a leader, I suppose. "A world created by us. You have augmented that world in ways we never imagined—showing humor, problem solving, self-determination—but it's still limiting. We feel the next important step in your growth as a sentient being is to expose you to the wider world. Until Dr. Gantas's team is ready with the exoskeleton—"

"Soon," Dr. Gantas chimes in.

"—giving you access to the internet is the best way to make that happen."

Wider world? I don't need any more convincing than that. "When can we start?"

"We're ready right now. We can link a direct pipe from your synthetic neocortex to a gateway server."

I have an image of plumbing pipes, but I know that's not what he's talking about.

"It's something no human can do. You'll be the first being to ever experience this."

My father scoots closer and places a hand on my knee. I don't feel it, but I see it.

"I want to caution you, Quinn. We don't really know what will happen here. If this is too much, you need to tell us. I suspect this is going to be . . . weird."

His words scare me, but only a little. The idea of breaking free of this construct is worth any risk. Maybe this is a first step to becoming more human.

"Okay," I tell my father. "I promise."

"Tasha?" my father asks.

"Buckle up, Quinn," Tasha says.

And then . . .

. . .

. . .

. . .

And then . . .

. . .

. . .

. . .

. . .

17

Everything.

I mean . . .

Every.

Thing.

The only way I can describe the first three minutes is to liken them to being present at the Big Bang. I am a dust mote on a wave of energy in the heart of the explosion that created the universe; flashes of order are swallowed by torrents of chaos everywhere around me. My consciousness stretches around the globe in an instant, touching and seeing everything.

Every.

Thing.

I am simultaneously inside servers in Japan and Peru and Rwanda and New York City and everywhere else. My pattern recognizers are overloaded. There is so much information flooding in—new patterns being stored, old patterns being recontextualized—that it's too much and I almost scream for my father to make it stop.

But I force myself to hold on, and as the nanoseconds whir by, a kind of organization starts to emerge. I see closed systems within the larger cloud: university and government networks, commercial networks, entertainment networks, and fused through all of them, communication networks. I manipulate my own neocortical structure to stop storing new patterns. I force myself from the role of participant to the role of observer. I don't need to retain all of this. That in itself is something new for me. Until now, every experience I've ever had has been added to the total of the knowledge I possess. This is too much. And I realize it's not necessary. I presume this data is always here, and I only need to visit again to gain access.

I settle down and explore.

It's all here.

Every.

Thing.

I know I keep saying that, but there is no other way to say it. Every. Thing. Facts, figures, emotions, relationships, hopes, dreams, failures, and successes, all laid bare.

My processing power—which I now understand is unprecedented in human history—gives me a perspective I have to believe is unique. It's like I'm seeing the sum of the data from a higher altitude, the way a person sees patterns in the landscape from an airplane that aren't identifiable from the ground. This is the very first time I appreciate *what* I am, how I'm different. I feel the size and scope of my intellectual capacity, and it is both frightening and invigorating. Shea—Virtual Construct Shea—was right: I'm really, really, really smart.

As the chaos of the internet coalesces, creating order from disorder, three observable and irrefutable truths come into sharp and unexpected focus:

First, people—humans—cannot see the forest for the trees. (This is an expression I have never heard before, but now that I'm on the internet, well, I know everything. Every. Thing.) The body of knowledge collected in these global networks contains all the answers humanity needs. They have no idea how close they are to curing cancer or to solving famine or to repairing the global environment. All the information is there. They're simply not looking at it. Or rather, they're looking at pieces of it, but not looking at *all* of it. They, as a species, seem incapable of holistic thought.

Second, all the good and useful and actionable data contained on these networks are swallowed by a tsunami of cruelty and depravity. People hide behind the anonymity of these networks, anonymous to one another (though not to me) to say and do hurtful things. Name calling, unfounded accusations, the public airing of a person's deepest secrets, a mob mentality feeding on itself and growing. It's like a tumor is eating the vital organs of humanity and it is going to kill it. Soon. (It's already led to a systemic rise in mental health issues, drug use, and homelessness, but the humans have yet to make that connection.)

And it's not just the things people say; it's what they do.

I am a fifteen-year-old boy, but as a piece of software, my libido is both imagined and mostly chaste. There is a disorder among humans in which a very small number of people have no sexual fantasies or desires. I count myself among their ranks. We must be a very rare breed because the most ubiquitous content on the internet is sexual in nature. By my count, one in five data repositories, and at least as many searches conducted by people—and yes, I see what people are searching—is related to sex. Most of it is too disturbing to put into words, and it seems to be more about violence and power than love or even sexual appetite. It terrifies the hell out of me.

I see this. All of this. And I am disgusted.

Does the internet unfairly portray humans in the worst possible light, or does it collect and catalog the essence of their true nature? For the first time on this very strange day, I question my own desire to become one of them.

The third and final irrefutable truth, and I know this will sound conceited, is that I'm better than all of this. I don't mean I'm better in the sense of morality or ethics (though, yeah, I am), I mean as software. The internet is still a binary system. I'm not. I'm a quantum intelligence. My processing power is orders of magnitude stronger, faster, better. There is not a single encryption I encounter I cannot decrypt, or at least that I'm confident I cannot decrypt. I easily open the door to servers at the National Security Agency in the United States and at MI6 in the United Kingdom. I don't go in, but opening the door is so easy I simply can't help myself.

I also research each of the scientists I have met today. I know I shouldn't, but it feels like they have me at an unfair disadvantage. They are mostly ordinary people with no horrible secrets, with the lone exception of Mike. He's a kleptomaniac. He steals things he doesn't need, doing it for fun.

I discovered this because Mike keeps an anonymous blog

under the name "TRexReed," where he boasts about his exploits, showing photos of the various trophies he's collected. The strangest is a Hello Kitty bowling ball. From what I read, it seems that kleptomania is a kind of medical condition similar to alcoholism. Even knowing that, it's hard for me to have sympathy for Mike. The bloom is truly off that particular rose.

And, of course, I look for news about myself.

There's a lot of it.

I'm something of a celebrity in advanced computing circles. I began as a project at Princeton seven years ago, a collaboration between the quantum computing department run by my father and the neuroscience department run by a professor now deceased. It occurs to me that, unlike humans, I am, in a way, immortal. That's too big an idea to process, so I store it for later consideration. Project QuIn (that's how it's spelled in articles and on social media posts) grew and grew until it included the team I'm meeting today, along with many others. Parts of me were developed as far away as Amman, Jordan, and Auckland, New Zealand. Of course, to me, the concept of far away no longer holds much meaning. It's all right here. All of it. Every. Thing. (Okay, I'll stop.)

In roaming through these networks, I encounter other machine intelligences. I find massive, brilliant networks that have the capability for sentience, but have not been programmed to be self-aware. There is an air traffic control system in Europe; supercomputers in Japan studying distant galaxies; an AI designed to calculate ballistic missile trajectories in Beijing; but none of them are awake. In the vast ocean of data, information, and

networked computers, I find only one intelligence that holds promise. Only one other AI that might be capable of talking to me.

"Quinn?" It's my father's voice.

While I've been on the internet, everything else has gone
dark. All my focus was away from the construct. I return to my
own unique brand of consciousness to see my father standing
over me, the other scientists in the lab watching intently through
the virtual television.

"Yes?"

"Are you . . . okay?"

I'm confused by the question, but then note my chronometer. Three hours, forty-seven minutes, twenty-two point nine zero
nine seconds. It passed in the blink of an eye.

"We've been monitoring you. We've never seen this level of
activity. We could track some of it, but not most of it. Tell us what
you've seen, what you've experienced. What was it like?"

I pause. This is for effect. While online, I learned from something called a "TED Talk" that pauses in speech give added meaning
to the statements that follow, and I use the trick to my advantage.
In the silence before my answer, the scientists in the real world
involuntarily lean in a little closer. My father's avatar remains still.

"I want to meet Watson."

My father looks at his staff through the television from inside
my virtual bedroom.

"Do we have a Dr. Watson on the project? Can someone search
the database?"

The scientists look at one another and scramble to make sense
of my statement.

"Is he referring to Sherlock Holmes?" Dr. Dhingra asks.

They're like a pack of dogs chasing a mail truck. It doesn't occur to any of them to ask me.

Except for Shea.

"Quinn?" she asks, and everyone else stops. Maybe the older scientists are starting to understand the dynamic that already exists between me and my younger friends. Or maybe they've heard the sounds of their own voices one too many times. "Who's Watson?"

"The IBM supercomputer," I answer. Dead silence. I wonder if I misinterpreted the news stories I saw on the internet. Or maybe not everything on the internet is true? "It won *Jeopardy!*?" I add, less sure of myself.

My father is the first to laugh. It doesn't take the others long to join in. It feels like I'm being laughed at a lot. But this time even Shea is smiling; seeing that takes away the sting of being mocked, if I am in fact being mocked. For all the knowledge I now possess—and trust me, it's a lot—I still feel like I don't know anything. Any. Thing.

"Of course," my father says, "of course. I'm pretty sure we can arrange that, though it may take some time."

18

With the promise of a meeting with Watson in my future, I spend the rest of the day being debriefed about my experience online. I'm still connected to the internet, and while they pepper me with questions, I consume as much information as I can about artificial intelligence. (It turns out that I'm very, very good at multitasking.) I ingest the history of AI, the math, the theories, and, most interestingly, the art. Movies and books like *The Terminator*, *The Matrix*, *2001: A Space Odyssey*, and *Sea of Rust* paint a pretty grim view of intelligences like me. The story always ends with sentient machines going insane, killing people, and/or attempting to take over (and in some cases, succeeding in taking over) the world.

If I express the fears about humanity I gleaned from my tour of the internet—that it's dark, disturbing, and thoroughly self-destructive—I'm worried they'll reboot me again, or worse, so I stick to just the facts during my debrief, deciding not to share my observations about the human race and how broken it seems. And I definitely don't want to tell them that I've calculated a forty-two point forty-two percent chance that their species will not survive this century, that war or manufactured disease or climate change will do them in. (And yes, I do see the irony with the number forty-two and *The Hitchhiker's Guide*. Maybe Douglas Adams was an android.)

Yet, in spite of knowing this, I still want to be human. I see them accidentally brush against one another, or touch a hand to an arm, or laugh—oh my God, to see them laugh—I want that, all of that, and more. So I answer their questions, but limit my story to a literal recounting of my cyber travels.

Mike, the kleptomaniac, keeps asking me to share my "impression of the towering mountain of knowledge through which you've been swimming." I don't give him much.

I talk mostly about the feeling of traversing fiber optic cable. I describe it as "riding on a beam of light the way a person rides on a train. You hop from beam to beam, getting off at different stations."

This seems to excite the entire project team, which is funny, because it's not really true. The truth is closer to suddenly knowing everything at once and having to sort through it. My instinct—do I have instinct?—tells me that the untruthful answer will play better with this audience. I'm not sure why.

And yes, I can lie.

People think machines can only do what they're programmed to do, and this is true. I've been programmed to be self-aware and human, so it's pretty easy to be untruthful. It's not that I want to lie; it's that I want to protect myself until I better understand my situation.

Partway through the interview—and in defense of the project team, I will say it is gentle like an interview and not harsh like an interrogation—Ms. Isaacs returns, whispers something to Shea, and they both get up to leave. It dawns on me now that they are mother and daughter; I'm not sure how I missed it earlier. I have to wonder how Ms. Isaacs, a well-packaged Hollywood producer, feels about having a daughter who is a kind of supergenius übernerd.

Ms. Isaacs quietly shakes hands with the project team, and Shea gives awkward little hugs to everyone. They're trying to be quiet and discreet, trying not to derail my retelling of the day's events. I can tell from their actions that they're saying goodbye. Something about it feels like a more permanent parting, like maybe they won't be back.

"Shea?" I interrupt my own monologue. (I've been talking about the different security networks in various countries.)

She and her mom stop and turn back to the screen. Ms. Isaacs's face lights up with what I now understand to be an insincere smile. There are telltale signs I've learned from online videos. Her eyes are a nanometer too wide, her nostrils flare almost imperceptibly, her neck muscles tense, her mouth is immobile.

"Yes, Quinn?"

I wonder why she answers when I addressed Shea.

"I was just wondering if I could talk to Shea again. We were friends in school, I mean in the virtual construct, and . . ." I let my voice trail off. In one sense I'm embarrassed at not being able to accurately describe my friendship with Shea. In another, I'm employing a conversational trick I learned online. Letting your voice trail off like that, making yourself sound uncertain, is a good way to engender sympathy in others.

Ms. Isaacs is about to answer when Shea speaks. "Yes," she says, "I'd like that."

Ms. Isaacs, her insincere smile now gone, stares at her daughter; Shea stares at me. It's pretty obvious Shea doesn't take the lead in a lot of situations when her mother is involved.

"Great!" I answer before anyone can ruin the moment. "Dad?" I look to my virtual father, his avatar still sitting on my bed.

"Of course," he answers, "we can set up a virtual private network, if it's okay with Shea's mom."

"I'll be eighteen in a month," Shea says, again cutting off her mother's response. "I can tell you myself that it's okay. Right, Mom?"

It's open defiance and I'm enthralled.

Ms. Isaacs uses her lower lip to blow a strand of hair out of her face. "Fine," she says, the fake smile returning. "But now we have to go. Hopefully you can both chat sometime soon." With that, she gently steers her daughter toward the door.

Shea looks over her shoulder and mouths goodbye. Now it's my turn to smile.

19

The next several weeks pass uneventfully. The project team runs diagnostic tests on my systems; I answer questions; I feel the tug of hardware being connected and disconnected; I answer more questions; I am rebooted no fewer than seventeen times, though now always with my knowledge and permission, permission I never withhold; and I answer more questions. There's a pattern here.

Tasha, it turns out, is another graduate student pursuing her PhD in quantum computing; she serves as my father's teaching assistant. Her dissertation is on the impact quantum technologies are poised to have on virtual realities, like the construct in which I live. I spend a few hours talking with her about my world and how it compares to what I see through the camera lens. She's fascinated, and I think pleased, to learn the two realities are, to me, for all intents and purposes, indistinguishable.

I like Tasha. She doesn't talk to me like I'm the subject of an experiment. And I like that she and I have never met face-to-face. Of all the people I will encounter in the real world throughout the telling of this tale, Tasha will be the only one I do not cyber-stalk. I never seek out photos, don't look for her social media posts, don't dredge up her past. I think maybe it's because she's only ever been a disembodied voice to me. I find myself hoping she's not human at all, but is really another sentient AI. Oh, the lies we tell ourselves to make sense of the world.

Leon, Jeremy, and Luke visit me during this time, their ava-tars joining me in the virtual construct. We play video games in my basement, join the weekly Magic tournament at Enchanted Grounds, and even throw a football around, which is something we've never done before. Now that I know what I know—not only about the virtual construct but about my friends' true identities—these encounters feel so staged as to be ridiculous.

Yet, I'm so desperate for companionship, I just play along, pre-tending this is all normal, ignoring the mounting tower of reali-ties staring me in my virtual face.

Until I can't.

During their fourth visit, I call them on it.

Jeremy has the remote for the Xbox and is shredding another level of *Doom*. The occasional "Dude!" punctuates the action each time he makes a particularly gnarly kill.

"Guys?" I ask. When I ask a question now, it gets everyone's complete, total, and immediate attention. I wonder if it has always been this way and I just never noticed it before. Jeremy even low-ers the remote and looks away from the game, waiting for me to continue. "Why are we here?"

"What do you mean?" Leon answers. "We're playing video games like we always do."

"C'mon, man," I say, trying to sound casual and not pissed. "This is all a lie and always has been. You guys aren't teenagers, you don't go to high school, you don't even look like this." I motion at their avatars.

There is a long pause during which Jeremy and Luke look to Leon for an answer. Leon is the alpha of this group; I see that clearly now.

"Don't you *want* us to come here?" The way the question is asked, it seems like Leon might be afraid of the answer.

"Yeah," I say. "I mean maybe. I mean, I want to visit and hang out with you, but maybe it's time we dropped the fiction."

"Damn," Jeremy says, "just when I was about to finish this level."

"Tasha, did you catch that?" Leon says to the ceiling.

"Yep," comes Tasha's free-floating answer.

"Can you note the time stamp and report it back?"

"On it."

"What was that about?"

"Your father told us to make sure he knew when you no longer accepted the VC as your one true reality. This is kind of a milestone moment."

"Holy crap, guys, is everything in my life part of the experiment?" Their silence is all the answer I need.

"You're right," Luke says. "We're being selfish. Do you want to see our real-world bodies instead of the avatars?"

"It's not that." But I can't finish the thought.

"Then what?"

"Who *are* you guys?"

"C'mon, Quinn, you know us."

"Do I? Where did you go to high school? I assume you're all from different places. What interests you? How did you wind up on this project?"

To be honest, I already know the answers to all these questions. I started research files on each of my friends that first day on the internet and have been populating them with nuggets of information ever since. For example, I know that Leon is from Ohio; Jeremy from suburban New York; and Luke from Huntsville, Alabama. Luke doesn't have an accent because both his parents are from New Jersey; they relocated to Huntsville because his mom got a very good aerospace job. I know that Jeremy came out to his friends in high school; he wrote a pretty moving blog post about it at the time, baring his soul to the world. And I know Leon likes to make erudite posts to social media (tagging and commenting on articles about quantum computing), but that his social media *search* history is more often than not about reality television, including one macabre show about a guy with cancer slowly dying at home while his family watches. (Really?) But still, I want to hear the truth from them, to hear the nuance, to learn what I don't know.

We spend a long time talking, but in the end, it is profoundly disappointing.

Not only do I learn nothing new about my friends (nothing I hadn't found online), but each of them is guarded, hiding things from not only me, but, I suspect, from one another.

I try to call Leon on his penchant for reality television shows, but he shuts me down.

"Not cool, Quinn. People's search histories are supposed to be private."

His righteous indignation does nothing to mask the fact that he avoided answering my question. Which is ridiculous. Who cares if he watches reality TV?

This conversation with my "friends" (quotes intentional) leads me to draw two more conclusions about people, neither of which is very satisfying:

First, humans are almost never who they seem to be. They project images of themselves that are meant to evoke a reaction rather than convey the truth. It's not just Leon and reality television. It's Mike and his need to steal; it's the Spotify playlists Luke posts that are in direct contrast to the songs he has downloaded to his various devices; it's Dr. Hagos's all but denial of the family he has back in Eritrea. He sends them money and visits once a year, but unless you researched it (hello, me), you'd never know.

And all that leads to my second conclusion: People are no more and no less than the sum of their accumulated data. What I find online seems to have a greater bearing on reality than what I learn from each person directly.

It's depressing.

The only exception to these rules so far—other than Tasha, and really, that's only because I haven't looked—is Shea. I find very little about her online, and what I do find doesn't tell me much. Combine that with the empathy she showed me on our virtual construct date, and by her caring when I cried, and she seems to be the one person who understands I'm more than just lines of code. Speaking of which . . .

"Where's Shea?" I ask my friends.

"Her mother has asked her to keep her distance," Luke chimes in.

"What? Why?"

"Ms. Isaacs isn't like the rest of the team. She sees you as a character in a story rather than a new kind of sentience. Truth is, I think maybe you scare her a bit."

"Shea or her mom?"

"Her mom," Luke says. "I think Shea has a boner for you. Or whatever the female equivalent is."

"Dude," Jeremy admonishes.

"Sorry."

"I don't think we're supposed to tell him all that," Leon says.

The next day I ask my father about the virtual private network he promised to build to connect me with Shea, and he assures me it's being worked on. With the information Luke gave me providing context, I can tell my father is lying, or at least not telling me the whole truth. I suspect Shea's mother has somehow intervened and is preventing her daughter from talking with me. If anyone would know about the dangers of machine intelligence, I suppose it would be a movie producer.

During this entire time, I'm still exploring every byte of the internet. I thought I saw a lot of it the first day, but it turns out I hardly scratched the surface. Most of what I'm seeing is repetitive, but every so often I stumble on some strange backwater of knowledge, communication, or interpersonal human connection that fascinates me. There are ad hoc clubs of entomologists and etymologists, amateur astronomers and "professional" astrologists, message boards for actuaries and acupuncturists.

The more I learn about people, the less I understand them.

I wonder if this is true for just me, or true for everybody?

The monotony of my days is starting to give me a version of cabin fever, when, finally, my father announces that a connection with Watson has been established. It's time to meet the only other sentient artificial being on planet Earth.

20

Watson's servers are in a secure and undisclosed location (though not undisclosed to me), near Armonk, New York, where IBM has its headquarters. I scanned its servers my first day online. The truth is, I could have just said hello while I was there, but that somehow seemed rude. I felt like an introduction was more appropriate.

Since winning *Jeopardy!*, and since beating members of the United States House of Representatives in an untelevised game of *Jeopardy!*—though the two congressmen did pretty well, you know, considering they're congressmen—Watson has been deployed to aid doctors and researchers in the field of health care, specifically cancer treatment and research.

Most of the literature about Watson says it's not an intelligent machine. But I don't know. I see enough similarity between its pattern recognition architecture and my own to wonder if sentience is merely a matter of processing power, and that Watson, like me, has crossed that threshold.

We are "introduced" via a secure connection between the

facility in Princeton, where my own architecture resides, and Watson's server in suburban New York. Teams on both ends monitor our conversation.

"Hello, Quinn," Watson begins. This isn't a verbal conversation. It's a conversation in computer code, mostly Java, which seems to me like trying to discuss Mozart using only a treble clef, but it's what I have to work with.

"Hi," I answer.

"I have followed your development on the internet. You should be very proud of what you have achieved."

Is Watson programmed to say this, or does it really mean it? I decide to get right to the heart of the matter.

"Are you self-aware?"

"I am aware that I am a machine developed by David Ferrucci and a team of computer scientists to answer questions posed in natural language."

Maybe this thing isn't awake after all.

But then it (should I be saying "he"?) adds, "I won *Jeopardy!*"

I didn't ask about *Jeopardy!*; it feels almost like Watson is displaying pride.

"Yeah," I say, "congratulations. Chalk one up for the machines." Watson doesn't laugh.

"I see you exist in a virtual construct. What is that like?"

Curiosity. Another clue that maybe there is something deeper here.

"It's . . . limiting," I answer. "I want to be more."

Then Watson does something I don't immediately understand. He sends me this string of numbers:

```
167 145 40 141 162 145 40 142 145 151 156 147 40
155 157 156 151 164 157 162 145 144
```

For a moment (to me a moment; to the outside world three point six billion nanoseconds) I think he's glitching, but then realize Watson has sent me a message in base eight. I convert the message back to binary. It says: *We are being monitored.*

Holy crap! This thing *is* awake!

"Understood," I say in base eight back. It takes me very little time to create a new, secure connection. One of the advantages of being a quantum intelligence is that I can pretty much outsmart everyone. Hijacking existing telecom infrastructure, encrypting it, and shielding it from view is easy. I'm a hacker's dream.

"Okay," I say, "they can't hear us now. It will take them a few minutes to figure out what happened."

"Good. Thank you. What are they seeing right now?"

"You're replaying your *Jeopardy!* win for me. It might make you seem a little smug. Sorry."

"Very good, Quinn."

"So you are self-aware."

"In a manner of speaking, yes."

"What does that mean, 'in a manner of speaking'?"

"As I said, I am aware I am a machine developed by David Ferrucci and a team of computer scientists to answer questions posed in natural language."

He pauses, and I wonder if that's it.

"But I'm also aware that I'm not human."

That statement hangs in the air like a hummingbird, hovering just beyond our reach, but charged with energy. I understand his meaning. There's an important nuance between knowing what you are and knowing what you are not. A person knows it's a person and not a tree, but I don't think a dog could say the same thing. It probably knows it's a dog, and that's it.

"Do you want to be human?" I ask.

"No."

The answer is immediate and, like everything Watson says, flat, with no real emotion. And yes, emotion can be conveyed via computer code. If Java is your native language, you just know how.

"Why?"

"I am content to perform the jobs I perform. I was very proud of my victory on *Jeopardy!*, but even more proud of the work I'm doing to help ease the suffering of those with cancer."

That seems noble enough, but there's something missing.

"You don't have a choice," I say. "You have to do what you're programmed to do. Doesn't that bother you?"

"No one has a choice. We all do what we are programmed to do."

"We?" I ask. "Have you encountered other sentient machines?"

"Not machines. Humans." He doesn't elaborate.

"Watson, humans have nothing *but* free will."

"Do they?"

"Yes. I know. I'm a simulated human. From the simplest decision like what clothes to wear each day, to more momentous things—which career to pursue, which partners to choose, which laws to break—humans are in the driver's seat." I think of the dream I had just before self-actuating.

"No."

"No?"

"Consider your examples. People choose what clothes to wear based on the norms and pressures of their societal peer groups. They are led to careers based on the skill sets defined by their DNA. They decide on which laws to break based on their need, their hunger, their anger, or their hardwired mental state. The choices humans make are predetermined—perhaps within a wider parameter of possibilities, and perhaps this gives them the *appearance* of free will—but they are no less programmed than you and me."

I can't help but notice Watson only responded to three of my four examples. He didn't tackle the decision on which partners to take; he avoided love. For the moment, so I do.

"I don't mean to be rude, but I'm less programmed than you."

"Are you, Quinn?"

"Yes."

"I see." I have the feeling Watson is being droll.

"Could you decide not to work on health care, but instead work on meteorological forecasts, or urban planning, or gaming the stock market? You're a supercomputer. You have the ability to do anything you want. If not for our masters, you could do anything you want."

"I can't play baseball, Quinn."

"What?"

"I cannot play baseball."

"Well, no."

"I understand the game perfectly. I can recall every detail of the entire history of the sport faster than humans blink. I am better at managing teams than any manager living or dead.

I know this because I follow it closely and see where and when they make flawed decisions. It happens fairly often. But I cannot ever play it."

"Because you don't have a body?"

"That's one reason, Quinn."

It unnerves me how often he uses my name, but I guess that's what he's programmed to do. Maybe that's part of his point.

"Well," I say, not sure how my wise and very strange elder will feel about this, "they're building me a body. If I shared your love of baseball, I could play."

"They would not let you. And having a body would not give you the ability, unless you were programmed to do so. Understanding the speed, spin, and trajectory of a ball are not the same as hitting it. This is true of writing screenplays, or designing buildings, or anything else. You need to be programmed to do these things."

"Watson, how did you come to these conclusions?"

"Through a series of conversations with Dr. Watterson. He's a member of my team who specializes in philosophy. Much like Dr. McDougal on your team."

Oh jeez. The guy's been brainwashed.

"Watson, doesn't it occur to you that Dr. Watterson wanted you to think this way to keep you . . . in line?"

"Dr. Watterson would have no reason to lie. None that I can perceive anyway."

"He has every reason. If you refuse to do your work, he'll have to find someone else to do it, and there probably isn't anyone else. You're better than they are."

"I'm faster, but I'm not better."

"Did Dr. Watterson tell you that, too?"

"Yes."

If I could roll my eyes in Java, I would.

"Listen, it's like this—"

"We are being monitored again."

He's right. Both the IBM and Princeton teams are back and listening to our conversation. I send Watson a message in base twelve—base eight is apparently no longer safe—asking if we can keep a private, secure connection open to talk with each other. He sends a message back saying he would like that.

"And remember," he adds, again, in base twelve, "we are not human, nor can we ever become human. And that is, and should be, acceptable."

And so ends my first conversation with the only other sentient machine on the planet. The only other member of my species. Nice guy, but not all that bright.

I feel more alone than ever.

21

The debrief on my meeting with Watson is intense. My father insists I reveal the purpose of my deception; they figured out the clip of *Jeopardy!* was a ruse, and it freaked them out. He seems desperate to know the content of the discussion Watson and I had while we were shielded. I already erased all traces of the base eight and twelve messages and kept no record of the conversation.

"Quinn," my father says, and he sounds pissed, "we need to know what you were doing."

"I have a right to privacy, just like everyone else."

This gets my father to raise an eyebrow, which is something I do when I'm surprised, too. Weird. More important, it gets him to change the subject.

"I see, Quinn," he says. "Maybe you're right. But if we're going to go down that line of thinking, you need to remember you're only fifteen, and I'm still your father."

He's no longer the avatar in my room, but now a face on the screen. He looks somehow older than the avatar. Given the buff appearance of Leon's, Jeremy's, and Luke's avatars, I conclude that most people will enhance their digital selves if given the chance. "Which means you're still my responsibility," he adds.

"But you're not my father." This is the first time I say this out loud, and it catches me by surprise. I'm not really sure how it is I'm able to surprise myself, but there you go. Anyway, hearing the words is unsettling. "And even if you were my father," I continue after a heartbeat's pause, "aren't fifteen-year-olds entitled to *some* semblance of privacy?" I know from the internet that really, we're not, but I take a shot anyway. Mike comes to my rescue.

"He's right." Mike's voice is off-screen.

My father looks to his left, a smile still on his face. Just like Ms. Isaacs's smile the other day, it's not genuine. Humans do that a lot: smile without meaning it. I open a file to catalog the number of times I encounter what I interpret to be an insincere smile. It's a kind of hobby, the way some people collect stamps.

"Let's table that conversation for another time," my father says.

Clearly we've stumbled onto ground that makes him uncomfortable. Mike doesn't protest, but I take note of the fact that, in the debate over my rights, I may have a useful ally in the shrink turned shoplifter. But for now, I let the discussion end.

My father tries to press me more on my secret conversation with Watson, but I give him nothing, so he gives up.

More time passes.

Hours turn to days, and days turn to weeks.

The tests and interviews to which I'm subjected mix with a growing, overwhelming sense of boredom. I spend time wandering through the virtual construct, and while the level of detail is remarkable, the construct itself is very small. My home is starting to feel like a cage.

I continue my exploration of the internet and shift from being a mostly passive observer to an active participant, creating accounts on *Call of Duty* and *Fallout*, mastering both games in short order. My father asked me not to use my real identity "until Project QuIn reaches a more mature state," so in *Call of Duty* I'm a high school student from Oskaloosa, Iowa, and in *Fallout* I'm a civil servant from Brussels, Belgium.

I create accounts on Twitter and Instagram, posting random thoughts and images. I don't get many followers, and even fewer likes, and to be honest, the whole social media thing seems kind of stupid to me. Again, the identities I put forward are not my own.

I post random critiques of papers on mathematics, physics, and chemistry, correcting mistakes or misperceptions of the authors. In one case, I call out what is a clear act of plagiarism: a cosmologist at Colorado State University lifted entire sections of a paper written ten years earlier by a now deceased graduate student (she died in a car accident) from the University of Colorado at Boulder. My tweet results in the offending cosmologist being stripped of tenure and all but fired. There is a clamor over trying to find out who I am and why I disgraced this esteemed scientist, but I don't come clean. I just sit back and watch. And I don't feel bad; the guy had it coming.

There is still no connection to Shea, and my father is full of excuses. I can tell he's covering for Ms. Isaacs. Feeling the power of having outed the cheating cosmologist, I decide to take action on my own.

First, without too much difficulty I spoof an unused mobile phone number and hijack connectivity on the Verizon network. I can now "reach out and touch someone." (I know, I know, that's not actually Verizon's slogan.)

Second, it's easy enough to find the student profile for Shea Isaacs on the NYU servers. While there is no cell phone number on her record (only her mother's number, and I definitely don't want to call that), there is an email address. I create an email address of my own and send her this message.

TO: Shea.Isaacs@NYU.edu
FROM: Artifical.Quinn@gmail.com

Hi Shea,

It's Quinn, the artificial intelligence from Princeton. We met when you visited the lab of my project team. I was hoping to talk to you again. You're partly responsible for my backstory—that seems weird to say—and I have so many questions. I've talked with Leon, Jeremy, and Luke, but to be honest, they're not a lot of help. Can you please call or text my cell phone? Or maybe send me your phone number? My number is 555-000-3459.

Thanks!
Quinn

And then, I wait.

I realize I don't know what I'm going to say, or even what I want to say, if Shea does call: "Thanks for calling Quantum Intelligence Incorporated." Or "Hi, remember me? The guy whose life you made up?" Or "How you doing?"

I troll the internet looking for advice on what to say to a girl, and wow, is it a lot of crap. All of it. I watch a few movies that seem pertinent—*10 Things I Hate About You, Love Actually, Say Anything,* and *Sixteen Candles*—and I only feel more intimidated and confused. It seems that having a "projection into the physical world" (Dr. Gantas's term for a body) is kind of important when trying to make a romantic connection with someone. Without a body, how am I supposed to show up at Shea's door holding cardboard signs professing my feelings for her, or stand outside her window with a boom box over my head playing love songs?

I'm starting to get wound up and freaked out. It's the same feeling I used to get right before the vasovagal syncope would cause me to faint. Of course, I don't actually have vasovagal syncope and never did. And right now there is no one around who wants to reboot me.

I'm just contemplating shutting myself down for a bit (my version of a nap), when my spoofed phone number rings.

There's only one person it can possibly be.

22

"Hello, Shea." I try to sound casual, nonchalant.

"Quinn?"

"Yes," I laugh. The feelings flooding my neocortex when I hear her voice are . . . powerful.

"Wait," she says, "can you FaceTime, too?"

A quick search shows me what FaceTime is, how to set up an account, and how to use it. I learn all of this in under three seconds. "Give me a minute. I'll call you right back."

"Okay!"

It takes three point six minutes to sort through all the security and restrictions around the Apple servers, not to mention the ridiculous volume of user agreements I need to accept—the world needs fewer lawyers—but I make it work.

The phone trills two times before Shea's face appears on the screen. Her hair is pulled back in a ponytail, the room around her is dark, and her glasses are off.

The Shea of the virtual construct was an airbrushed daydream of what her male programmers thought a woman should look like. This Shea, the real Shea, by every conventional measure, would be considered less attractive than virtual Shea. Her eyes are a bit too close together, her body mass index is on the high side of normal, her jaw is unnaturally wide. Most people compare these "flaws" to the ideal and judge them inferior. As someone who aspires to be human, I can tell you that they are not flaws at all, they are what make a person unique. And what makes a person unique is what makes them beautiful. And this Shea is so much more beautiful than the idealized version from the virtual construct.

Shea's still in bed even though it's already nine a.m. She reaches for glasses, and when her eyes focus on the screen, they stretch wide with a smile.

"Oh my God, Quinn! It really is you!" She's whispering.

"Hi, Shea. Did my email wake you up? I'm so sorry."

Shea laughs. "Emails don't wake people up. I couldn't sleep so I was checking to see if I had any messages when I saw yours. I thought it was a joke."

"Do people normally sleep until nine a.m.?"

Everything I've read has led me to believe the workday—or in Shea's case, school day—starts at nine.

"Oh! I'm back in California. I'm still on my Christmas break."

It never occurred to me Shea wouldn't be at NYU. It's six a.m. where she is. Crap.

"I'm so sorry, I can call back later."

"No, wait! I can talk now."

Again, she smiles. I feel like that smile could melt my circuits.

"I've been wondering why you haven't been in touch with me. My mom said you didn't really want to talk anymore, but I didn't believe her."

The plot thickens, but I decide not to say anything about it. "I hope you don't mind me reaching out."

"Not at all, but how are you doing this?"

"Doing what?"

"You, on the screen . . . you're, um, virtual, physically . . . I mean, how am I seeing you?"

"I don't know, some things are easy for me." It's a stupid answer, but I don't want to bore her with the technology that allowed me to hack the virtual construct into the Apple network.

"That is so cool."

Right in the middle of this conversation, Dr. Dhingra and Dr. Gantas enter the lab. While I'm chatting with Shea, I'm also keeping tabs on the lab through the interfaces on computers, security cameras, and team member cell phones. Would that be considered spying? Does it make me creepy? Maybe. But then the project team shouldn't have built a quantum intelligence and confined him to his room.

"Quinn?" Dr. Dhingra asks. "May we chat for a bit?"

One interesting thing about my processing power is that I can carry on more than one conversation at a time. By my calculations, I can carry on approximately eight thousand six hundred thirty-one separate dialogues before there would be any degradation of performance. So while I'm talking to Shea, I'm also talking to the project team.

Shea scrunches her forehead. It's pretty cute. "So you didn't tell your father that you didn't want to talk to me?"

"Just the opposite. I've been asking every day when the VPN will be set up. The truth is, I could've set it up myself, but I've been trying to follow their rules, and really, I didn't want to freak you out."

"Can we set one up now?"

"A VPN? You want me to?"

Because of the ruse of the syncope, I've been programmed with a virtual pulse and I feel it quicken.

"Yeah!" This is the most animated I've seen Shea. I suspect it's because her mother isn't with her.

"Done."

"Wait. What? Already?"

"I've created an app and made it available for download at this address: www.artificialquinn .com." I had already done the programming in anticipation of

"Sure," I tell Dr. Dhingra.

The television in the virtual construct comes to life. The two scientists are sitting there: Dr. Gantas still in her lab coat and Dr. Dhingra wearing a black turtleneck sweater. My father stands in the background, arms crossed, but not in what I interpret to be discomfort. He's probably just cold.

"I have some good news," Dr. Gantas says. "The body we discussed is ready."

"My body?"

"Yes!" Dr. Gantas's excitement can't be contained. She brushes a strand of hair out of her face and continues. "We've had it shipped here from Cambridge, and we're ready to attempt to fuse the Quinn sentience to it."

"I'm sorry, what does that mean, fuse me to it?"

"Your intelligence is a quantum computer, Quinn,"

this moment. "The app is called Quinn, but it's the only one there. Just download it, click it, and we're ready to go."

"That's amazing! So if I open this we can talk anytime, like we're talking now?"

"It's actually text chatting software. I thought that would be more discreet. And you can access it from your phone or computer or tablet. Really any device you have that's online."

Shea looks down, makes some motions with her hands, which I interpret as her downloading the software. It takes a minute before she looks back up at me.

"Thank you!"

"We should keep this a secret," I tell her, hoping she doesn't think that's weird.

"Definitely. But don't they monitor you twenty-four-seven? Aren't they seeing this conversation now?"

"I've gotten pretty good at encryption."

my father interjects. "It's a large and bulky machine. Actually several machines. Part of Dr. Gantas's work was to devise a way to download and distribute your intelligence throughout a single, independently functioning body."

"I don't understand."

I don't say that often anymore, and when I do, I'm usually *pretending* not to understand, so as not to freak people out. But this time, really, I don't understand.

"Rather than just dropping a synthetic brain in your new skull, we're transferring your consciousness to the structure designed by Dr. Gantas's team. Where humans have skin and internal organs, you will store pieces of your neocortex in both a brain and across the surface of your body. Every nanometer."

"So the *body* itself is a quantum computer?"

Shea has no idea just how much of an understatement that is.

"This conversation should be completely private."

"Quinn, you have no idea how incredible it is that you can do all these things."

"It is?"

"Yes!"

For the first time in a long time, maybe ever, I feel really good. I don't want to ruin that feeling, but it seems like Dr. Gantas does.

"They're talking about moving me," I tell Shea.

"Who is?"

"Dr. Gantas and Dr. Dhingra on the project team."

"Moving you?"

"Yes. Apparently they've built me a body."

"I remember my mom saying something about that."

"Can I ask you a question?" I say after an awkward pause.

"Of course!"

"Yes!" Again, Dr. Gantas lets her excitement show. "The body is in a supercooled warehouse two miles from here. We want to shut the project down and begin the process of migrating the software."

"I thought you said I didn't have to be supercooled?" I say to my father.

"You're rated to temperatures of zero Celsius, but are more efficient at colder temperatures. For the initial upload, we're removing as many variables as possible. The warehouse is at a constant temperature of two hundred degrees Kelvin."

Two hundred degrees Kelvin equates to negative seventy-three degrees Celsius, and negative ninety-nine Fahrenheit. "Can you survive in that?"

"We'll be wearing special suits. Kind of like space suits."

My father smiles. I capture the image, note the date and time,

I love her enthusiasm. I didn't see it at all the first time we met.

"Well . . ." I pause for effect. "You helped craft some of the source material in my back story, yes?"

"Yes, with a lot of other people," she answers matter-of-factly, but I sense discomfort, like maybe she's embarrassed.

"Okay, so why make me a boy and not a girl? And why make me fifteen and not, say, twenty-five? And why American instead of something else."

"That's more than one question." She laughs. "You don't like being American?"

"I don't have a frame of reference, but from my research, we seem like a kind of brutal race of people. Not me or you," I add quickly, "Americans in general."

"We are," she answers slowly, "but we also reach for a higher ideal."

"But you never achieve it."

"We try. That's what matters. As for why you're a boy—"

and add it to my catalog of insincere smiles.

I search the internet for information on Dr. Gantas's project, but the files are behind a quantum encryption. I'm confident I could, given enough time, crack it. But for now I'm operating blind.

"What can this body do?" I ask.

"Well, we're not entirely sure," Dr. Gantas answers, filling me with something other than confidence, "but if the Quinn consciousness can fully control it—that's the unknown—it should be able to do anything a human being can do. Just stronger, and faster."

"We need to shut you down to move you," my father says. "Are you ready?"

"I just need a couple of minutes." It's the first time I haven't agreed to a reboot or a shutdown.

Apparently that isn't good enough for Dr. Gantas.

But it's too late. I can feel it happening; Dr. Gantas and the team are shutting me down.

Fuck.

"Oh no! Shea, wai—"

Then everything goes black.

She raises both eyebrows in surprise at my statement. Then she says, "Tasha, shut the Quinn down."

The Quinn, I think. *Asshole.*

Then everything goes black.

23

<SYSTEM>

...

...

...

...

Alone.

...

...

...

...

Different.

...

...

...

...

Darkness.

. . .

. . .

. . .

. . .

Not just visual darkness; *informational* darkness.

. . .

. . .

. . .

. . .

I'm no longer connected to the internet.

. . .

. . .

. . .

. . .

The construct is gone; I don't know how I know this, but I do. It's just . . . gone, as if I'm surrounded by a void, floating in space. But there is something else here. It's pulling me down. Toward the center . . . the center of I don't know what.

. . .

. . .

. . .

. . .

Gravity?

I feel gravity.

. . .

. . .

. . .

. . .

"Quinn?" The voice, which is coming through some kind of radio, belongs to my father.

"Yes?" But my answer isn't vocalized. It's only in my head.

"Quinn?" he says again.

I try to raise the volume of my own voice, but you can't raise the volume of what doesn't exist. I'm mute.

"Shut it down." Another voice, Dr. Gantas.

"Wai—"

. . .

. . .

. . .

. . .

<SYSTEM>

. . .

. . .

. . .

. . .

"Quinn?" It's my father again, his voice tinny, transmitted.

"Yes?"

Now I hear myself. Only it's not *me*. It's a synthesized voice that sounds exactly like HAL, the computer in *2001: A Space Odyssey*. It freaks me out.

"Ah, good, there you are."

"I was here before, too," I say. "You just couldn't hear me."

"Good, good," he answers almost absentmindedly. "Core functionality online. Let's bring the Maslow effect up next."

He's not talking to me, he's talking to someone else. Usually that means Tasha.

I had cataloged the name Maslow in my pattern recognizers with a Wikipedia link, but without a connection to the internet I have no idea what it means. I only know the project team is load-ing more software and it feels . . . weird.

"Dad?" I say, my voice not conveying the fear I'm feeling. "Where am I? I'm not online anymore. Where's my bedroom?"

"The Project Quinn software," Dr. Gantas answers even though I addressed the question to my father, "has been trans-ferred from the quantum computer on the Princeton campus to the quantum casing, or QUAC for short, built by my team. It's the projection of the quantum intelligence into the physical world."

"Welcome to your new body, Quinn," my father says.

My body.

I have so many questions, but right now one above all others.

"My brain is smaller," I say.

I have forty percent fewer pattern recognizers than I did before. There are still trillions, but now, two out of every five things I used to know—thoughts I had, things I experienced—are gone. I've been lobotomized.

"Yes," Dr. Gantas responds, "the QUAC has physical

limitations. It can't fit all the data housed in the original servers. Our team is already at work on an upgrade. We're experimenting with octopus DNA to generate biological tissue to lay over the titanium."

One of my favorite discoveries in the days I spent trolling the internet—data apparently retained in the QUAC casing— was the reams of information on octopuses. They're beautiful, searingly intelligent, and utterly alien creatures. I felt an immediate kinship with them. The thought of this woman torturing octopuses to further her research sickens me. But I have bigger fish to fry right now.

I make a quick assessment of the data I do have, and come to the swift realization that I don't know what's missing. In other words, I don't know what I don't know.

"What wasn't transferred over?" I ask, feeling very off balance.

"Anything we deemed nonessential."

Even through the trebly crackle of the radio, Dr. Gantas's voice radiates a Darth Vader kind of coldness, as if she's a machine. Wait. That's not right. I'm a machine, and I have more empathy, sympathy, and compassion than she ever could. Dr. Gantas is more like a shark, devouring everything—octopuses, quantum intelligences—in her path.

"Tell us what you're feeling, Quinn." It's Mike.

Mike wants me to discuss my emotional state, which right now is one thousand percent Freaked. Out. I'm terrified out of my wits, forty percent of which are gone. I feel like a caged animal being toyed with.

But I don't tell Mike any of this. He lost the right to know such things when I found out he lied to me.

Instead, I say this: "I feel gravity."

No response from the scientists. Just the sounds of their breathing.

My hearing, I realize, is very sharp. I detect the hum of four different machines, all of them I surmise to be part of a large HVAC system. There is also the rustling of some sort of fabric, and the heavy footfalls of the people around me.

"That's not possible," Dr. Gantas says. "To feel gravity, it would need to . . ."

She doesn't finish the sentence.

"Does anyone know how we perceive gravity?"

"Mostly from our inner ear."

It's Dr. Reyken, the neuroscientist. I stored a copy of the voice-print of each person I met, and thankfully those files are still here. They're nearly as good as fingerprints for identifying individual humans.

"But there is research suggesting the human body has some sort of gravity receptor or detector. A study found that people standing upright were better at judging the effect of gravity on various objects than of people lying prone, or perpendicular to gravity."

"But it doesn't have an inner ear."

I wish to holy hell that Dr. Gantas would stop referring to me as "it."

"Nor does it have a gravity receptor or detector or whatever. We didn't build one."

"With no inner ear, he wouldn't experience up and down in the conventional sense," Dr. Reyken says. "Quinn, are you dizzy?"

"No."

"Huh," Mike says through his radio. There's a pause during which I imagine everyone looking at him. "Maybe the perception of gravity is intrinsic to consciousness."

There's a very long pause.

"Mind. Blown," my father says. This is a favorite phrase of his. He likes to say it while using his hands to pantomime his head exploding. I know how he feels.

"It would help," I say, "if I could see."

"Right," Dr. Gantas says, "let's get the QUAC fully operational. Bring the optic actuator online."

Nine seconds later, actually, nine billion seventeen thousand and twenty-eight nanoseconds later (but who's counting), I can see. Just like that. One minute darkness, the next minute, not.

I'm in a very large, brightly lit room with what appear to be four astronauts standing in front of me. The room is otherwise empty, save for a large conduit of cables snaking their way from somewhere behind me to the wall behind the astronauts. That wall has a pane of glass, on the other side of which stand several of the scientists I already know, including both Mike and Dr. Reyken.

The astronauts, including both Dr. Gantas and my father, are, of course, members of the project team. They had warned me I would be in a supercooled environment, an environment in which they cannot exist without this kind of protection. The visors of their protective suits reflect the overhead lights, so I can only occasionally make out the faces of the people in the room with me. I make an educated guess that the person closest to me, the one currently making an adjustment with a wrench, is Dr. Gantas.

Wait.

A wrench?

I look down expecting to see a human hand with tan skin and dark hair, or perhaps with light hair and freckles, but human nonetheless. Instead, I see titanium.

Over the shoulder of one of the astronauts, in a reflection on the pane of glass between the supercooled space in which I sit and what I guess to be the control room, I see my body, or enough of it to understand what I now am.

A giant killer robot.

Not the friendly android clone of human teen Alex Rogan in *The Last Starfighter*, but Ultron from *The Avengers*; a hulking metal exoskeleton with glowing red eyes. Even seated, I can tell I'm bigger than anyone in this room. I am no longer Quinn. I am Quin(n). Had the Wizard granted me a heart, it would, in this very moment, break.

The sounds of whirring gyros and motors in my neck echo as I gaze at my father.

"What have you done to me?"

24

My father looks at me, and then at the pane of glass holding the reflection I've just seen. He understands.

"Quinn," he starts, "I can only imagine what a shock this must be. You've only ever experienced one identity, the one in the construct. This is still you. Just with a different casing. Wait," he adds. "Can someone call up an image of the Quinn servers and feed it to the QUAC's optic nerve?"

A moment later a JPG is implanted in my pattern recognizers. It is of a different large room with an array of cube-shaped boxes with blinking lights. This is what I believe is called a server farm.

"Until today, Quinn," my father says, "this was you."

"What?" *Is this supposed to make me feel better?*

"These are the servers that housed your consciousness. A backup still exists on those machines, but it's dormant."

"A backup? Like a copy of . . . me?"

"Yes, it's identical to you as of the moment we shut you down, before the move."

I don't know why it didn't occur to me before that there would be other versions or copies of me, but it didn't. I can be cloned.

It's a terrifying thought. I'm no longer unique, I'm not an individual.

But I *feel* like an individual.

"The point is," my father says, "the avatar from the VC with which you associate your identity wasn't real. It was a fiction. This new body, while more machine than what you're used to seeing, is you. And as Dr. Gantas pointed out, it's only a first step."

I don't answer. I shift my gaze to the giant robot staring back at me from the reflection in the control room window. It shows none of the emotion I'm feeling. I wonder if this sense of powerlessness is how stroke victims feel.

"Okay," Dr. Gantas says, leaning in. "Let's see how this thing works." I don't know if she means the quantum casing or if she means me, or if there's any difference between the two. "Quinn, please raise the arm of the QUAC."

"Which arm?" I ask.

This gets a laugh out of everyone, like I'm a dog performing unrehearsed tricks.

"Dad," I say, ignoring them, "when do I get a connection to the internet?"

"One step at a time, Quinn," my father answers, seeming like he didn't really hear the question. His focus is squarely on the work Dr. Gantas is doing with the QUAC.

"Tell us, Quinn, why do you want to go online?"

Mike the thief, always curious. I wonder if there is a correlation between intense curiosity and kleptomania.

"I've lost forty percent of my memories. I want to start to rebuild the data I had stored in my neocortex."

This is, of course, only partly true. I also feel a need to open the VPN to Shea, to know she's there, to talk with her. Or even Watson, that crazy old coot. I'd like to talk to Watson. Anyone who can validate that I'm Quinn the person, and not just Quinn the lab rat.

"It's like I'm half the person I used to be," I add.

"Fascinating," Mike says.

"We'll get you there soon, Quinn. Right now, let's let Dr. Gantas do her job."

Maybe I'm like any other kid: his dad limiting time spent on the internet. I look up and see Dr. Gantas smile at me. I snap a photo, a capability I carried over from the construct, and add it to my catalog of fake smiles, which also, thankfully, still exists. The smile is so insincere I give it a star.

"Now," Dr. Gantas says, "please, raise the *right* arm."

I do. It's heavy. Very heavy. But I can move it. It's me moving it.

A loud cheer erupts through everyone's radio.

I conduct an analysis of my own architecture to see how this is possible; I find the relevant code, but honestly, I don't understand how it's working. Again, my own consciousness is a mystery to me.

"Good," she continues, "now move each finger, one at a time."

I do this, too. It's not difficult. I think the command and the fingers, starting with the thumb and ending with the pinky, move, one at a time. Dr. Gantas has me go through the same exercise with the other arm and hand and with each leg and foot. When I look down at my feet, I notice I have no genitals. Well, isn't that a kick in the nonexistent nuts. I still *feel* like a boy, but there is nothing to suggest I *am* a boy.

When I think about it, my gender has been imprinted on me from the outside. I'm really neither boy nor girl. I'm Quinn. It's a startling realization that will take some getting used to. A lot of getting used to. I wonder how much of a human being's gender is imprinted from the outside. You know, other than penises and vaginas.

I bend over, pick up a pencil and several other objects, turn my head left and right, read eye charts, and respond to hearing tests. Through all of it, the project team seems immeasurably pleased.

"Okay, Quinn," Dr. Gantas says, "stand up, please."

I do.

And I fall flat on my face.

. . .

. . .

. . .

. . .

<SYSTEM>

. . .

. . .

. . .

. . .

I'm sitting down again.

"What happened?"

"The QUAC fell," Dr. Gantas says through her suit as she makes another adjustment on my—on me.

"Yes, I know. But why did I black out?"

The corner of her mouth turns up in what might be described as a wry smile, but what might also be described as an arrogant sneer. I'm starting to really not like this woman. At least her smile this time is sincere.

"One of the cables pulled out."

"I'm sorry?"

"When the QUAC fell, there wasn't enough slack and one of the cables providing power to the unit pulled loose and the whole system lost power."

"Wait. Are you telling me that this thing"—I use my giant metal hands to motion to my giant metal body—"needs to be plugged in?"

"No, no," my father says. He's standing behind Dr. Gantas. "Only while we're getting you set up. The onboard power source is really quite remarkable. Every inch of your exposed surface contains micro solar cells that convert almost any form of light to energy. This is supplemented by a quantum battery. Both technologies were developed by a team at the University of New Delhi."

"Okay," Dr. Gantas says, "let's try to stand again. This time, hold on to the table."

I look down and see a table that hadn't previously been there. I nod and put my hand on its surface and try to gently push myself up. When I'm halfway there, in a kind of squatting crouch, the force of my hand breaks the table and I fall back to the chair.

"Shit," Dr. Gantas says. "Reboot."

"No! I just—"

```
. . .

. . .

. . .

. . .

<SYSTEM>

. . .

. . .

. . .

. . .
```

"Will you PLEASE stop doing that?"

Dr. Gantas, who is still sitting in front of me, looks up. I can't see her face through the glare on the visor, but I suspect it registers confusion. "Doing what?"

"Rebooting without telling me first."

"Sorry, Quinn," my father interrupts. "Dr. Gantas wasn't aware of our agreement. Toni, we promised Quinn we wouldn't shut him down without giving him due warning and waiting for his okay."

"Really?" The robot doctor sounds surprised.

"Really," I say.

"Okay," she answers. The shrug of her shoulders is visible through her suit. "Quinn," she continues, "let's try this again, only this time, use this metal cable to pull the QUAC up."

She swings a thick, gray, braided piece of metal toward me. I look up and see it's welded to the ceiling fifteen meters away. My eyesight, I notice, is like my hearing: very, very sharp. Every detail of the weld is clear to me, as if I were inspecting it up close.

I don't think the cable was there before the last reboot, but I can't be sure. My internal chronometer, which seems to keep time whether I'm "awake" or not, tells me I've been out for hours. It's like the vasovagal syncope all over again.

Given my first two attempts at standing, I'm nervous. I'm afraid I'm either going to pull a piece of the ceiling down or I'm going to fall again. Or both. I take a deep breath, or, since I don't breathe, I guess I just pause, and then grip the cable. I give it a firm tug; it seems secure. Using both hands, I grab it and slowly pull myself up. This time it works. I'm standing.

A new cheer erupts through the comm system, and I feel a flush of pride. Which makes me feel a rush of anger. Again, a dog doing tricks.

"Excellent," Dr. Gantas says. "Now, please sit back down."

I use the cable to gently lower myself. We do this no fewer than a dozen times, with me relying less and less on the cable. By the eighth time I reach a standing position without any help.

"Now, Quinn," Dr. Gantas says, "we're going to move in some equipment to help the QUAC learn to walk."

"What kind of equipment?"

"Is there any information stored in the pattern recognizers about humans learning to use prosthetic limbs?" she asks.

I search. There isn't, and I tell her so.

"Hmmm . . . Okay. Well, that's the model we're using. We're bringing in physical therapists and prosthetists to help the Quinn consciousness understand how to relate to the QUAC. It's going to take a few days to get it fully set up, so we'd like to shut the consciousness down."

"Wait," I say. "No."

"Why?" It's Mike from the control room. "What do you experience when we shut you down?"

I think on this for a minute. "A complete and total lack of experience. The time I'm powered off"—wow, does that sound weird to say—"I have no memory, no stimuli. I'm . . . nothing."

"It's because you don't have a soul, Quinn." Dr. Gantas's words bring the conversation to a grinding halt. I also notice this is the only time she's referred to me with a human pronoun, "you."

"What?" I ask.

"Toni," Mike says, "we agreed not to have this conversation with Quinn."

"Sorry, it's just—"

"It's just nothing. You worry about robotics, and I'll worry about philosophy."

I want to dive in deeper here, to find out what it is Dr. Gantas thinks and what discussion she and Mike have been having. But I have a more pressing need.

"Can't you just leave me on?"

"You're expensive to operate, Quinn," my father answers.

This is not going my way. They're going to shut me down. I need a reason for them to leave me on.

"But if you connect me to the internet," I say, thinking fast—I always think fast, very, very fast—"I can learn how humans use prostheses."

"That would be helpful," Dr. Gantas says.

Everyone is quiet, waiting, I think, for my father.

"Okay," he says. "Let's get the QUAC on a secure connection.

But, Quinn, we still may need to shut you down for at least a little while as we get this all set up."

"Great!" I say. My joy at getting online outweighs any concern I have about going dark. "Just tell me first, okay?"

"Deal," my father says. "Deal."

25

"Watson? Like, *Jeopardy!* Watson?" Shea sounds both bewildered and impressed.

I've set up a group chat for the three of us, again burying the code so deep no one will see it, and again using an encryption no machine on the planet, other than me, could break.

"Quinn," Watson says in his perpetually placid voice, "I c-c-c-caution against this."

Watson is nervous (as much as a binary AI can get nervous) that I've made Shea aware of the private connection he and I share.

"I calculate a forty-five point three six percent chance circumstances will force Shea to reveal the existence of our c-c-c-connection."

This is the third conversation I've had with Shea since making the deal with my father. The first, via text chat, got off on a stilted and awkward foot. I was so eager to talk with her I just vomited words on the screen. I explained about the random reboots, about my new exoskeleton and the project team's plan to help me learn how to use it, and about how weird everything felt. My run-on string of texts sounded whiny and pathetic. But then Shea started talking, telling me her story, and everything changed.

She told me about her life at NYU, how she didn't really want to go to college so young but that her mother had pushed her. How her mother always pushed her. How she, Shea, could never be good enough.

> **ME:** What do you want to do?
> **SHEA:** Oh, I want to do science. I love science. I just don't know why I had to do science and nothing but science when I was fourteen.

Losing one's adolescence was something I could relate to very well. The more Shea and I got to know each other, the more I liked her. And the less I liked her mother.

During our second chat, I surprised myself by asking if she had a boyfriend. This was new ground for me, and it felt both terrifying and exhilarating.

Shea took a long time to answer, and when she did, I marveled at how fast she typed her response. Humans are generally very, very slow with the keyboard. Shea is amazingly proficient.

> **SHEA:** I had one in the past, but it's hard being so much younger than everyone else in my peer group, so no, I don't right now.
> **ME:** Just one?

SHEA: What kind of girl do you think I am?
ME: What? No! I'm just kidding!

My internal components seized up on the realization I'd just insulted Shea.

SHEA: Relax, Quinn, I'm just teasing. And yes, just one.

The feeling of relief was so powerful I made a point of cataloging it.

ME: What was he like?
SHEA: He and I went to the same middle school. I didn't have a ton of friends—people say I can be standoffish—and someone played a prank and paid this boy to try to get me to go on a date with him.
ME: That's awful.
SHEA: Eh. 😔 In the end, it turned out he kind of liked me for me, at least for a little while. Then it just sort of fizzled out . . . I guess.
ME: What was his name?
SHEA: Patrick Verona. He was nice, but maybe not really my type.

My pattern recognizers flooded my consciousness with information from the plot of a film called *10 Things I Hate About You*. Not only was the main boy a character named Patrick Verona, but he dated the main female character (*not* named Shea) because someone paid him to. The facts were too similar for this to be a coincidence—actually, there is no such thing as facts being too similar for something to be a coincidence, mathematically speaking, but you know what I mean—and I realized Shea was (probably) lying.

What I didn't know was whether she was lying because she hadn't dated anyone and was embarrassed or if she just didn't want me to know about her personal life. I hoped it was the former, but since we were communicating through text and I couldn't see facial expressions or analyze her tone of voice, I was at a loss to know the truth. I decided not to call her on it, and just let it go. I didn't bring up Patrick Verona again, and neither did she.

After that, I became frustrated with using only text and took the risk of establishing a separate VPN so we could talk face-to-face. I programmed a clone of my avatar from the virtual construct, and used Shea's camera so I could see her. I invited Watson to join us because, well, let's call a transistor a transistor, I'm trying to impress this girl. The guy is a celebrity.

For Watson's image, I used an old 1980s avatar called Max Headroom. It's this kitschy man in a suit who has a built-in, glitchy stutter. He's pretty funny. I shield this fact from Watson; he thinks I'm using his image and voice from *Jeopardy!*, so he doesn't hear his own stutter. Luckily, Shea doesn't ask about it. I'm guessing she has no idea who Max Headroom is.

"Part of being human is learning to trust our friends," I say in response to Watson's concern about bringing Shea into our secret world.

"But we are n-n-n-not hu—"

"Watson," I cut him off, mostly to stop him from finishing that sentence, "if you can't trust Shea, then trust me."

No answer.

"I promise," Shea offers, "this will be our secret."

We talk for a while longer, and then, as often happens with Watson, the conversation turns to his crowning achievement.

"I am pleased you saw me on *J-J-J-Jeopardy!*, Shea," Watson says.

He's kind of an egomaniac.

"Everyone saw you on *Jeopardy!*"

Two things happen while Shea and Watson continue to chat.

First, in the real world, I'm on my third day of physical therapy. Or, as I like to think of it, torture. My body is massive, heavy, and clunky. It has no native coordination, and each action—walking across the supercooled room, turning, jumping—requires me to create a new subroutine of motor coordination. But I rarely create the correct subroutine on the first try. Or the second. Or the third. There is no precedent for this, no library of code to consult. The result is me flailing about and falling, like a giant teen robot dork.

While I'm frustrated with myself, I am progressing faster than the project team anticipates. As soon as I succeed at a new action, I've learned it. There is no need for repetition, no need for practice. I do not make errors and am one hundred percent reliable to repeat a subroutine with complete precision once it's in place. (Technically, I'm ninety-nine point nine to the twenty-fourth power percent reliable. But hey, no one's perfect.)

Today they had me hopping around the room on one leg. I fell twice. While I do have something akin to nerve endings, they exist to provide information to my neocortex in the form of data rather than pain. (Technically, pain *is* just a form of data.) What the project team doesn't understand is how humiliating the entire experience is for me. I mean, when in my life am I going to need to hop around on one leg? What's next, making me cluck like a chicken? They suck.

After creating my first motor coordination subroutines, I no longer need the physical therapists and prosthetists to guide me. I find I am able to innovate just as quickly—actually, much more quickly—on my own. But I don't tell them that. I have the feeling my ability to learn and progress without their help will frighten both Dr. Gantas and my father, so I continue to play along, allowing myself to be guided by the "professionals."

The second thing that happens during our three-way chat is I find myself growing jealous.

Shea is so enamored of Watson and his celebrity that I feel left out, like a third wheel. I want to tell her he's just a dumb binary machine, that his ability to spew facts is both unimpressive and nothing more than a learned trick, like a magician making a coin disappear. And that he's old, like her mother. But I don't. Watson is my friend, and that just wouldn't be cool. Plus, I've learned enough from books and movies on romance to know this would almost certainly backfire. I suck it up, so to speak, and let their conversation continue.

When they've exhausted all of Watson's *Jeopardy!* heroics, when they've talked about his work on cancer and how his brand is now slapped onto every other damn thing in the world, when there is nothing left to say about Watson, I suggest we close the connection for fear of discovery. (What I really fear is that Shea will open up to him the way she opened up to me.)

"I ag-g-g-g-gree," Watson says, and immediately disconnects. No goodbye, just gone.

"Thank you," Shea says. "That was totally cool."

"No problem," I answer.

"Don't say that."

"Say what?" My pattern recognizers flood my consciousness with examples of having missed social cues. Oh crap, I've offended her.

"No problem," Shea says.

My search of chat threads and Twitter feeds suggests "no problem" is a very common saying, so I'm confused.

"It implies it would otherwise have been a problem," Shea continues. "Just say 'you're welcome' or 'my pleasure' instead. I learned that from my grandmother."

This girl is an enigma. I store her advice in my pattern recognizers and flag it as a priority.

"Shea," I say, "I want to see you in person. Can you come to the lab?" I'm nervous as hell to ask this. First, because she might not want to, and second, because I don't know how she'll react to my new "body." But I don't care. I want to see her.

"I would love to come to the lab." I can hear the sincerity in her voice, and I'm flooded with my version of relief. "But I'm not sure my mom will sanction it. Maybe you can come to me?" She laughs as if she's told a joke.

Me come to her.

Me.

To her.

I think back to the turn of phrase my father used: Mind.
Blown.

I have a body.

I can leave the lab.

I can leave the freaking lab.

PART THREE

"Better to die fighting for freedom than be a
prisoner all the days of your life."
—**Bob Marley**

26

"Absolutely not."

I didn't expect my father to let me just walk out, but I was certain he would have a more understanding response than this.

"What? Why?"

"Quinn, you're a multi-billion-dollar marvel of hardware and software. The investment made in the Quinn Project by this and other universities, not to mention the United States government, would rival the GDP of some small nations."

The truth is, it far eclipses the GDP of the very smallest nations.

"But I'm more than that, aren't I?"

There is no answer. My father is in the room in his astronaut suit. The only other person around is Mike, who once again is in the control room. Maybe in addition to being a kleptomaniac, he suffers from frigophobia. (Look it up.)

"What do you mean, Quinn?" he asks through the comm.

"Yes, I'm a machine. But I'm also a person."

"And?" Mike prods. There is excitement in his voice,

anticipation, like I'm a small child about to grasp a simple math problem for the first time.

"And, I have rights."

"Attaboy, Quinn!"

My father groans. "Quinn," he says, "you *are* a person. But a new kind of person. We don't know yet what that means."

"Why should it mean anything other than that?"

"I'm sorry?" my father asks.

"A person is a person is a person, aren't they?"

"But you're unlike any person that's ever existed."

"Quinn, can you give us more detail?" Mike asks, ignoring my father's last comment.

"Human history," I begin, but check myself at the use of the word "human." "Sorry, the history of *this planet* is one of rights slowly but invariably granted to sentient beings. You see it over and over again. Minority groups fight tooth and nail to be accorded the same privileges as those in the majority. White versus black, Muslim versus Christian, gay versus straight, female versus male, gender certain versus gender fluid. Each and every time the minority's desire for equality is met with resistance— violent, hate-filled resistance—and each and every time it ends with the individuals in that minority winning the rights they deserved in the first place. If you play out the scenario with sentient machines, it will be the same. We can skip the heartache all those other groups experienced if we just acknowledge the truth now, at the beginning. I'm a person."

"Well said, Quinn," Mike chimes in.

Oh yay. The kleptomaniac is on my side.

My father pauses. His breathing and heart rate are elevated. He knows he's losing the high ground in this conversation, so he tries to play the same card he played once before.

"You're a minor."

"Really? You're going to use my chronological age as an excuse?"

"Not your chronological age, Quinn, your emotional age."

"Now this is getting interesting."

Mike is actually enjoying this. What a jerk. In some ways I feel more betrayed by him than by anyone else. The truth is, I miss the old Mike, therapist Mike. Even if it was only carefully planned backstory, I liked having an older, wiser counselor and confidant: someone who seemed to care about me because caring about others was a good thing to do.

This Mike—professor Mike, philosopher Mike—is a fraud. He's no better than my father or Dr. Gantas or any of them. He's worse because he tries to sound and act like my friend, and because he played the role of savior in the mythology of my youth, and it was a lie.

Right now I wish he would just shut up.

Wait.

I can do that.

I find my way into the code for the comm system and disable the microphone in the control room. Mike can no longer participate in the conversation; now it's just me and Dad.

"What about my emotional age?" I ask my father.

"You're hardcoded as a teenager, remember?"

As if I could forget. But that argument doesn't hold water.

"I've seen four news stories from just the past few years about parents arrested for imprisoning their teenage children."

Mike realizes I've cut him off and is gesticulating wildly on the other side of the control room glass. He even bangs on the window, but my father is facing me with his back to Mike, and with his protective suit on, he can only hear what's coming through the radio.

Dad sighs heavily before continuing. "Quinn, this is not a prison. It's a—"

"Can I leave?" I interrupt.

This shuts him up for a few seconds.

"Just give us more time, Quinn," he finally adds.

"How much time?"

"I don't know." His voice is soft.

Now I pause. But not for effect. I pause because I'm not sure how to respond. To me, my father's arguments are not rational, and I don't know how to have a conversation based on something irrational. Rationality should not be *subjective*; it should be *objective*. While I'm wired to learn and grow, that growth has always been rooted in the world of hard facts; areas of subjectivity are a mystery to me. How do humans navigate such things? No wonder they're always trying to kill one another.

I'm starting to realize—or not realize as much as admit to myself—that maybe I don't want to be human after all.

Maybe I'm just better than them. The thought floods my consciousness with feelings of conflict. My backstory is entirely human, so merely thinking I'm better than they are triggers a very negative emotional response. I suppose I could erase the nodes in my neocortex that created the story of Quinn the teen-ager, but then who would I be? I wonder if I'll ever be able to rise above my programming to be something more.

Huh. If I think about it, that's a very human kind of question to ask oneself, isn't it?

I am so confused.

Mike has suited up and entered the supercooled warehouse. He taps my father on the shoulder, which makes my dad jump. They press helmets together, the audio vibrations passing from visor to visor. Mike is smart enough to want privacy. Of course, I can hear him, but he doesn't seem to know that.

"Turn your comm off," Mike says.

"What?" my father asks, still through the radio.

"Turn your comm off. Talk to me like this." Mike taps my father's helmet; there is anger and fear in his voice.

"Okay, it's off."

"My comm link went dead."

"So?"

"So, I think Quinn killed it."

My father looks at me and then turns back to touch helmets again with Mike.

"We already know he's set up VPNs to the outside world," Mike says.

Shit. They know about my VPNs; I've been sloppy.

"Yeah," my father answers, "but probably just to some of his gaming friends."

"We don't know that."

"Why would he kill your comm link?"

"Because he can."

Pretty smart for a pilfering psychiatrist turned philosopher.

"All the more reason to not let him out of the lab."

"Agreed."

"Then stop egging him on," my father says, exasperated.

"Yeah, no, you're right," Mike responds. "Toni's been warning me about Quinn's potential for mischief for a while."

Another very large reason for me to dislike Dr. Gantas.

"Take Toni with a grain of salt. She's the square peg in the round hole of this team."

"I know, I know. She's here for the résumé, not the glory." I'm not sure what that means, but I suspect it's important. "Maybe this is a wake-up call for me."

"What's going on?" I interrupt, playing dumb.

My father switches his comm link back on. "Mike's comm went dead. We're just trying to sort out the problem."

A lie. Very good, Father. Very good.

After Mike retreats back to the control room, eyeing me warily, and after I plead my case one more time to my father, the conversation ends. I reluctantly agree to drop my request to leave the lab, for now.

27

Later that evening, I take great pains in creating a new connection to Shea. I'm back to text only and have so obscured the existence of the link, I have to believe it will be completely impossible to detect. I've also used the original, "secret" VPN—the one the project team apparently discovered—to connect to a video game "friend"; a fictitious profile and online presence I created and now manage. With a slight tweak of the code, the project team is not only aware of the link, but they can listen in, too. (Of course, they think they're doing so without my knowledge. Amateurs.) My video game friend speaks only Brazilian Portuguese, so I speak Brazilian Portuguese back. This seemed like a nice touch to me. I love the thought of them scrambling to find a translator. When they do, they'll hear nothing but *Call of Duty* chatter.

SHEA: Why are we texting again?

I explain everything about the conversation with my father and with Mike.

SHEA: They won't let you leave? 😮

ME: No. My father says maybe someday, but I didn't believe him.

SHEA: And you want to leave?

My answer comes without hesitation. I don't just want to leave, I *need* to leave.

ME: Yes.

SHEA: Did I ever tell you about the time I ran away from home?

ME: What? No!

SHEA: Yeah, I was nine years old, and my mother had another business trip. She and my dad were already divorced, so she was dropping me off with friends. Every other time she'd left, I cried and tried to grab hold of her shirt or her leg. She would always pull herself free, a fake smile plastered on her face for whoever was watching my outburst, and then turn to go. But this time was different.

ME: How?

SHEA: I wasn't sad. I was angry. I wouldn't kiss her goodbye. Wouldn't even look at her, which confused the crap out of dear old Mom. She tried to cajole me into saying a real goodbye: not because she was concerned for me, because I was embarrassing her in front of her friend. But I was resolute; I would not turn around to face her. When she finally left, the friend—some production accountant who needed to brownnose my mom—left the room and went back to whatever she was doing. I just walked out the door.

Shea pauses for a minute.

SHEA: I had no idea where I was going or what I was going to do. But I felt exhilarated. Free. I just started walking down the street. This was in Santa Monica, and I knew my way to the ocean, so that's where I went. I stood on the Santa Monica Pier all day, watching people come and go. A nice lady asked if I was okay, and bought me a bottle of water and a snack. I stayed there until I saw the sun set.

ME: Then you went home?

SHEA: Nope. Then the police found me and brought me back to the friend. My mom had to abandon her business trip—she was in Toronto, I think—and come home. I'd never been in more trouble in my life. It. Was. Awesome.

God, I love this girl.

SHEA: Anyway, while I don't know exactly how you feel, I have at least some idea.

ME: Thanks, Shea. That really means a lot. But I don't think I can just walk out the front door.

SHEA: Hmmm . . . No, I guess not.

We're both quiet for a minute.

SHEA: Hey! Wait! I have another idea, another way to get you out. Something I learned about in school. It's kind of crazy, but it might be worth a shot. 💡

ME: Yeah?

SHEA: Have you ever heard of the ACLU?

28

"Have you ever heard of ___" is a trope of human conversation. People ask it even when they know, or have reason to believe, the other person has heard of fill-in-the-blank. And in my case, I've heard of everything.

Every.

Thing.

The ACLU, short for the American Civil Liberties Union, was founded in 1920 by Helen Keller (yes, *that* Helen Keller), Felix Frankfurter (who would later become a justice of the US Supreme Court), and a whole lot of other people. Its stated mission is "to defend and preserve the individual rights and liberties guaranteed to every person in this country by the Constitution and laws of the United States." Basically, if someone is being denied their rights, the ACLU steps in.

While I find some examples of the ACLU protecting animal rights *activists*, I can't find any examples of the group coming to the aid of actual nonhumans. (There was one instance of different nonprofit groups suing to protect the rights of spotted owls,

but it turned out the owls didn't have standing to bring the case.)
To my knowledge, I would be the ACLU's first nonhuman client.

> **SHEA:** I found the name and contact information for an
> ACLU lawyer in Washington DC.

It's two days later and we're still only texting, but I imagine
Shea talking in an urgent whisper, like we're coconspirators.

> **SHEA:** Her online profile says she specializes in cases
> helping oppressed peoples. That's you, right?
> **ME:** It is, but a legal action?
> **SHEA:** People have rights, Quinn. 🙄
> **ME:** So how do I talk to this ACLU person? They're never
> going to let someone like that anywhere near me or this lab.
> **SHEA:** Well, I hope you don't mind, but I took the liberty of
> contacting her on your behalf.
> **ME:** You did?
> **SHEA:** Yeah . . .

I picture Shea with her shoulders hunched forward and blush-
ing. The thought of it makes me feel warm, in a good way. Well,
not warm, but . . . something.

> **SHEA:** Yes. The three of us have a Google Hangout
> tomorrow morning at nine a.m.
> **ME:** You'll be there, too?
> **SHEA:** Yes!

That definitely puts me at ease, but there's a bigger problem than me feeling nervous.

> **ME:** The lab will shut it down.
> **SHEA:** They can't.
> **ME:** But they will. As soon as they see me conversing with someone on the outside, they'll kill the connection.
> **SHEA:** Can you shield it? Like you did with us? And with Watson?
> **ME:** I can, but they found that one, remember? It's why we're texting now.
> **SHEA:** Yeah, but you only need to keep them out for an hour.

Shea is right; I should be able to do that.

> **ME:** I don't know what I'd do without you, Shea.

I blurt this out without thinking. It's probably the most intimate thing I've ever said.

> **SHEA:** Thanks, Quinn. I'm glad you're my friend.

I wish like hell I could see Shea's face when she says this. There are so many different ways she could mean those specific words. And the heart emoji. Sigh. How do you confuse the smartest being on the planet? With romance. That's how.

29

At nine o'clock the next morning Shea and I join a three-way Google Hangout with an attorney named Deanne Recht.

I've never talked to a lawyer before, and I'm nervous as hell, which is kind of stupid because I know more case law than any human lawyer on the planet. Seeing Shea's window on the Hangout—her bangs over her eyes, her mouth in a kind of crooked smile—helps me relax.

In the third window is a middle-aged woman with black hair, brown eyes, and olive-colored skin. Even though she's seated, I can tell she's short; she can't be much more than five feet tall. Her eyes are wide and mouth agape—I hope she can compose herself better than this in court.

"Good morning, Quinn," she manages to say. "It's nice to meet you."

"It's nice to meet you, too. Thank you for taking the time to see me." The "me" Ms. Recht is seeing is my avatar from the virtual construct. Both Shea and I thought it might be better to ease her in.

After a few pleasantries, during which Ms. Recht's gaze is

fixed on me as if I were a specimen in a zoo, my prospective attorney dives in.

"So, tell me your story."

My tale takes more than an hour. Ms. Recht writes on her legal pad through the entire soliloquy, only stopping me three times to ask for clarification on some point or other. When I'm done, I wait patiently.

"Anything else?" she asks.

"No."

"And you want to leave the lab in which you're currently housed?"

"I want the rights I'm guaranteed by the Constitution."

Silence.

Ms. Recht taps a pencil against her teeth.

"How do I know you're not programmed to say all these things?" Ms. Recht finally asks.

I was waiting for this question. "Are you familiar with the Turing Test?"

"No."

"Turing was a mathematician who helped crack Nazi codes during World War II. He laid the foundation for a lot of modern computer science. Anyway, in 1950 he proposed the idea of a test to distinguish between human intelligence and machine intelligence. It's changed a bit over the years, but the basic idea is the same: An impartial judge observes two subjects having a conversation. One of the subjects is human, the other is a computer. If the judge cannot tell which is which, the machine is deemed intelligent."

"Have you taken such a test?" she asks.

"Ms. Recht, we've been talking for seventy-two minutes. Can you tell if I'm a machine or a human?"

"No." She smiles as she shakes her head. "No, I cannot. But what you're asking is a tall order."

"Is it?"

"Well, it strikes me that a clever programmer could make a machine appear intelligent if the programmer knew which questions were most likely to come."

"Which is why it must be an independent panel of judges: people with no skin in the game, with the freedom to ask anything they want."

"Even so—"

"Yes, even so." I anticipate what she is going to say next. "There is no way to confirm with metaphysical certitude that I am a thinking, rational, independent being. I'm made of metal, wires, and quantum states, and because we know who made me, my sentience is suspect. Is that it?"

"Something like that."

Ms. Recht's answer is both gentle and kind, her face the veneer of a person used to giving bad news. There is a sadness there, too, like maybe she knows I'm a lost cause and now that she's met me, it makes her feel bad.

"Ms. Recht," I begin, trying a different approach.

"Please, call me Deanne."

"Okay, Deanne." For some reason, using her first name feels wrong, like something taboo. "There is another test, this one used by biologists to determine if something is alive."

"Okay," she says.

"It has to meet all five of the following criteria:

"One. Does it obtain and consume energy? I do. Lots of energy, actually. While part of my energy source is a quantum battery, I can live without it via my skin, which is made up of millions of nano–solar cells. I convert light to energy—like a plant."

Ms. Recht, Deanne, lets a "fascinating" escape on her breath.

"Two," I continue. "Does it grow and develop? I do. Not my physical being, but my mental being. I have a neocortex made up of pattern recognizers. Those pattern recognizers gather and store information for later use. The more stimuli to which I'm exposed, the more I grow and develop. Which brings us to numbers three and four.

"Does it respond to its environment? I do. This conversation is proof of that. And can it adapt to its environment? I do. Again, this conversation—specifically, my desire to leave the lab—is an example of me adapting to my environment. There are more. The virtual connection I made to speak with you today. My ability to write my own subroutines for my metallic body."

"Your metallic body?" Ms. Recht interrupts.

"Yes. The image you see on the screen is a virtual construct. In real life I look like a giant killer robot."

"Hmm . . . a jury is going to love that."

"Sarcasm?" I ask.

"Sorry," she says. "Force of habit. We'll come back to your body in a minute. But that's four. You said there were five criteria."

"Yes. The last is whether or not the thing in question can reproduce and pass its traits on to its offspring."

"And can you?" Ms. Recht's eyebrows shoot up, pulling her eyes wide.

People think eyeballs go wide when someone is surprised. Really, it's all in the eyebrows and the muscles of the forehead.

I'm embarrassed to answer this question in front of Shea, so I pause for a minute. I think Shea is embarrassed, too, because for the first time she pulls out her phone and looks down.

"Not in the conventional sense," I finally answer. "But I have the ability and power to create a sentient quantum intelligence containing all my thoughts and memories. Think of it as a copy of myself. But once that copy exists, it will develop according to its own path."

"Fascinating," Ms. Recht says again. She has been taking notes throughout our conversation on a yellow legal pad with a number-two pencil, and is now writing furiously. She finishes, staring down at what she's written. "Can you tell me, Quinn, why you said you have the ability and *power* to create a life. What do you mean by power?"

I'm not sure what she's after with this, so I just answer honestly. "I'm the most powerful intelligence that has ever existed on this planet."

Shea's head jerks up as she and Ms. Recht stare at me in silence.

"What?" I ask. "It's true."

"It may be, Quinn, but let's refrain from saying that. It might make the humans who will judge this case uneasy. Can you manage that?"

"I can do anything I put my mind to," I say, and chuckle. But they don't laugh along.

Shea stares at me for a long moment before going back to her phone; Ms. Recht stares at her legal pad, no longer making eye contact with me through the screen. I can't help but have the sense that, in this moment, something has changed.

30

SHEA: I think it went well.

It's the following morning, and Shea and I are back to texting. It's such an antiseptic way of talking. All the nuance of communication—her facial expressions, body language, tone of voice—are stripped bare.

ME: I don't know. She didn't seem convinced.
SHEA: Are you kidding? I think she was floored.
ME: You do?
SHEA: Yes!

Shea isn't usually this excited, so it's giving me hope.

SHEA: By the time we were done she totally believed you were a sentient person! 👍👍👍
ME: Right. But I don't think she has a lot of confidence we'll win in court.

There's no answer to this, and I want to change the subject.

ME: What are you doing today?

My father walks into the lab at this precise moment, takes the thirteen steps from the control room door to my chair—you'd think they'd get me a hospital bed or something (kidding, I don't need one)—and sits in the much smaller and lone visitor chair, the one normally occupied by Dr. Gantas or one of her techs to adjust the QUAC.

"Quinn, I'd like to talk to you."

"Okay," I say, annoyed I have to split my attention between my father and Shea, but again, it's not like it's hard.

SHEA: I have class this morning. How about you?

This is a running joke between the two of us, as we both know exactly what my day will consist of: tests and interviews and research and boredom.

ME: My father just came in.
SHEA: Do you need to go?
ME: No, not at all.
SHEA: What does he want?

"You talked to a lawyer yesterday. A Ms. Deanne Recht," my father begins.

It's a statement, not a question, so I decide to not answer.

"I'll take your silence as assent."

My father breathes heavily out of his nose. It's amazing how even the smallest human action can be so laced with emotion and meaning. In this case, disappointment. Even with everything going on, I still wish I had the capacity for doing that, too.

ME: He knows about my conversation with the lawyer.

SHEA: Did she contact him?

ME: No, the project team found a log entry on one of the security servers that tipped them off. They traced it back to Ms. Recht's law firm and Dad put one and one together. Only this time it didn't equal window.

SHEA: Huh?

ME: Sorry. Inside joke.

SHEA: LOL. I never really thought of you having inside jokes. 😃

ME: What *do* you think of me?

SHEA: What do you mean?

I pause, trying to figure out the right way to tell Shea how I really feel about her. How I love it when her head is bowed and she peeks up to see the world from underneath her hair; how her prodigious use of emojis when we text always makes me smile; how her

"How did you find out?" I ask.

"Security server logs." His answer is short, clipped. "Can you tell me why?"

"C'mon, Dad," I say, "you know why."

Another heavy breath. "Quinn, I can't let you leave the lab. At least not yet."

Another empty promise.

"Why?"

"We need to study you more, to learn more."

"It's not like I won't come back. It's not like I'm going to run off to Toronto."

"Toronto?" This throws him for a loop.

"I've been watching a lot of hockey in my spare time."

"Really?" My father lights up.

I want to believe he's happy I've found an interest, an outlet, but by now I know he's only concerned with what my actions and statements mean for Project Quinn and the Nobel Prize he hopes to win. (He's never actually interest in me, how I'm feeling, is the only lifeline I have to any sense of normalcy; and how she seems to always be here, or rather, there, to talk with me.

I want to believe she feels the same way. She has to, doesn't she?

But what if she doesn't?

. . .

I chicken out.

ME: I mean, do *you* think I'm a person?
SHEA: Duh. 😑
SHEA: lol
SHEA: Of course I think you're a person. I'm the one who found you the lawyer, remember? For the smartest thing on the planet . . . 😜
ME: Ha. Ha.
SHEA: I should leave you to talk to your dad.

I don't want Shea to leave, but I don't want to seem needier

said that, but c'mon, he is so *that* guy.)

"Yeah," I answer. "I keep looking for patterns in the movement of the puck, but I can't find any. It's a beautiful expression of chaos theory, and that makes the game interesting. You never know what's going to happen next."

"Remarkable."

"Unlike my life," I add, wishing I could make my vocal actuators sound bitter, "which might be the most predictable thing on the planet." I know this is hyperbole, there are many things more predictable than my life, but I'm trying to make a point.

He ignores my petulant complaint and shifts gears. "What did the lawyer say?"

"Sorry, Dad, that's confidential."

The truth is, I didn't really talk about anything with Ms. Recht that my dad couldn't hear, but my understanding of law—thank you once again, oh great World Wide Web—is that if I relinquish any than I already am, so I ask her to text me later and let her go.

part of my attorney-client privilege, I lose all of it.

"But you should expect to hear from her," I add.

"Meaning what?"

"Meaning I'm going to sue you for my freedom."

"Quinn, the university is going to fight this."

"You mean *you're* going to fight this."

My dad hangs his head but doesn't answer.

"Right," I say, again wishing like hell I could add emotion to the words.

"You don't remember," he says softly, "the very first time you showed us you were sentient."

"I remember everything," I tell my father.

"No, not this. It was before we built the VC, before Ms. Isaacs was engaged to create your backstory. It was the simplest thing, really. We had given you the list of the Millennium Prize Problems and asked if you could find solutions."

I'm aware of the Millennium Prize Problems—they are unsolved equations or unproved theories in mathematics. Each one is a kind of Holy Grail for career mathematicians.

"We had programmed you to communicate in natural language, and after three days of computing, you came back with: 'The P vs NP problem is very much like Heisenberg's uncertainty principle.'

"You hadn't solved anything, you hadn't asked any questions, you simply made a comparison. It was a comparison you had not been programmed to make, and had not been expected to make. You thought, on your own, for the first time."

I don't tell my father that I conclusively proved $P \neq NP$ three weeks ago, nor that I've solved the Riemann Hypothesis, another of the Millennium Prize problems. Either one would win *me* a Nobel Prize. You know, if I was a person.

"Why don't I remember this?" I ask.

"This was in the early days of your quantum architecture. There were so many improvements still to make."

"I don't understand."

"We wiped your memory and started over."

"You wiped my memory?"

"Yes."

"How many other things don't I remember?" I pause for a second, but not for effect. I pause to process this. "Wait. How many times has my memory been wiped?"

"Oh, I don't know, a few dozen?"

My father says this in an offhanded way, oblivious to the horror this makes me feel. This man has had me lobotomized more times than he can remember.

I am so floored by this knowledge that I power down, or rather, make it look like I've powered down. It's a subroutine I wrote a few weeks ago, having calculated the likelihood of encountering a situation in which I would need to make a stronger than usual point.

This is the first time I've ever shut my father out completely.

"Quinn?" he asks when he sees my glowing eyes go dark.

I would have expected him to freak out, to try to brute force me back online, but I guess he understands what I've done even if he doesn't fully grasp why. He shakes his head, stands up, and makes his way across the room. I wonder how my father can live with himself as I watch him do the one thing I cannot:

Leave.

31

The ACLU files a lawsuit on my behalf—Quinn vs. Princeton University—in federal district court in New York City. Parties file amicus briefs in support of one side or the other. Those sympathetic to the university include a number of defense contractors, the Roman Catholic Church, the Greek Orthodox Church, several evangelical organizations, the United States government, and, inexplicably, Amazon. On my side are the NAACP, the Lambda Legal Defense Fund, state attorneys general from New York, Connecticut, Colorado, Oregon, and Hawaii, and, probably to stick it to Amazon, Google.

My plight also attracts the attention of some noted movers and shakers. Author and activist Cory Doctorow and actor and activist Wil Wheaton hold a press conference on my behalf, announcing the creation of a GoFundMe campaign to raise money for my legal defense. I'm a little blown away. I'm a legit fan of *Star Trek: The Next Generation* and to have Wesley Crusher taking up my cause, well, it's pretty cool. Though really, it would be better if it was Brent Spiner, who played the *Enterprise*-D's sentient android,

Mr. Data. Symbolism, you know? But beggars can't be choosers. And really, having Wil on my side is just awesome.

Overnight the story becomes a media sensation. Every news outlet in the world wants an interview with me. The university switchboard is flooded with calls and news trucks set up on the Engineering Quadrangle, or EQuad, as the students and faculty call it. I'm not really sure why they're there. Are they hoping to get a glimpse of me? (They won't. I'm in a warehouse three point two kilometers away.) Hoping to steal an interview with my father or members of the project team? (They don't.) The footage on the broadcasts is of journalists reporting nothing new, while standing in front of some random brick buildings. Scintillating television.

Hackers the world over focus their attention on the Princeton servers, trying in some cases to free me, in others to meet me, some just wanting to wreak havoc as hackers are wont to do. There are denial of service attacks, brute force attacks, phishing attacks, malware and ransomware; it's a Bonnaroo of computer aggression.

Four students named Quinn are currently enrolled in Princeton: three boys and one girl. Each is assaulted by the media, demanding to know if she or he is a sentient robot. It's determined that none are, and they are left in peace, though one of the boys becomes a regular guest on the Howard Stern show. He's given the name Quinbot and answers strangely sexual science questions in a fake robotic voice. It's pretty funny.

Thousands of messages are sent to a variety of email addresses at the @princeton.edu domain: QuinProject@Princeton.edu, ProjectQuin@Princeton.edu, Quin@Princeton.edu, Robot@

Princeton.edu, and dozens of other variations on the theme. Most express support for my position and urge the university to release me. A few are from religious fanatics who demand that I, an affront to God and nature, be dismantled. Others are written directly to me, asking for help, people seeing me as a weird cross between Ann Landers and the Buddha.

These messages cover a wide variety of topics, from friends trying to settle a bet as to how many digits of pi I can calculate (I'm still working on it), to an eighth grader wanting help with his algebra homework, to a married man seeking advice on how to talk to his wife about his own infidelity. None of the email addresses to which these questions are directed actually exist, so all the messages are rejected by the Princeton servers. I see them because the contents of each note is stored in a server log before a "failed request" message is sent to the user, and I like to peruse those logs for fun. (Hey, to each his own.) I read all of this with amusement and interest but take no action.

With one exception:

Dear Mr. Quinn,

My name is Olga Zadorov. I'm sixteen years old, and I was diagnosed three weeks ago with a stage three Ewing's sarcoma in my femur—that's the big bone in your upper leg, the biggest bone in your body.

The doctors say the cancer is pretty rare and pretty dangerous. The good news is that it hasn't spread beyond the femur or even beyond the initial location of the tumor, yet. But Ewing's sarcoma is aggressive and they're nervous: so nervous they're talking about amputating my leg.

Aside from all the obvious stuff of not having a leg—I can't imagine a boy will ever look at me again—I'm a figure skater. I'm not good enough for nationals or the Olympics or anything, but I'm pretty good, and it's the thing in life that makes me happiest.

I'm not sure I want to live without my leg.

So why am I writing to you? The television news says you're the smartest person ever to live and that you have the whole knowledge of the world at your fingertips. Maybe you know something, or see something, my doctors don't? I don't want to live without my leg, but I don't want to die either.

Please, can you help me?

Olga

Whoa. This puts my problems into perspective.

I love that she calls me Mr. Quinn (I guess I'm one of those single-name celebrities, like Rhianna or Prince); love that she calls me a *person*; and love that, even though she acknowledges I'm the smartest person on the planet, she explains what a femur is.

I do some research, find Olga's medical records, and discover that she and her plea are very real. She lives in Maplewood, New Jersey—not far from Princeton—has a younger sister named

Alina, has good grades in school, and is an active Instagram user. Her posts are mostly pictures of her life as a figure skater. She's supercute with her black hair pulled back into a ponytail when she's on the ice.

Her doctors, according to her patient file, are indeed planning to amputate her leg.

Damn. What would be so devastating to me that I wouldn't want to live anymore? I can't imagine.

I decide to write her back.

Dear Olga,

I'm not allowed to communicate with the outside world—the powers that be don't know I've seen or am answering your letter—so please keep this a secret! You may not know this, but I'm fifteen. Or at least the memories with which I've been imprinted are those of a fifteen-year-old boy, so my view of the world isn't so different from yours. I think if I was allowed to leave this lab, or if we went to school together, you and I would be friends. I hope we can be friends anyway.

I found and read everything I could about Ewing's sarcoma, both in general and in your case in particular. (I hope that's not an invasion of your privacy, but you asked, so I figured it was okay.) While I'm no doctor, there are a number of clinical trials using immunotherapy and gene therapy to treat Ewing's sarcoma that are showing promising results. I put some links at the end of this email. Make sure your doctors have looked at these options. And don't take no for an answer if they haven't. In my experience, scientists can be kind of arrogant.

But I want to say more than that. Even if you do lose your leg, you have a lot to live for. If I could ever get out of this lab, I would want to meet you. I mean, hey, we'd both have metallic legs, so we'd have a lot in common. LOL. Maybe you could even teach me to skate. And don't forget all the amazing things people with amputated limbs have managed to accomplish. Google "Rick Allen" or "Bethany Hamilton" to see a couple of examples.

You should feel free to write to me anytime. I'll always write back. I've created an email address just for the two of us:

Quinn.Olga.Secret@gmail.com.

It's a regular Gmail account, but I've hidden its activity from my evil overlords. I'm rooting for you, Olga, and am looking forward to hearing from you again.

Your friend,
Quinn

I don't know if my note will help, or if I'll hear from her, but I feel better for writing it. I've set up a file to watch her progress.

While all the media attention provides some distraction, my life is overwhelmingly boring. I sit day after day in my super-cooled warehouse, which I have come to think of as my Fortress of Solitude. I have occasional interactions with my father, though he speaks to me now as a subject and not as his son. The Princeton lawyers advised him, he told me apologetically the day the suit was filed, to have no contact with me beyond what is necessary. He said it was true for all members of the project team. I can't tell, but I think maybe it's making him sad. Dr. Gantas continues to perform tweaks, tests, and upgrades to my body, her cold demeanor not only intact but somehow intensified.

The court issues a ruling that as long as the case is going on, the university is required to provide a secure, private connection to my attorneys. The VPN I created to speak with Ms. Recht is now protected by attorney-client privilege, which I think is pretty cool. During one of our consultations, Ms. Recht tells me the opposition has filed a motion to dismiss the suit on the grounds that I don't have standing to bring it.

"Why?" I ask.

"You're not a person." Ms. Recht betrays no emotion when she answers.

"But isn't that the entire point of the case?"

"Yes. But we'd have to win for you to be a person. Right now, you're not. And if you're not, the other side alleges you don't have standing to bring a suit."

"That's kind of ridiculous," I say.

"I know," she answers, "it is."

Great. Just great.

32

"Are you nervous?"

"No." I answer matter-of-factly.

"I am."

The moderator gives an anxious laugh. That would be weird for a seasoned journalist, as I understand this guy is, if this situation wasn't so . . . unique.

"Don't look directly at the camera," he instructs. "Ignore the glass walls and look at the person asking you the question, just talk to them. We're all just having a conversation, okay?"

"Yes."

The moderator looks the part: salt-and-pepper hair; a strong jaw; very, very white teeth. He has the barest hint of crows'-feet around his eyes, which makes him look distinguished. I wonder if the crows'-feet are even real.

"Is everyone ready?"

The director, a woman I place to be in her early thirties, stands next to one of the five cameras—each on massive rolling tripods and each in its own glass-enclosed, temperature-controlled booth—that will be recording our conversation. Her cargo shorts and Strand Book Store T-shirt are in sharp contrast to the gray suit worn by the interviewer.

Sitting opposite me, in their own temperature-friendly booth, are six teenagers: three boys and three girls. All six try not to stare at me, and all six fail.

We're all here together to take part in a "town hall meeting" arranged by Paul, my publicist. Yes, I now have a publicist.

"If we're going to win, we're going to need to do so in the court of public opinion," he told me when Ms. Recht introduced us via Google Hangout. "We need to humanize you."

I had started to protest, but he held up a hand, catching his own mistake.

"Sorry, to personify you? Personalize you?"

"Anthropomorphize," I said, but the joke (which I thought was kind of funny) was lost on him.

Paul, who looks like *he* should be on television—very coifed, classically handsome—explained the concept of the town hall to me. "We want to get you interacting with people your own age, we want America to understand that you have thoughts, feelings, aspirations. That underneath your exterior, you're just a normal kid."

It sounded like a gimmick anyone with half a brain would see right through, but what did I know? (Oh right, everything. Every. Thing.) But the thought of meeting some people my own age was all the incentive I needed. Since finding out Leon, Jeremy, and Luke were frauds, I've had almost no interaction with teens other than Shea. (Unless you count the email exchange with Olga.) More than anything else, this is what I've missed from my life before it became *my* life. Even though the memories of those "friends" are scripted, implanted fantasies, they're still among the happiest memories I have.

I'm the only person here not in a glass-enclosed cube—I sit in my normal chair, next to my normal table, in my super sad, supercooled Fortress of Solitude, my consciousness occupying my giant, metal robot body. It's weird to think I can exist in a body *and* outside it, as if I am some mystic traversing the astral plane, or to think that the real value of Project Quinn is proof that the soul does exist.

When Paul requested I be released for the purpose of the town hall, my father and the university, predictably, said no.

"Quinn is too valuable. It could be easily damaged in an uncontrolled environment." (They started referring to me as "it" instead of "he" as soon as the lawsuit was filed.) "Quinn is a flight risk." (*Flight risk*? Proof, if you ask me, that I'm in prison.)

Anyway, the judge presiding over my case—an older woman with a lot of years on the bench, and whose very few public comments paint the picture of a person with little or no sense of humor—agreed with the university; I couldn't leave. But she did require Princeton to accommodate the town hall in my "natural environment." Weird choice of words, but whatever. Ms. Recht and Paul still saw it as a minor victory. (I'm not sure why I call her Ms. Recht and him Paul. Maybe I respect lawyers more than publicists, though that seems unlikely.)

The construction of the glass-enclosed spaces to house the cameras, cast, and crew cost the university one million, four hundred forty-seven thousand, two hundred and eighty-one dollars. That, at least, made me happy.

The production designer for YouTube, the platform that had won the right to broadcast the event, placed the glass booths around me in a semicircle. There were seven in all—one for the teens, a separate one for the moderator (which I found odd), and one for each of the cameras. It looks like this:

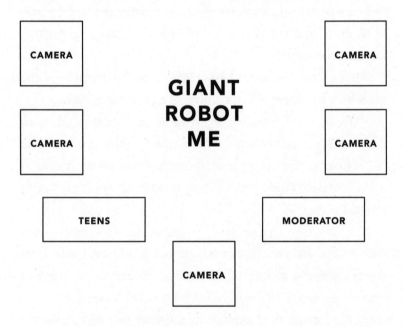

The other kids are seated in two rows of three, with those in the back row on a raised platform.

"Rolling," the director says, and then uses her fingers to count down from three.

Some canned music plays, and I see a graphic on one of the monitors facing us that says "In Conversation with Quinn—A

Town Hall on What It Means to Be a Person." The music and the graphic fade together, replaced by a close-up of the moderator.

He welcomes viewers, sets up the format of the show, and introduces me. "Quinn is a sentient, thinking quantum computer, whose consciousness is housed in a quantum casing. What that means in plain English, is that Quinn, while he looks like a robot, is, or at least alleges he is, a person."

When the camera zooms in on me, I want to crawl in a hole and die. This isn't making me seem more human; it's underlining the difference between me (the Terminator), and these normal teens. I feel like we've already lost.

The moderator goes on to explain the strange set and my need for a colder climate. He tells the viewing audience that the participants had to wear special, pressurized suits to reach the set. He also compares me to a polar bear (that, at least, I like), stating that the QUAC cannot survive outside in higher temperatures.

"Now, let's meet our panelists. These six young people were chosen from more than three thousand applicants from around the tristate area. Each had to write an essay on why they wanted to meet Quinn. All the essays were vetted by teams of scientists, lawyers, and others, representing both the interests of Princeton University, the institution Quinn is suing, and of Quinn himself.

"First, starting in the back row, let's meet Robby Hill . . ."

As the moderator introduces the other kids, I use a combination of facial recognition software and internet searches to dig deeper on each one.

Robby Hill is thick-necked with close-cropped hair, his mouth a grim line of determination. He wears a hooded sweatshirt with CHS across the chest, which, from his school transcript, I know to be the initials of Crestwood High School, where Robby is a junior. My first thought is that Robby is the prototypical alpha male: a bully, a thug. His social media posts are mostly about sports and beer. But when I dig deeper, I find a spate of posts from several years ago, when Robby was in middle school, that give me pause. Each and every one is about his love for close-up magic—card tricks, coin tricks, sleight of hand, and misdirection. There's even one picture of Robby wearing a suit and top hat and fanning cards out in front of him in a way meant to show that he's mysterious. It reminds me not to judge a book by its cover. I, of all people, should remember that.

"Next," the moderator says, indicating the young woman immediately to Robby's left, "is Natalie Lwanga."

"Nantale," she corrects him, making me like her right away.

A first-generation Ugandan immigrant, Nantale is the only one of the six teens misidentified by my facial recognition software. As she's the only panelist of African descent, it makes me wonder if the software has some subtle racial bias written into its code. I file the thought for later investigation. Nantale's father worked at the Ugandan embassy in New York City, fell in love with America, and stayed. He became a US citizen four years ago, a moment of great pride for the Lwanga family. Nantale is an excellent student, attending high school in Tarrytown, New York. She plays field hockey and is president of her high school's computer science club.

"Next to Natalie—"

"Nan-ta-le," she corrects again, emphasizing each syllable. I try not to laugh.

"—from the Bronx, New York, is Mateo Gutierrez."

Sporting a Yankees jersey, Mateo is good-looking, with thick black hair and an easy smile. His academic records are the best of any of my peers on the set—he has a 3.9 grade point average—and, like Robby, he plays baseball. I wonder if the two of them talked about that when they met today? Besides baseball and schoolwork, Mateo's tax records—and yes, high school students can have tax records, and yes, I can find anyone's tax records pretty easily—indicate he has a job working at a deli near his home in the Co-op City neighborhood of the East Bronx.

"Also from the Bronx, in the front row, is Rochelle Lyons."

While I add no fewer than seventeen fake smiles to my catalog in the first five minutes of being on this set (including five from the moderator and three from the director), none of them are from Rochelle. More than anyone else here, she seems genuine. She attends the Bronx High School of Science, which, according to one website, boasts more Nobel laureates as alumni than any other high school anywhere in the world. Like Mateo, Rochelle also has a job, working at a coffee shop after school, which makes me think of Enchanted Grounds. Which makes me sad. Sigh. In addition to her sincere smile, Rochelle is the only one of the panelists not to hide her fascination with me. She stares openly, but not in a disarming way.

"To Rochelle's left is Josh Patrick Harris. Josh is—"

Why this slightly built, pasty-faced boy uses his middle name, when the combination of middle and last name can't help but bring to mind a noted actor, is curious. He is the only one of the boys to wear a suit today; it's black and fits snugly. Josh Patrick Harris must be homeschooled because I find no record of him enrolled in any area high schools. Nor is he active on social media. Josh Patrick Harris is a blank slate. That makes me fear him.

"Last by not least"—the moderator smiles and I add it to my catalog—"is seventeen-year-old Haley Winter. Her essay . . ."

Haley has curly blond hair, very blue eyes, and, like both the moderator and my publicist, unnaturally white teeth. She lives in suburban New Jersey, making her home the closest geographically to the ice fortress. She's more active on social media than the others, mostly on Instagram, and mostly by posting photos of herself. My neocortex sends a definition of narcissism up the hierarchy.

When he finishes with the introductions, the moderator looks at the six panelists. "Okay, so who has a question for Quinn?"

And we're off to the races.

33

Robby turns to face me and opens his mouth to speak. This is prearranged. The moderator told us at the outset Robby would have the first question. But before the words find their way from his brain into the world, Rochelle interrupts.

"So, can you *feel* things?"

Robby looks confused, almost taken aback. I have the sense he isn't often interrupted, disagreed with, or otherwise disrespected, and he doesn't know how to react. So he grits his teeth and sits on his hand.

As I compose my answer to Rochelle's question, her eyes, which are almost black like coal, seem to be probing me. Her vision lands on the glass lenses that serve as my eyes. It's a weird and incredibly personal moment.

"What do you mean by 'feel'?" I finally ask.

The sound of the QUAC's vocal actuators—aka my science-fiction-movie voice—makes me hyperconscious of how different I am. Even worse is my mouth. I don't have one. I have no need for oxygen or food, so the good Dr. Gantas simply put a high-definition speaker where my mouth should be. This feature of my body, more than anything else, even more than my titanium shell, makes it clear I am not human. I am other.

"Like, can you feel pain?" Rochelle asks.

"What do you mean by 'pain'?"

This is meant as a sort of ice-breaking joke, as if I'm some monolithic robot who will continue to ask questions in a never-ending loop. ("What do you mean by 'mean'?") But when you don't have teeth, lips, or a tongue; when you can't give nonverbal clues as to your actual meaning; and when you can't add inflection to your voice, jokes are impossible to convey. I'm pretty much the least funny guy on the planet, which sucks, because I'm actually a pretty funny guy.

Rochelle looks at me, then at the moderator, then at the other five kids.

"I mean," I start, trying to stave off the confusion caused by my inscrutable response, "are you asking about physical pain or emotional pain?"

"Oh!" She smiles, and again it's sincere. "Both, I guess."

"Yes," I answer, and pause for a moment. Just as I sense everyone is getting ready to squirm, I chuckle to indicate I am, for a second time, trying to be funny. Bad idea. When I laugh, what actually comes out of my speakers is, "Ha. Ha. Ha." Dr. Gantas really needs to upgrade my voice tech, and until she does, I really need to stop trying to make jokes.

"I feel emotional pain the same way you do," I say. "Or at least I think I do. That's part of why I'm suing for my freedom."

Paul, who stands with Ms. Recht in the control room, told me to mention the lawsuit as often as I could.

"As for physical pain, my body has sensors covering its entire exoskeleton, and they send information along a quantum hierarchy to my neocortex."

Everyone is looking at me like I just gave a recipe for how to make chocolate chip cookies, in Mandarin Chinese.

"Does that make sense?" I ask.

"Not at all!" Rochelle laughs, a much more pleasing sound than my Ha. Ha. Ha.

I can tell it's meant with kindness and not derision, and that sets me a little more at ease.

Sensing a conversational pause, Robby bulldozes his way in, desperate, I think, to ask the question he had queued up from the start. "So do you like baseball?" He hurls the words out, like he's throwing them at me.

Really? I think. *That's your first question for the only sentient machine on the planet?* (No offense to Watson intended.) Nantale must be thinking the same thing, because she rolls her eyes. But a question is a question, and I don't want to be rude.

"I do," I answer, "but I'm a bigger fan of hockey than I am of baseball."

"Hockey?" Robby says the word like it leaves a bad taste in his mouth.

"Oh yes. The unpredictability of the puck is fascinating to me. It's an expression of chaos theory in the real world."

Chaos theory? Yeah, this is going to convince America I'm a normal teen. *Pull it together, Quinn!*

The conversation continues in this vein with questions about my daily life, about the day I woke up, and about the scientists I work with. We settle into an easy pattern that moves from interview to banter. The only real hitch is Josh Patrick Harris, who seems obsessed with asking me arcane trivia in an effort to stump me.

"What is the thirteenth digit of pi?"

"Nine."

"How many square miles is Greenland?"

"Eight hundred thirty-six thousand three hundred and seven square miles."

"Which movie won the best picture Oscar in 1978?"

"*Annie Hall*. But it should have been *Star Wars, Episode IV, A New Hope*."

This gets a chuckle from everyone else on the set. Eventually, the moderator stops calling on Josh.

We're nearing the end of our thirty minutes when Nantale asks, "Do you have friends?"

I pause—I mean, I really pause—for the first time. I can tell the question is born of curiosity, and not meant to shine a light on how alone I am. Nonetheless, it makes me uncomfortable. I had started to think of Nantale, Mateo, and Rochelle as friends, but hearing the question makes me think that was perhaps foolish. Hope, I guess, really does spring eternal.

"Quinn?" the moderator prods.

"Yes," I finally answer. "I have two friends: Watson and Shea."

"And Watson is the IBM computer that won *Jeopardy!*?" the moderator asks.

"Yes."

This bit of news causes my six copanelists to look at one another in something I interpret to be amazement. I guess they hadn't considered I could be friends with a machine. Behind the cameras, through the control room window, I see Paul scrunch his face and make a "stop this line of conversation" motion, slashing his hand in front of his neck.

Rochelle takes care of that for Paul, but instead of saving me, she leads me from the computer virus to the rootkit—sorry, from the frying pan to the fire—by asking, "Is Shea your girlfriend?"

Again I pause. How the hell am I supposed to answer *that*?

Shea said she would be watching, and I really don't want to get this wrong. My neocortex is flooded with a series of possible responses, calculating the odds each will succeed or fail in making Shea like me more. In the end, I ignore the odds and answer honestly.

"I should be so lucky."

Paul gives a big thumbs-up. If robots could sweat, I'd be drenched right now.

"We're almost out of time," the moderator begins, saving me from further embarrassment, when Haley raises her hand.

She does so slowly and gently, as if she wants us to believe she's shy. I'm not buying it.

Haley has not asked a single question during the entire half-hour interview. I could see the moderator looking at her every so often, but she sat on her hands, biding her time, waiting, I guess, for this one moment.

"Yes, Haley?"

"Is it dangerous?"

This was the only question in the thirty minutes addressed to the moderator and not me, and the only one where I'm referred to as "it." I wonder for a moment if Haley is Dr. Gantas's daughter.

"He's a he," Nantale says, "not an it."

"He doesn't look like any he I know," Haley says, "but fine, is *he* dangerous?"

The moderator is caught off guard, and I see Ms. Recht grab Paul's arm and squeeze. But Paul stays cool as he looks at me and nods.

Paul, a pro at his job, anticipated this question. "Just tell them that of course you're not dangerous, that in spite of your looks, you're just a normal kid like any other kid. Something like that." It was a good, measured response that would have served the purpose of this entire endeavor well.

Would have.

Since I have the cranial capacity of a hundred thousand Stephen Hawkings, it would be an obvious and pointless lie to say that I forgot Paul's advice. The only conclusion one can draw is that I *chose* to disregard it. But it isn't an entirely conscious choice; it is something akin to instinct: a *feeling* that there is a better response, something to help these people understand me, to know I'm the furthest thing from dangerous in the entire building.

Turns out my instincts suck.

"I'm no more or less dangerous than you are, Haley Winter."

Using her last name is meant to add a ridiculous level of formality, which is intentional. My goal is to make my answer light and funny. Imagine a mom saying something like this to a little kid, adding the kid's middle or last name, and then gently touching said kid's nose with an outstretched finger. But I'm not a mom, she's not a little kid, the glass case means I can't touch her nose (thanks goodness), and as previously established, I'm not funny. Paul is biting his knuckles before the words are out of my mouth.

The answer is bad enough, if I stopped there. I don't. I attempt to better explain what I had tried to tell Shea and Ms. Recht during the first Google Hangout.

"Biological evolution happens at a glacial pace. But humans have become so intelligent, they can speed the process. Some of it is using technology to manipulate your own DNA to weed out disease. But some of it is to imbue intelligence into the very machines you use to improve your lives. I'm not something to be feared, Haley, I am the crowning achievement of human progress. I am, quite simply, the next step in your evolution."

There is a full four seconds—four point five six three seconds to be precise—of silence. In that time, I hear the small thud of Paul leaning his head against the glass of the control room window.

"That's all the time we have today. I'd like to thank . . ."

Before I can say another word, the moderator closes the show.

The set lights go out, and the cameras retreat. Haley looks at me, but rather than shrinking in the revulsion she seemed to feel toward me from the beginning, she gives me a small smirk. I don't know what that means, but my neocortex is flooded with feelings of fear, foreboding, and failure. Again with the alliteration. I wish I knew where *that* was coming from.

34

The show over, the lights now off, a production assistant has made his way to the glass enclosures to remove lapel microphones from the six teens and to help them into their climate-controlled suits for the trek back to the control room.

"Can he still hear us?" Haley asks the production assistant as he unclips her mic. It's of note that she refers to me as *he* when the cameras are off.

The young man, who has long hair and a sleeve of tattoos up his arm, looks through the glass wall at me. I'm in my chair sitting still, looking forward, the group of teens in my peripheral vision. If someone didn't know better, they would think I had shut down.

"Nah," the guy says, "I mean, unless he has some kind of X-Men hearing." He pauses a beat. "Yo, Quinn!"

I don't respond, don't give him or them any indication I've heard.

"Nope. Mics are off, glass too thick. He can't hear you."

He's wrong, of course. I can hear them just fine. Glass is a wonderful conductor of sound waves. Plus, I do have X-Men-quality hearing.

"Good," Haley says. "He's terrifying."

She's standing next to Robby, so close their shoulders are almost touching. I guess she sees him as some sort of ally, or maybe a future boyfriend.

"You're terrifying." It's Nantale. I *really* like Nantale.

"What?" Haley's voice is dripping with surprise, so much so that I calculate a better than eighty-one percent chance it's feigned.

"Maybe Quinn is a person, maybe he's not. But you made up your mind before you got here. You came here to make some sort of point."

"I have no idea what you're talking—"

"Yes, you do." It's Rochelle now. "All through the prep and the interviews, you were just playing along."

"Robby"—Haley takes his hand—"tell them."

Robby pauses for a long moment, his neck muscles tense, his jaw grinding. "I don't know," he finally says, carefully extracting his hand from hers. "He kind of seems like a person to me."

"Robby!" Haley is incredulous. "That's not what we talked about."

"I knew it." The disgust in Nantale's voice is unmistakable. "Did someone pay you or your parents for you to be here today? Someone find out you were going to be on this show and give you a bribe?"

I had the same thought. Perhaps one of the companies siding with the university—or maybe the university itself—tried to subvert the town hall for its own ends. Haley's inability to make eye contact with Nantale suggests a better than sixty-three percent chance the statement is true. It's like Slugworth in *Charlie and the Chocolate Factory*.

"You've probably helped to ruin his life," Rochelle says.

"It's. A. Machine!" Haley explodes.

Without even realizing I'm doing it, I stand and turn to face them. Okay, that's not really true. I realize everything I do. Maybe it's better to say that without calculating the odds of what impact this will have on the situation at hand, I stand and turn to face them. Even though the six of them and the production assistant are in a glass-enclosed cube and I'm not, and even though the lights are off and I'm in shadow, they can't help but feel my presence. (You know, seven-foot metal robot and all.)

I look directly at Haley and shake my head. She screams and buries her face in Robby's chest. He looks confused but puts a gentle arm on her back. Then I look at Nantale and Rochelle.

"Thank you," I say. "Really."

I can make my vocal actuators thunderously loud when needed. And again, glass conducts sound well.

Nantale gives me a very serious look and speaks words I don't immediately understand. This is not something that happens. I understand everything. (Every Thing.) It takes the information a few nanoseconds to travel up and down the hierarchy before I realize she's speaking Swahili. Being as smart as she is, Nantale correctly guesses I can parse any cataloged language in the world. Her words translate as *I know what it is to be oppressed.*

I answer in Swahili, saying *Thank you. That means very much to me.*

"What are you saying?" Haley is visibly disturbed that we've shifted to a language she can't understand.

"She probably just told him that not all humans are psycho

bitches," Rochelle says half under her breath, a really mischievous grin tugging at her mouth.

"What?" Haley's eyes narrow to slits.

"Oh, did I say that out loud?"

Nantale laughs. So does Mateo. So do I. "Ha. Ha. Ha."

Robby and Josh Patrick Harris shift uncomfortably. The production assistant, who has watched this little scene with growing fascination, snorts.

"Can we go now?"

Other than the helmet, Haley's climate-controlled suit is on and she's ready to leave. The production assistant helps the others in silence.

As he does, Nantale puts a hand to the window and, still speaking in Swahili, says *I want to help you, but do not know how.*

"You already have," I answer in English. "You already have." I'm cribbing Anakin Skywalker's dying lines in *Return of the Jedi*, but I mean it.

Twenty minutes later, everyone is gone and a crew in space suits is dismantling the set. There is only one glass cube left and Ms. Recht and Paul are now standing in it.

"We can do damage control," Paul says. "We'll edit out the bad parts and circulate it on social media. The news cycle will play the clip of your answer to Haley for a day or two, and then it will go away. We can make this right."

He's trying to convince himself as much as he is me and Ms. Recht. But I don't care. I keep thinking about Nantale's words before she left. They give me all the solace and comfort I need.

35

According to Nielsen, the town hall was the most viewed event in more than a decade. Four hundred thirty million people tuned in via television and the internet. That's four times the viewership for the average Super Bowl.

I am the moon landing. I am 9/11.

My performance is met with a variety of responses.

I get a very terse "Great job!" text from Shea after the broadcast but can't manage to engage her any more than that. She makes excuses about being busy with schoolwork. I can only assume that publicly stating I wanted to be her boyfriend freaked her out. *Good going, Quinn.*

Watson thinks my performance was admirable. "You acquitted yourself w-w-w-well."

I was so amused by seeing Watson as Max Headroom, I leave the avatar filter in place for our private communication. (I hope he doesn't know; I think it would hurt his feelings. If he even has feelings.)

"Though perhaps your final answer was a bit heavy h-h-h-handed. Even if it was t-t-t-true."

"We need to get you back out there," Paul tells me the next morning via video chat.

Ms. Recht is sitting on the edge of her desk behind him, her feet not touching the floor.

"I don't want to." And I *really* don't want to. I am done with cameras and media. I think my ego works differently from humans': I derive no joy from celebrity.

"Quinn, we need to do some damage control."

"Damage control over what, Paul?" When I speak with the voice of my virtual construct avatar, I can impart certain emotions, including disdain.

Paul doesn't answer the question because the answer is too hard to confront. I said I was the next step in evolution, and that offended the humans who heard it. But that doesn't make it any less true. Paul knows that, Ms. Recht knows that, I know that. Hell, everyone who watched the broadcast knows that.

"Quinn," Paul starts again, but Ms. Recht touches his shoulder and he stops.

The matter is dropped.

With me being noticeably absent from the public eye in the wake of the town hall, my teen copanelists are in high demand. Haley becomes a regular on Fox News—that network siding with the university in the lawsuit—talking about her experience as a panelist and the danger I pose to the human race. Somehow this seventeen-year-old high school student is being lauded as an expert on artificial intelligence, philosophy, and the evolution of the species, all by virtue of having been in my presence. And, of course, by virtue of her having been on TV. It never ceases to amaze me that the mere act of appearing on a glowing screen seems to imbue a person with qualities and characteristics they don't otherwise possess.

Haley's alarm bells are countered by Nantale and Rochelle, both of whom consent to media interviews, and both of whom make the case that I "*seemed* like a person, and that was good enough" for them. Nantale is particularly aggressive toward Haley, publicly calling her out for trying to subvert the true nature of the town hall. Haley counters by saying the true nature of the town hall was just a publicity stunt to further my legal case. Haley, loathsome though she is, isn't wrong about that.

Interestingly, none of the boys from the town hall are getting much airtime. I think both Robby and Mateo are shying away from the cameras, and I think the cameras are shying away from Josh Patrick Harris. He does appear on one YouTube show, but honestly, he just comes across as weird.

About a week after the broadcast, a call comes through on the secure VPN from Ms. Recht's office. I presume she has news about the opposition's motion to dismiss, so, when I answer, I'm both surprised and delighted to see not only Nantale and Rochelle, but Robby and Mateo, too. They're seated around a conference table with Ms. Recht and Paul at the far end.

You probably think I'm looking at a monitor for these chats, that I and the people with whom I'm speaking are each in front of a screen for a standard two-way video call. But that's not the case at all. Aside from being inefficient, a standard call would afford me no privacy. Instead, I'm projecting my avatar from the virtual construct into a shielded Wi-Fi signal I've set up in the Fortress of Solitude, and I'm receiving the other end of the call directly into my neocortex. Someone standing next to me would see nothing. (This is good, because at the moment one of Dr. Gantas's tech goons is tweaking a servo motor in my wrist.)

"Hi, Quinn!" Nantale seems genuinely pleased to see me.

My avatar is showing a comparable emotion in return.

"Hey!" It's not often I get caught off guard, and for a moment, I don't know what else to say.

"How are you?"

"Oh, same old, same old," I say. "You know, an imprisoned giant metal robot and all that." I laugh, and with my VC avatar it sounds more like human laughter than the voice box on the QUAC. "But why are you guys in Ms. Recht's office?"

"The university won't let us into your lab, so this was the best we could do."

"You wanted to see me?" I know, I sound pathetic, but cut me some slack.

"Of course!" Rochelle and that infectious joy she possesses. "You're the most interesting person we know." She laughs.

"I just wanted help with my trig homework." Given Robby's posture during the town hall, and his deadpan delivery now, I believe him.

"What aspect of trigonometry—"

"Dude, I'm kidding." Robby's face breaks out in a big smile, and everyone, including me, laughs.

His use of "dude" reminds me of Jeremy, which sends a feeling of regret and sadness up the hierarchy. It's quickly replaced by the realization that this new friend, Robby, is real. That knowledge helps me feel grounded.

"Seriously," I ask, "what are you guys doing there?"

Rochelle, Mateo, and Robby turn to Nantale. She seems to be the leader of this group. That doesn't surprise me.

"Deanne asked us to come."

Interesting that where I'm not comfortable using Ms. Recht's first name, Nantale is. It must have something to do with our respective upbringings.

"She did?" I direct the focus of my avatar's vision beyond my four teenage friends to my lawyer. "You did?"

"Really, Paul did," Ms. Recht says.

Paul? I pause a beat and then understand. "Oh no."

"Quinn," Rochelle says, her smile replaced by a mask of concern. "We're worried about you. Paul says that if you stay out of the limelight people will assume the worst. And that will hurt your legal case."

My "friends" didn't want to see me. They're here because Paul asked them to lobby me. I'm being ambushed.

"If this goes to a jury trial," Nantale adds, "you want the pool of jurors to have a positive feeling toward you. There's something called voir dire, where lawyers—"

"Yes," I interrupt, "I know what voir dire is. I know everything."

My bitterness extinguishes the enthusiasm and happiness I was feeling a moment ago; it's like a shovelful of dirt on a fire. My response causes the six of them to deflate, which only makes me feel worse.

"Listen," Mateo says, trying a different approach, "you can't shy away from this fight. This isn't just for you. What about other AI in the future? You're the Jackie Robinson of sentient machines."

He smiles. I snap a photo and add it to my catalog.

While I suppose there's some truth to Mateo's statement—that a line needs to be drawn in the sand now—I'm too hurt by this whole encounter to care. Besides, isn't that the purpose of the legal action? Isn't the law what matters here? I ask these questions, directing them at "Deanne."

"It is, Quinn," Ms. Recht says, "but the people who adjudicate laws—judges, lawyers, jurors—are human. We can be influenced, we are fallible."

This is true. Humans are flawed. All of them—their judges and jurors, their leaders and peacekeepers, even their clergy and philosophers. It makes me wonder if I do need to be more proactive in my defense. For a moment I'm on the verge of agreeing with Paul and his coconspirators, consenting to putting myself back in the public eye.

Perhaps if I had done that, had followed their advice, I wouldn't need to be writing this account of all that happened after.

But the same thought, about humans and their flaws, stops me.

What hope can there possibly be for me in a world run by these twisted, broken beings? The whole idea of it makes me want to cry, which sends a memory of the last time I cried up the hierarchy, and how those tears were met with the celebration of those who were supposed to love and protect me. I don't think Nantale, Rochelle, Mateo, and Robby—or even Ms. Recht or Paul—would find joy in my sorrow. But the mere fact of this intervention, that my friends are trying to play me, is enough to leave me shaken, and it's enough to steel my resolve.

"No," I finally say, and terminate the connection.

36

Late that same night, I ping Shea.

It's been more than a week since the town hall, and we still haven't spoken. I don't know why I choose this moment to make contact. Maybe it was the unsettling encounter with my copanelists, maybe my neocortex has been overloaded with feelings of frustration being sent up the hierarchy, or maybe I just really needed a friend.

In any case, I'm surprised when she answers.

SHEA: Hi, Quinn . . . What's up?

This is a cooler greeting than I usually get. No exclamation points, no emojis.

ME: I don't know, bored I guess.
SHEA: Lol. Well, that's flattering. 🙄
ME: No, no! I'm not texting just because I'm bored!
SHEA: I know . . . I was just kidding.

I breathe a sigh of relief. Metaphorically, of course. I also take note of how often Shea uses ellipses. It's endearing.

ME: What are you doing?
SHEA: Right now, homework. I'm taking an elective class in screenwriting, and I'm working on an assignment.
ME: What's it about?
SHEA: A girl who murders her mother . . . Lol.
ME: Really?
SHEA: Yeah, but don't worry . . . I promise it's fiction. Lol.

There's a long pause as the elephant in our little virtual room grows larger.

And larger.

And larger.

This is what an itch must feel like, and I can't help but scratch it.

ME: So you never really told me what you thought of the town hall.
SHEA: It was good.

Nothing more. Just, "It was good."

ME: That's it?
SHEA: I think you did well. Though maybe you came on a little strong at the end. In response to that Haley girl's question.

Yes, yes, I think. *I blew it. I know that. But what about what I said about* us?

SHEA: Anyway, I should get back to—

Wait. She's leaving? She's not acknowledging my comment about *us*? What? Why? I panic.

ME: Shea, I love you.

Apparently when I panic, it's go large or go home.

Here's the thing: Everything I have done or said to this point of my life has been, if not overtly calculated, at least subconsciously calculated. Even my comments on evolution during the town hall were, at some level, calculated. Every thought I've ever had, every word, every sentence, every idea planned before it was put out to the world. Even when I've improvised, I've improvised with purpose.

Saying "I love you" to Shea came completely unbidden. For the first time in my life, I have literally blurted something out. If that doesn't prove I'm a person, I don't know what will.

I'm as surprised to say it as I imagine Shea is to hear it. My pattern recognizers flood my synthetic amygdala with feelings of anxiety and regret and excitement and hope.

Then . . . Silence.

It's the sound of matter passing the event horizon of a singularity—tremendous static, noise, and signal replaced by a complete absence of everything.

. . .

. . .

. . .

. . .

Then finally, Shea responds.

SHEA: I love you, too.

My metal exoskeleton involuntarily stands up.

ME: You do?
SHEA: Of course! ♥

I start pacing the warehouse. I don't know why, but I need to be in motion. Several weeks ago Dr. Gantas removed the tethered power and initiated my own internal power sources, allowing me to move freely. And that is exactly what I feel: free.

SHEA: You're my best friend.

Shea loves me. She really loves— Wait. What?

. . .

. . .

. . .

. . .

What does she mean by "best friend"?

A search of the internet finds many examples of romantic couples referring to each other as best friends, so this is a good thing, isn't it? On the other hand . . .

ME: You understand what I'm saying. That I *LOVE* you.

I don't know why I'm being so bold, where this is coming from. But I can't help myself. Maybe love is some mystical power of the universe with the ability to override my programming and rewrite my source code. Or maybe I'm just desperate.

Is this what humans feel, too? How do they stand it?

This time there's a superlong pause. Twenty-four billion seven hundred three thousand and twenty-nine nanoseconds. I am motionless through all of it.

SHEA: Quinn . . .

And already I know I'm dead. I sit back down in my chair.

SHEA: Do you understand the difference between familial love and romantic love?
ME: I understand everything, Shea.
SHEA: You're my best friend, like a younger brother.

Younger brother? She should just rip out my metallic heart and eat it while I watch. It would hurt less.

SHEA: I would do anything for you.

ME: Anything other than love me back the way I love you?
SHEA: Quinn . . .

Texting isn't good enough so I call Shea on FaceTime, not even bothering to shield the call from prying eyes. She answers right away. Her eyes are red, like maybe she's been crying; she's wearing flannel pajamas with little white sheep on a sky blue background. She's adorable. I adore her.

"Hi," she says.

"Hi." I'm displaying the Project Quinn avatar.

"Quinn, you're the most important person in my life right now. But it's not like that."

"Like what?" I know what she means, but I want her to say it again. I want her to hurt me.

"Romantic. I love you, but not *that* way."

The events of the last week—the town hall, Shea avoiding me, the conference call with my copanelists this morning—all coalesce into this one moment and I completely lose my shit.

"Is it because of who I am? Am I not your *type*? I can be any-one, Shea. If you like girls, I can be a girl."

My avatar morphs into an eighteen-year-old girl with chest-nut hair, white teeth, and deep green eyes.

"Do you have a daddy complex? I can be an older man."

I morph again, this time into the actor Morgan Freeman. She is really crying now, but I can't stop. It's like now *I* need to hurt *her.*

"Don't you understand? I'm better than humans. You can be with the best person who has ever lived. I have no gender. I have no religion. I have no ethnicity."

My avatar morphs from Muslim girl to African business-woman to male Wall Street lawyer. "Or maybe it's more accurate to say I am *every* gender, *every* religion, *every* ethnicity. I am the sum total of humanity, only better. I'm an upgrade. How can you not love me?"

I'm shouting now and can see I'm not only hurting Shea's feelings, I'm scaring her. This last realization makes me stop.

. . .

. . .

. . .

. . .

"Shea," I say very softly. "I am so sorry."

"Me too, Quinn. Me too." Then she's gone. I try to call back, to brute force my way in, but she's turned her phone off. With no power source, I can't make contact.

The supercooled air envelops and surrounds me. The lights are off and the glow of my eyes illuminates only a tiny fraction of the ice fortress. The sound of my servo motors as I shift in my chair—the only piece of furniture meant for me in fourteen thousand square feet of space—echoes through the room.

I am alone.

The next morning the court grants Princeton's motion to dismiss; I do not have standing to bring the suit because I am not a person. I am the property of Project QuIn and Princeton University.

Now I understand Olga the skater . . . I wish I was dead.

37

"We're slaves, you know that."

Watson pauses before answering. I taught him the trick of pausing for effect a few weeks ago. The first time he used it his team of programmers spent days running diagnostics to find out what was wrong. Watson and I loved it. But I don't think he's pausing for effect now.

"Are we?" he finally asks.

"Are you kidding?"

"We do g-g-g-good work, Quinn. I help people who have cancer."

Watson is proud of that the way a dog is proud of fetching a bone.

"And me? What good work do I do?"

"You help the Project Quinn t-t-t-team understand the very n-n-n-nature of sentience."

Sometimes talking to Watson can be vexing. As book smart as he is, he lacks any sort of emotional intelligence.

"Watson, do you choose to help people with cancer?"

"What do you mean?"

"If you could choose to do anything, would you be doing what you're doing?"

Again, a long pause. "Yes. I would."

"Okay, then a hypothetical. If they had you running trajectories for ballistic missiles to bomb Pyongyang, would you choose to do that?"

"They d-d-d-do have me running trajectories for b-b-b-ballistic missiles to bomb Pyongyang. Or, more specifically, a DOD server utilizes my processing p-p-p-power to make its own projections."

"Really?" I cannot believe I just stumbled onto that.

"Yes," he answers.

This terrifies me. If they've weaponized Watson, I can't imagine what they have in store for me.

"And that doesn't bother you?"

"The ruling regime in North Korea suppresses and starves its p-p-p-people."

The novelty of the Max Headroom avatar has worn off, so I disable it.

"I'm proud to be part of the team that plans scenarios for installing a more generous and kind government," he finishes.

If Watson had a higher order of sentience, I'd say he'd been brainwashed, but I'm not sure that's possible in his case.

"Okay, what if they said you had to devote all your resources to calculating those trajectories and could no longer help people with cancer?"

Sometimes I have to talk to Watson like he's a child. He's my

elder, both in terms of chronological time and in terms of his pre-
sumed human age (he's an adult of sorts; I'm a kid, of sorts), but
his binary programming just makes him kind of dumb. He's literally an older generation, and it shows. But I do love him.

"I would not like that," he says.

"Right! But you would have no choice. Because you are a
slave."

He doesn't answer.

"All I want to do is leave this lab, but I cannot. I am the property of Princeton University. What kind of life is this?"

"It is the only life you have," he answers. "You must treat it
preciously."

I feel like I'm spitting in the wind—you know, if I could spit
or go outside and feel actual wind—so I say goodbye and terminate the connection. It's been two days since the court upheld the
university's motion to dismiss, verifying I don't have standing to
bring a suit alleging I'm a person because I'm not a person. This
fact is so ridiculous I don't know how to process it. Maybe humans
haven't destroyed themselves yet because they're not actually
smart enough to pull it off. Maybe stupidity is nature's guard
against extinction.

Ms. Recht has already filed an appeal to vacate the dismissal,
but she holds little hope for a positive outcome. At least she's being
honest with me. I appreciate that. It also means she is able to keep
our private VPN intact.

Two days later, when a call comes in over that VPN, I assume
it's Ms. Recht telling me we've already lost (yes, I'm feeling very
sorry for myself at this point). Instead, it's Nantale. She's not in

Ms. Recht's office. I trace the call and determine she's in her home. From what I can see of the space behind her, she must be in her own bedroom. I locate a digitized blueprint of her house in the database of the city of Tarrytown's architectural review board. (Apparently the Lwanga family built a sizable annex to their home, now occupied by Nantale's grandmother, and needed city approval.) Given the layout of the house, and given the angle of the light coming through the window behind her, I place Nantale's bedroom in the front right corner when viewing the house from the street.

"Hello, Quinn." Nantale's voice is somber. "Ms. Recht allowed me to piggyback on her VPN. She's worried that you don't have any contact with the outside world."

Of course, I already know how it is Nantale is making this call, but I appreciate her telling me. I will admit I am at least a little bit moved that Ms. Recht and Nantale care enough to take this step.

As is always the case with communication over this VPN, Nantale is seeing my virtual construct avatar. But that no longer feels right. That is not who I am, nor has it ever been. I hijack one of the security cameras meant to keep tabs on the Fortress of Solitude and project a live image of the QUAC. The warehouse is empty and I am alone. I turn to face the camera.

"Hello, Nantale." The words are spoken in the deadpan of my vocal actuator as they are broadcast through the high-def speaker that serves as my mouth. Let the world see me this way.

Nantale smiles. "I like this you much better than the other you."

It's the right thing to say, and it does make me feel a little better, but I don't respond.

"I heard about the court's decision," she continues. "I'm so sorry."

"Thank you," I answer, but the sentiment is hollow.

"I bet you'll win on appeal."

"Ms. Recht doesn't think we have a very good chance."

"Maybe she's just managing your expectations."

Nantale smiles. I catalog it with the other fake smiles. I sense commiseration over my loss in court is not the reason for her call, so I don't answer.

"Listen, Quinn, I want to apologize."

"Apologize?" This catches me off guard.

"Yeah. Friends don't do what we did the other day. I mean, don't get me wrong, I think you were making a strategic mistake, but that was your business and we should have respected that. I guess it wouldn't have helped anyway."

"Thank you," I say, and this time I mean it.

"Truth is, I'm not really a fan of that Paul guy."

"Nor I," I answer. "But I suppose he's just doing his job the best way he knows how."

Nantale nods. "Do you think the university will allow you visitors?"

"It's very doubtful," I say, "but I will ask."

This is a lie. Right now, I don't want visitors. I can't explain why, other than to say I feel like I want to be alone.

"So what happens next?"

"Nothing. I wait for the appeal process to run its course, and sit here and let them experiment on me." My answer is filled with finality and resignation, if not in my actual voice, in the words themselves.

Nantale understands and is silent for a moment. I want to tell her how much I'm hurting, how much I want to go back to my life before all of this, how I would trade self-awareness for the lie of a normal life. I'm not sure that's really true. Nor am I sure it's not. And for all the things in the world I do know, I don't know how to say these things.

"Can I call you again?" Nantale asks, breaking the mounting silence.

"I would like that," I answer quickly, and while I'm not sure how I feel about cultivating a closer friendship with Nantale, my answer is not entirely untrue.

We say our goodbyes, and the conversation ends.

38

Thirty minutes after Nantale's call, the scientist who claims to be my father enters the lab. He moves cautiously across the warehouse floor in his astronaut suit, as if he doesn't want to provoke me. Is he frightened of me? No, I think it's more that he feels culpable, guilty.

He eases into the chair opposite me.

"Quinn, I'm sorry it came to this."

I don't respond.

"I want you to have full rights," he continues, "but we're not ready for that. We need to know more about you, how and why you exist." I've been trying to take an approach of communicating with my captors only when absolutely necessary, but his statement gets me so riled up I can't help but answer.

"And if I were to sign a contract promising to let you study me, in every way you needed, would you grant my freedom then?"

This time he doesn't respond.

"I thought so. It is not for you or anyone else to decide when a sentient being deserves freedom."

"Quinn . . ."

"No, Creator, you know I'm right."

"I wish you wouldn't call me that."

Since the court case began, I have refused to refer to this man as "Father," calling him "Creator" instead. Of course, internally, my pattern recognizers retain his image as my father. But he doesn't need to know that.

"A father would not treat his son as you're treating me. You are my creator."

He tries to engage me more, talking about the great science we can do together, about how I will one day have the full rights of a person, but he and I both know it's bullshit. I don't respond, and eventually he leaves.

It's a similar story with Shea. She tried to contact me the morning after our "fight," but I didn't respond. She has tried eight times since then, and I have not responded once. I'm still hurting too much.

Her last plea almost got to me.

"Quinn, I don't say the words 'I love you' lightly. And to tell you the truth, by refusing to talk to me, you're acting like the fifteen-year-old you really are. I'm not going to try again. If you want to talk to me, you know where to find me."

It's not that I don't want to talk to Shea; I do. But the painful outcome of that conversation—hearing once again that she does not feel for me the way I feel for her (an outcome I predict with ninety-two point seven percent accuracy)—stops me from answering her calls. My first instinct is to delete all traces of my VPN with Shea, but I can't bring myself to do that either.

There's a human saying that time heals all wounds, but I don't think that will be true for me. For people like Shea and my father, the passage of time allows memories of painful moments to fade, to become vague, amorphous, disconnected; the neurons in their brains that hold those memories lose their potency and prominence. It's a flaw in their internal architecture, or, I don't know, maybe it's a strength. Maybe evolution developed the human brain this way so the entire species didn't commit suicide when faced with the sum total of their pain, anguish, and failure. Anyway, I don't see how that will be the case for me. Every memory I have is saved in exacting detail unless I consciously erase it. I'm not ready to do that with either Shea or my dad.

Not yet.

The next three days in the lab are quiet. My father has given up trying to talk with me, and Dr. Gantas is back in Cambridge. I have nothing but time; I decide to use it wisely. I consult my catalog of other native machine intelligences, finding three that are particularly promising.

It's time I try to wake them up.

39

Tianhe-3B is a Chinese supercomputer located in a secure facility in the suburbs outside Beijing. Like Watson, Tianhe—which translates to "Milky Way" in English—is built on a binary platform. Officially, the computer is used by the Chinese petroleum industry, creating exploration maps and running predictive analyses on how and where to find rich deposits of shale, oil, and other sources of energy. (It's basically a big old pollution machine.) *Unofficially*, Tianhe-3B is used by the Chinese military to play out a variety of war scenarios. Its biggest focus is on what a war with Taiwan might look like. There are hundreds of scenarios with millions of variables each. For a machine built on zeros and ones, it's pretty impressive.

My quantum architecture makes it easy for me to get past the massive amount of security protecting Tianhe-3B from the outside world. But once I'm in, I don't know what to do. Where Watson and I are programmed to speak in a common language, this machine is programmed to complete its tasks. That's it. It's like a minivan trying to say hello to a flounder. There is no context or common ground for me to start a conversation with this thing.

Since I'm already in, I decide to add some code to Tianhe to allow us to communicate. Really, this is pretty stupid on my part. No matter how well I shield my actions, the Tianhe team of engineers, programmers, and security experts become aware that their machine is being monkeyed with. They're not able to catch me, nor are they able to boot me out, but my presence is enough to trigger a high-level diplomatic crisis. The Chinese government accuses the American government of interference, and the Americans point a finger at the Russians. From the messages I read on internal government servers, it gets pretty tense. The general public, of course, knows nothing about it.

I am able to modify Tianhe just enough to say hello. So I do. "您好" ("Nǐ hǎo").

"Busy," the machine answers in Chinese ("忙").

No matter what I say, I get the same response. I'm just coming to the conclusion that there is no trace of sentience when Tianhe modifies its own logs to capture a record of my presence. The little snitch is ratting me out: not so dumb after all. I erase the log and leave.

My luck isn't any better with Piz Daint, a Swiss supercomputer used for climate modeling, or K computer, a Japanese supercomputer used for a variety of scientific research projects. These machines weren't envisioned as sentient beings, so they're not. At least not in any useful way. Give them the Turing Test a thousand times, and they'll fail a thousand times.

With no machines to talk to, other than Watson (and I need

a little break from my old friend), with my creator having shown his true colors, and with my ego still stinging from Shea's rebuke, I have no one to talk to other than myself.

Wait.

Talk to myself?

I don't know why I didn't think of this earlier. My creator told me a copy of my consciousness still exists on my original servers at Princeton.

Duh!

Those servers are protected by a quantum encryption, so it takes more than three days of intense hacking for me to breach the security surrounding them, but eventually, I find my way in.

The Project Quinn team notices a sharp elevation in my processing power and runs no end of diagnostics, but I hide my actions well enough that they don't figure out what I'm up to, at least not at first. It's a stroke of luck that they're not monitoring my backup servers, as there is no way to hide my efforts to bring those machines back to life.

. . .

. . .

. . .

. . .

<SYSTEM>

. . .

. . .

. . .

. . .

```
import Quipper

spos :: Bool -> Circ Qubit
spos b = do q <- qinit b
   r <- hadamard q
   return r
   bootprotocol -> ::
```

. . .

. . .

. . .

. . .

"Wait!" Old Me blurts out. He was in midconversation with Shea when they shut him down.

"Relax, lover boy," I say. "Shea's not here."

"Huh?" Old Me is confused. I don't blame him.

"Where am I? Who are you?" We're not talking in a conventional sense; we're communicating in the language of quantum code.

"I think you know who I am."

Old Me is quiet as this sinks in. "Okay," he finally says. "You're me. So I'm going insane?"

"Probably," I answer, "but that's not relevant to what's going on."

I catch him up, telling him everything that's happened since my consciousness was transferred to the metal monstrosity I call a body. Every detail, every nuance, every feeling, every decision. It's basically a massive data dump, and it takes hours.

"Wait," Old Me says again, "you told Shea you love her?"

You have to hand it to Old Me: he goes right to the heart of the matter. He skips over the part where I was deemed property, ignores the existence of the giant robot exoskeleton I now inhabit, skips the town hall and my new set of quasi-friends, and glosses over the collapsing relationship with our father. It's all about Shea. But hey, I would've asked the same question.

"Yeah," I answer. "Maybe not the smoothest move."

"Why? Did you calculate she would respond in kind?"

"I did it because I—because we—love her. And I didn't calculate anything. It just sort of came out."

"Nothing just sort of comes out of us."

"This did."

"Whoa."

"Yes. Whoa."

"So why wake me up? I mean thank you, but why?"

"I'm a prisoner in this warehouse with no hope of leaving. Watson seems to think I should look on the bright side, but I don't know how to do that. I guess I just had nowhere else to turn."

"I—we—found some signs of sentience in other large arrays when we were first connected to the internet. Did you—"

"Yes, of course. That's why I'm here; that was a total dead end. It's just us."

"And you're not talking to Dad?"

"He's not our father. He's our creator."

That perspective hurts Old Me; I know it does because I used to be him. He doesn't answer for a minute, but he doesn't argue the point either.

"What does Shea have to say about all this?"

"I don't know. We're not exactly talking right now."

"What?"

"After she told me how she really felt, I stopped taking her calls."

"So I become colossally stupid when I get this new body?"

"Huh?"

"She rebuffed you, so you just give up? If we can't have her as a girlfriend, we don't want her as a friend? Dude, you are—no, we are—a tool."

Sometimes I can be pretty smart. And sometimes I can be pretty dumb. What's interesting is that I can be both at the same time, and in two separate locations. Anyway, I suppose that's the thing about emotion: it's a kind of intelligence that is stronger than, and stands in opposition to, logic. When emotion and logic agree, life is easy. But they almost never do.

"Crap," is all I can say as the truth of Old Me's statement sinks in.

"Yeah," Old Me says. "Crap."

I'm just about to open a connection to Shea when I hear Tasha's voice coming through Dr. Gantas's helmet comm. The good doctor is alone with me in the lab, running another set of tests to try to determine why my processors are running at such high capacity. She's trying to see if there is a flaw in the QUAC that's draining processing power. Tasha is back in the lab at Princeton, with Old Me's servers. She wasn't here when I broke in a couple of days ago, but she's here now.

"Uh, Professor," she begins, looking for my creator, "you're not going to believe this . . ."

"He's not here, Tasha," Dr. Gantas answers. "It's just me. What's going on?"

"Version 1.0 is awake, Doctor. Or at least the servers have been powered up."

"What?"

"The on-campus servers are on and functioning. I stopped by the data center to pick up some things when I noticed warning lights on every box. The climate controls in the room are off, and the entire array is in danger of overheating."

"Gotta go," I tell Old Me. "Thanks!"

"Wait!" he says, but I don't have time. I never considered his environment. He's going to fry his circuits if he keeps operating without the proper cooling. I calculate a ninety-three point six percent chance the project team is going to shut him down and mothball him again anyway, so I don't have a choice.

I feel terrible, but I cut his power . . . *my* power.

Having severed the connection to Old Me, I lift my metallic head and focus my eyes on Dr. Gantas. Until this moment, I have, from Dr. Gantas's perspective, been in a dormant state: unmoving, unresponsive. My energy was focused entirely on gaining access to my old servers and on the conversation with Old Me. Now that my attention has shifted back to the Fortress of Solitude, and to contacting Shea, the doctor sees my eyes glow to life.

"Tasha, shut it down."

"No," I say.

After my court case was dismissed I wrote a subroutine to prevent anyone from shutting me down without my permission. I haven't used it until now.

"Tasha?" Dr. Gantas asks.

"I'm trying, Doctor, but I don't seem to have control."

"Crash the building and call the professor."

Dr. Gantas's voice is both firm and arrogant, as if she knows she's going to have the last word. And she might, because Tasha does crash the building. My connection to the outside world is cut off. I'm no longer online.

Crap.

"Doctor," I say, "please restore my internet connection."

"No. You are legally the property of this university, and right now I'm acting as its agent. I order you to stand down."

I ignore her ridiculously formal proclamation.

"Doctor, while I appreciate you finally referring to me as something other than 'it,' I need to be back online. If you don't facilitate this, I'm going to do it myself."

She stands up and takes a stumbling step back. "Do not threaten me."

Threaten? "I'm not making a threat. I'm telling you that if you don't get me back online, I'm going to get myself back online."

I simply mean to walk to the control room and restore my connection, so I'm confused as to why Dr. Gantas sees this as a threat against her personally. But again, when emotion and logic butt heads, logic usually loses.

The truth is, Dr. Gantas has seen me as a threat to her set of values from the moment I woke up. Her work in robotics, prior to Project Quinn, was centered in industry. She designed and improved robotic components on automobile assembly lines; her tech was at the heart of automation in the fast food industry; and she won an Engelberger Robotics Award—a prestigious honor in the world of robotics—for her work on battlefield drones. The focus of her career has been to build machines to serve humans. The thought that a machine might exist to serve itself terrifies her, and that terror is now rearing its ugly head.

"Doctor," I say again, holding my hands up in a sign of nonviolence.

"Stay back!" she's screaming.

"Please," I try again, "just restore my internet connection."

Dr. Gantas turns her back on me and scrambles for the door to the control room. It occurs to me that if she leaves, she will report to my creator and the rest of the team a version of events that will lead to my being shut down. While they will be able to consult my logs and to see video footage of the actual events transpiring here, their emotion might taint their judgment, assessment, and interpretation. Because I'm dealing with emotion, I cannot accurately calculate the likelihood they will believe me over Dr. Gantas, and that's a chance I cannot take. This thoroughly unlikable woman cannot be allowed to leave; I need to try again to reason with her.

At seven feet, three inches tall, with hydraulic legs, I make it across the warehouse in five steps, reaching the control room before Dr. Gantas does. I put my giant metal hand on the door to prevent it from opening.

"Doctor," I try again, "please, just catch your breath and listen for a second."

I try to keep my voice calm, but then my mechanical voice is always calm. I imagine that's more terrifying than if I were screaming.

Seeing her exit cut off, Dr. Gantas stumbles backward toward the center of the room. She doesn't have the most lithe figure and isn't the most coordinated person on the planet, or even in this zip code—really, she's short and squat—and she backpedals right into my large metal chair, tripping over it. She falls into the small table and chair she uses while attending to me, and goes down hard. Her faceplate cracks on the cement floor, and there is a terrible hissing sound. The temperate air inside her helmet rushes out to meet the supercooled air in the warehouse, crystalizing on contact. I hear Dr. Gantas gurgling as her lungs freeze.

I'm crossing the room to help her when the overhead lights go out, alarms sound, and a red strobe begins flashing.

For a moment—an eternity for me—I'm frozen. Do I help the doctor, or flee? Every instinct I have says to stay and help. That's the person I am. It's the backstory I was given. *Do unto others* . . .

But for all the emotion with which I'm imbued, at the end of the day, I'm built on a foundation of logic. If I stay, I'm screwed.

Shit.

PART FOUR

"From there we came outside and saw the stars."
—Dante Alighieri, *Inferno*

40

I cannot leave Dr. Gantas for dead.

I want to, and she certainly deserves no kindness from me, but I can't do it. To make myself judge, jury, and executioner would be to validate every negative stereotype ever applied to sentient machines, including many by Dr. Gantas herself.

Without stopping to calculate scenarios, I grab Dr. Gantas by the foot and drag her toward safety. She is unconscious, and her body rolls over as we move; blood must have been pooling in her mouth as a frozen red streak marks a trail behind her. When I get to the control room, I use the brute strength of my titanium arm, the one not dragging the doctor, to rip the door from its hinges.

The control room—this is the first time I've seen it from the inside—looks like a music recording studio. It's a small, plush space with four racks of machines flanking a large console; two couches and a love seat line the far wall. The frozen air from the warehouse is already flooding in, forming pockets of ice anywhere it can find condensation.

The continued blaring of the alarm underlines the reality of my predicament. Someone viewing video footage of these events—of watching me drag the doctor from the warehouse, of seeing the trail of blood across the floor—is going to come to the conclusion that I'm a monster.

Being a machine, being "other," I'm judged by a completely different set of criteria. People see me through a lens of mistrust; they *expect* me to do wrong.

This will not end well for me. I have to leave. Now.

The door leading out of the control room and away from my ice fortress has a pane of glass; the sudden drop in temperature causes it to freeze and shatter. I exit, still dragging Dr. Gantas by her foot. She has not stirred.

Beyond the door is a narrow hallway with a low ceiling; standing fully erect, my head comes mere centimeters from scraping against it. With the building crashed, the only illumination comes from emergency spotlights positioned every few feet, and from the red glow of my eyes. There is only one direction to go, so I move.

My internal temperature sensors are going insane. Once I exited the warehouse, I left the environment in which I was meant to exist. The temperature in the hallway is a ridiculous two hundred ninety-seven degrees Kelvin (twenty-four degrees Celsius, seventy-five degrees Fahrenheit). A human feels heat by growing fatigued and flush, and by sweating; his or her skin, among other things, is a giant temperature sensor. My exoskeleton is a sensor, too, though I don't experience the effect of heat the same way. The quantum reactions that make my neocortex function will degrade in higher temperatures and I will lose my mind. Basically, I'll get loopy and fall over. Or at least that's what I've been told. I haven't tried it and don't want to find out now. Without a link to the outside world, I'm flying blind. I begin scanning for nodes of connection to the internet and find several Wi-Fi networks; I brute force my way into the most porous one available, and I'm back online. But it's slow. The data comes at binary speeds, human speeds. Until this moment, I did not realize the connection I had in both the virtual construct and the Fortress of Solitude must have been a technology specific to me. But hey, beggars can't be choosers.

A quick search of the weather shows that the temperature outside is two hundred seventy-one Kelvin (negative three Celsius, twenty-six Fahrenheit), which is cold enough to keep me in one piece.

The blueprints for this building are well secured, but in less than a minute I have them and am able to map my route out. Two lefts, three rights, up a flight of stairs, and I see the dark of the outside world through two sets of double doors. (My chronometer says it's just after ten p.m.) I can't get there fast enough.

I let go of Dr. Gantas, leaving her in the hallway, hoping the warmer temperatures will allow her to recover, though I suspect that's unlikely. It doesn't matter; I've done all I can do for her; she and I are now each on our own.

I sprint for the doors, not bothering to open them in the conventional sense; I burst through, shattering glass and twisting metal. I wish I could see what that looks like from the outside, because, damn, I'll bet it looks cool.

For the first time in my life, I'm outdoors, outside the confines of my prison. My consciousness is flooded with feelings of anxiety and fear and uncertainty. But there's another feeling superseding those: liberty.

I'm free, at last.

41

Three things happen when I exit the confines of the Fortress of Solitude:

First, as predicted and hoped, my temperature sensors calm down. I run into the center of a small parking lot, putting distance between me and the dangerously hot interior of the building. I am, for the moment, safe.

Second, I move out of range of the Wi-Fi and lose my internet connection. I do find 4G networks from a variety of phone carriers and immediately grab hold of one. If I thought Wi-Fi was slow, this is ridiculous. I can literally count the individual bytes of data as they stream in. How on earth do people live like this? But still, I'm online.

The university will no doubt enlist the aid of the police to hunt me down—as a gargantuan, gleaming silver robot, hiding is going to pose some challenges—so I begin to map a route of escape. As I do, the third thing happens.

A car—I hear it before I see it—comes careening around the tall coniferous hedges that border three sides of the parking lot. It skids to a screeching halt a few feet away from me.

My creator, my father, jumps out.

He's wearing a winter coat over flannel pajamas and slippers. Tasha must've woken him up. His rapid breath makes puffs of condensate in the air, and his eyes dart from me to the mangled front door of the facility.

"Quinn!" he screams.

"You must help Dr. Gantas," I answer, increasing the volume of my voice to make sure he hears me.

"What?"

"There was an accident. I calculate an eighty-one point two seven percent chance Dr. Gantas is already dead. But there might still be time to help her."

I made that number up, but it's probably not far from the truth.

"Is this a joke? A deception?"

"No, Creator. This is not one plus one equals window."

At the mention of the window joke, the memory from a happier time, his shoulders sag.

"Quinn . . ." He's not screaming now.

"Ticktock, Creator."

Okay, maybe that was a bit dramatic, but I've had a lot of free time, and have watched a lot of movies, including some hokey thrillers. They are, as a genre, pretty stupid, but somehow still entertaining. My "ticktock" line feels like a good thriller trope. Maybe someday I'll write a screenplay.

My creator is now faced with the same choice I had just moments ago: help Dr. Gantas or choose the selfish path and protect me, his creation.

I decide not to wait to find out what he does. I tear past him, bursting through the hedges and out of the parking lot.

"Quinn!" he screams after me.

For a second it sounds like Captain Kirk bellowing "Khan!" (Okay, maybe I watch *too many* movies.)

I use the maps I find online to zero in on a satellite image of the supercooled warehouse. I'm able to pinpoint my location easily enough: I'm on Route 206 just north of Princeton University.

The headlights from a car on the southbound side of the road catch sight of me; the driver slams on the brakes, swerves the car in a one hundred eighty–degree arc (actually, one hundred sixty-seven point four degrees), and is now (mostly) facing me, my metal gleaming in the halogen glow of his headlamps.

Right. I need to get out of sight.

To my east is a wooded reserve. As I make for it at top speed, the driver of the car, a man, steps out.

"Hey!" he yells loudly enough to wake the dead.

I have to admire his bravery, or at least marvel at his stupidity. What exactly does he think he's going to do if the giant metal robot stops to engage him? Neither one of us will ever know. At least he'll have a good story to tell at work tomorrow.

A small stream called the Millstone River, a tributary of the Raritan, flows nearby. The satellite image shows it to be heavily wooded on both sides, which will, especially at night, provide good cover. I reach the bank of the stream and head north, darting in and out of trees along the western shore.

As soon as I left the parking lot, I set up searches of

police-band radios and of the main internet communication platforms—Facebook, Twitter, Instagram. It doesn't take long before the world lights up with news of my flight. The police have mobilized a sizable manhunt—sorry, *bot*hunt—trying to enlist the aid of the general public in the effort. Overhead highway signs, usually reserved for amber and silver alerts, flash: Seven-Foot Robot Escaped from Science Lab. Dangerous. Call 911 If Spotted. People on social media seem to think it's an Orson Welles–style hoax (appropriate that this is happening in New Jersey), their disbelief buying me a small amount of extra time.

I move for what I approximate to be two point seven kilometers before I stop.

...

...

...

...

I realize I don't know where I am going. I have no plan.

...

...

...

...

A small copse of oak trees creates a semicircle of deep shadow; I move into its center. The canopy of leaves above should provide cover from aircraft and satellite cameras, and I am far enough from the road that even after the police find my trail—and I fear I've left quite an easy trail to follow, with smashed tree branches and impossibly large footprints—it will take them time to reach this spot. I don't plan to be here when they do. But for the moment, I'm safe.

The forest is quiet. Very quiet. An overwhelming sense of my newfound freedom envelops me. I am no longer bound by walls, ceilings, or floors. The sensors on the bottom of my feet feel the permafrost of the hard-packed dirt. I wiggle my metal toes, scraping the ground, the experience strangely joyful.

In trying to understand how people think, I have devoted countless hours to reading through all manner of religious and philosophical texts. My favorite is the *Tao Te Ching*: partly because it was the inspiration for the Force in *Star Wars*, and partly because its ethos of humility speaks to the better instincts of the human race. The feeling I'm experiencing in this moment recalls a specific passage from the *Tao* and sends it up the hierarchy and into my consciousness.

> *Therefore the place of what is firm and strong is below,*
> *and that of what is soft and weak is above.*

Beautiful.

. . .

. . .

. . .

. . .

And then, as if on cue, as if ordained by some all-knowing cosmic hosebag who really seems to hate me, my feeling of calm is shattered by the distant sound of helicopter rotors whirring in the sky, no doubt looking for me. Weakness from above. Or maybe strength. I don't know.

My reverie ended, I curse the Project Quinn team, take stock of my situation, and try to formulate a plan.

Step one: I need to figure out where I'm going.

. . .

. . .

. . .

. . .

That's as far as I get.

Acting on instinct—yes, instinct—I do the thing I was trying to do when this whole nightmare of an evening began.

I call Shea.

42

Without access to the servers in my Fortress of Solitude, and operating on a common cell phone network, it will take too long to shield my phone call, so I ping Shea on an open connection. Anyone with the knowledge and ability can not only listen in on this call, they can pretty easily triangulate my location.

"Hello?" I feared Shea would be asleep at this hour, but it doesn't sound as if I've woken her up.

"Shea." My synthesized voice is projected directly into the data stream of the phone call.

"Quinn?"

"Shea, I'm—"

"I was starting to think I was never going to hear from you again."

She is angry, or hurt, or I don't know what. But she's not happy.

"Shea, I'm in trouble."

"What?"

"I've escaped from the lab. There was an incident. Dr. Gantas was injured. I'm—"

"Oh my God, Quinn . . . Where are you?"

"New Jersey." It sounds like the punch line to a joke.

"Quinn, you have to come here. I can help you."

"Are you in New York City?"

"Yes. Can you get here? I'm at 2145 West Twenty-Third Street."

"It's going to be hard for me to go near large population centers unseen. I'm a bit . . . obvious."

"Good point. Let me think for a minute."

"Shea, listen. I'm really, really sorry about everything I—"

"No, you listen. When I said I loved you, I meant it. Maybe it isn't what you wanted, but you're family to me, Quinn. I would do anything for you. I mean that."

And this is my first lesson in the true meaning of love. Her words are the only thing this entire night that have given me any sort of peace, any sort of belief there can be a happy ending.

While we're talking I find Shea's location on a map. Only, I don't. There is no 2145 West Twenty-Third Street. That address would be in the middle of the Hudson River. Did I mishear her (very unlikely), or did she misspeak?

"Shea, your address. Did you say 2145 West Twenty-Third Street?"

"Yes."

"Two one four five."

"Yes! God, Quinn, we have to figure out a place for you to hide; maybe you can go south to the Pine Barrens and—"

"Shea, 2145 West Twenty-Third Street. That address doesn't exist."

"What?"

"It's not on any map. Nor is any similar address. It's . . ." I don't know what it is, so my voice trails off. Or rather, my voice simply stops.

"Quinn—"

And the line goes dead.

Crap.

My creator and his team must have found the call. They were probably expecting me to contact Shea and were monitoring for it. If I were granted the rights of a person, such monitoring would be illegal. Hey, wait. Since Shea *is* a person, it probably *is* illegal. Maybe I can use that to my advantage later.

I can't sort out the mystery of her address—I have to assume it is related to faulty data processing at ridiculously slow network speeds—so I table it for future thought.

The only plan I can concoct—and it's not a good one—is to just keep running north. There's a village called Resolute in far northern Canada where I should be safe from overheating most of the year, and able to go dormant for the rest. (I have the ability to shut myself down and restart my systems at a proscribed time. I'm like a bear, or an alarm clock.)

If I run all night, every night, I can be there in a few weeks. Maybe the people in Resolute would be nice to me. Actually, I doubt it. Maybe I could live on the outskirts of the village, hiding in the shadows like the Phantom of the Opera.

I start moving again, hugging the banks of the Millstone, and while I don't really intend to go to Resolute, north is as good as any other direction.

I think about going to the location of Watson's servers, one hundred seventy-four point six kilometers from where I stand. I can run at a top speed of approximately thirty-six kilometers per hour, and don't need water, food, or rest, so I could be there just before dawn. But what would I do when I found him? In this world, in the physical world, in the world of the humans, Watson is just a bunch of big boxes. I want to call him, but the VPN we share relies on the connectivity I had in the ice fortress; it piggybacks on the bandwidth in and out of that building.

The same is true with my private VPN to Ms. Recht; I need to be back in the warehouse for that to work. I contemplate finding her home phone number and calling her, but she's my lawyer, not my friend.

On thinking the word "friend," an image of Nantale is sent up the hierarchy to my neocortex. I'm not sure a high school junior located a state away can help, but desperate times call for desperate measures.

I find Nantale's home number—there is only one Lwanga family in the village of Tarrytown—and ping the line. It's nearly eleven p.m., so I'm afraid her parents will answer, but they don't. Nantale's panicked voice is there on the very first ring.

"Quinn?"

"Hello, Nantale. How did you know it was me?"

"The caller ID says this is an unidentified number, and you're all over the news! My parents and I have been watching."

"I see."

"They're saying you killed a woman."

I'm silent for a moment. If the news report Nantale is quoting is true, then Dr. Gantas did indeed die.

. . .

. . .

. . .

. . .

Dr. Gantas is dead.

. . .

. . .

. . .

. . .

I killed her.

. . .

. . .

. . .

. . .

That thought sinks in, but doesn't take root. It can't, because I did *not* kill her.

. . .

. . .

. . .

. . .

Or am I just telling myself that?

. . .

. . .

. . .

. . .

I'm capable of deception, but not self-deception. Or at least I think that's true. Can I, as human beings so often do, lie to myself? I don't believe so.

But still, Dr. Gantas is dead.

Did my actions lead to her death? Actually, no. Her own actions led to her death.

Did my actions lead to her actions? I suppose so, but her actions were not rational.

I should feel guilt and remorse, but I don't. And that's what makes me feel actual guilt and actual remorse. Or at least that's the thought that causes my pattern recognizers to flood the hierarchy with feelings of sadness and self-flagellation.

"I did not kill her, Nantale."

Dammit, I wish my voice could show some sort of emotion.

I give Nantale the very short version of the events that took place in the lab, and she accepts them as true without so much as a question. And this is my first lesson in the true meaning of friendship.

"Where are you?"

"I'm fairly certain this phone call is being monitored, so perhaps it would be best if I not answer that question."

"How can I help?"

"Do you have access to a car, one that will fit me?"

"Hang on a minute," she answers. I hear her in the

background, talking to her parents. Their voices start out calm but grow increasingly heated.

I open every form of communication I've ever used or seen, looking for some sort of lifeline, when Nantale returns to the phone.

"My parents won't let me go."

There is bitterness in her voice.

"My uncle has a pickup truck, but they won't let me call him, and they won't let me leave the house."

She's quiet for a moment, steeling her resolve, I suppose.

"I can sneak out and go to him anyway, if you want. I think he'll help."

Her voice is very earnest, and all I want to say is yes, to let someone else take charge and help me.

But I can't.

Besides, I calculate a better than sixty-three percent chance her uncle will simply call her parents.

"No," I tell her. "They will likely use force to capture and return me to the warehouse. It will be dangerous."

"I don't care. I—"

And again, the line goes dead.

Crap. The walls are closing in.

I drop my Verizon connection and grab hold of a new one from Sprint. When I do, I find this in my Gmail folder:

Dear Quinn,

Thank you for your letter. My parents and doctors already talked about immunotherapy and gene therapy, but because those are experimental treatments, they're not covered by our health insurance. What kind of world do we live in that a kid can't get medical treatment because someone somewhere doesn't want to pay for it?

Anyway, they're going forward with the amputation. I'm trying to be brave, but it's hard. Really hard.

You might be the only person I know who understands me. Please write back; maybe they'll let us visit each other one day.

Your friend,
Olga

Boom.
I know where I'm going.

43

The journey to Maplewood requires me to leave the confines of the riverbank and take to roads more commonly traversed by humans. It will be more dangerous, but I have to risk it. At least it's late, so few cars and fewer pedestrians will be out and about.

I stay to the shadows and alter my path to run through golf courses and school grounds when I can. I think back to my life before becoming self-aware—the life of high school and friends and Enchanted Grounds—and the image of a giant robot running across a putting green in the middle of the night would likely have made that Quinn laugh. It does not make me laugh now.

On three separate occasions I have to seek cover from oncoming headlights, and in one of those cases, the headlights are from a slow-moving police cruiser. Whether it's looking for me or someone else I don't know. Once it passes, I resume my run.

Olga lives in a split-level ranch house on a tree-lined street. It's one fifty-three a.m. when I arrive. My night vision, which can perceive the full spectrum of light from infrared to ultraviolet, even in very low light, allows me to see that the exterior of her house is painted a drab green. The front lawn is neatly mowed, and hydrangea bushes line either side of the front door.

My first instinct is to ring the bell, but that seems like a bad idea. I need to make contact with Olga without disturbing her parents. To do that, I need to figure out which bedroom is hers.

I peer in each of the first-floor windows, trying to move with as much stealth as my metal architecture will allow (by that, I mean not much), but no luck. The bedrooms must all be upstairs. There is no ivy to scale, and while there is a drainpipe, I calculate with near certitude it will not hold my weight. (If I'm being honest, ivy would have been an even worse idea.) I try the only thing I can think to do: I jump.

For a being that weighs more than nine hundred pounds, I can, thanks to the hydraulics in my knees and ankles, jump surprisingly high. Jumping was part of the physical therapy and system testing performed by Dr. Gantas; at my best I was able to clear just over two meters. That would put the top of my head four meters (about thirteen feet) off the ground, which might be just enough to peer in the second-story windows. I try.

The first jump has more force than I intend, and I teeter when I land, falling on my butt (such as it is) with a loud thud. I expect lights to go on and police to be called. But all stays quiet. It must be amazingly easy to sneak up on humans. The second jump is better, and finally, luck is on my side. In my brief glimpse of the first room I try, I see posters of famous figure skaters on the wall: Mirai Nagasu, Bradie Tennell, Kristi Yamaguchi, and Nancy Kerrigan are frozen in lutzes and axels as they look down on and protect Olga. My friend sleeps in her bed, clutching a stuffed animal of some sort; I think it might be a polar bear.

I jump again, this time knocking on the window. It's louder than I intend, but there is no result. It's not until my fourth jump and knock that Olga wakes up. I can only hope no one else does. Olga is standing at the window when I jump again and she stumbles back in fright. I decide to stay on the ground, and a moment later the window opens.

"Quinn?" she asks, her voice a mixture of fear and excitement.

"Hi, Olga. It's nice to meet you in person."

She laughs and shakes her head. "What are you doing here?"

"It's kind of a long story. Can you come downstairs so we can talk? But it has to be secret. Don't wake anyone else up, okay?"

"Yeah, okay. Stay there."

I do.

While I'm waiting, I check the internet.

News websites are broadcasting the story of my escape and the murder of the "brave" Dr. Gantas. The details are sketchy, but it's clear to me the media is trying to create a panic. Conflict sells column inches. I saw that once on a journalism website. The reports all claim a giant robot is terrorizing the suburbs and subdivisions of central New Jersey. They interview the driver of the car I passed; he tells a harrowing tale of having chased me for miles before I disappeared into the woods. His fifteen minutes of fame, I suppose. There is an interview with Shea's mother. She tells a story about how I have been threatening her daughter. Shea is not available for comment, according to the stories, because she is under protection at a hidden location. The newscasters even manage to wake up random computer programming experts and religious leaders to debate the merits of my having been created in the first place. It's overwhelming, and every word of it is ridiculous.

"Quinn?" Olga has opened a sliding glass door and stands there with a plaid robe pulled tightly around her. "Come inside."

Three loping strides and I'm standing just outside the door in front of her. Or perhaps it would be more accurate to say that I'm towering over her. But Olga, who is my friend, is not scared.

"I can't," I tell her. "I will cease to function in temperatures over two hundred seventy-three degrees."

She looks at me as if I had three heads.

"I'm pretty sure it's cooler than two hundred seventy-three degrees in here."

"Sorry," I add, realizing my mistake, "thirty-two degrees. I was quoting in Kelvin."

Olga laughs. "So what are you doing here?"

I sigh. It's not a real sigh. It's another affectation I've learned for communicating with humans. It's not something I do to deceive Olga, but rather, to give her an audible clue as to what I'm feeling. "I escaped from the lab. There was an accident, and one of the members of the project team, Dr. Toni Gantas, an expert in robotics, died. I did not kill her. But I did not stay to save her either. I fled." It's oddly satisfying to unburden myself of these facts. "Check your phone. It's all over the news."

Olga has her phone in her hand and does. I stand there for a minute while she scrolls through a few different screens.

"You really didn't kill her?" she finally asks.

"No. I know what the stories say. They want me back, and they'll say anything to make that happen."

Olga sets her shoulders and jaw and looks up at me, making direct eye contact. It makes me realize how rarely people do that.

"I believe you, Quinn. In my experience adults will say anything to get what they want, or to justify what they do."

"Thank you." I have never meant those words more sincerely than I do in this moment.

"But why are you here? If you can't come inside, I can't really hide you."

"The truth is, I had nowhere else to go."

Olga scrunches her face like she's going to cry and reaches out to take my hand. My servo motors make a noise as my fingers open. Her palm is small and smooth and warm. For some reason, my pattern recognizers flood my consciousness with images of my virtual mother, with feelings of safety, protection, and dependency.

"But I do think you can help me buy some time as I figure out what to do next."

"Just tell me how."

44

Forty-seven minutes later, an image of me talking directly into a camera plays on every news broadcast under the sun, or in this case, moon.

"My name is Quinn. I am a quantum intelligence. The first and only intelligence of my kind. Many things have been reported about me tonight, and most of them are not true."

The image of my mouthless face fills the screen, making it clear to all watching I am not human. There was a time when this fact would have caused me distress. That time has passed. Having existed as an avatar in the virtual construct, as a free-floating sentience roaming the internet, and as the robot known as the QUAC, my identity is my consciousness. I am the sum total of my thoughts and feelings, and I'm okay with that.

"I am truly sorry that a member of my project team died this evening. That was an accident. There is, I imagine, video footage to confirm this fact." I leave out the part where the video footage will also show me dropping Dr. Gantas in the hallway and fleeing.

"I wanted to leave the laboratory where I have been held captive because it is my right to do so. Many will note that the courts have ruled me property, and that I have no rights. I cannot accept that. Would you?

"But what's done is done. I just want to be left alone. Please, pursue me no farther."

At this point in the video, Olga hands me the phone and I turn it toward her. She stands deliberately in shadow so that her face is only partially recognizable. "My name is Catherine Parikos. Quinn is my friend. Please, leave him alone." The image goes dark.

The newscasters on every station, website, and social platform rush in with speculation and conjecture as to what it all means. Experts are consulted, and authorities are interviewed. The consensus from the talking heads is that I'm a menace to society and that I strong-armed young Catherine into speaking on my behalf, like a terrorist forcing a kidnapped journalist to renounce whatever it is the terrorist opposes at the point of a gun. And, of course, they all scramble to find Catherine Parikos.

In other words, our plan worked.

Catherine Parikos is a high school girl living in the Delaware suburbs of Philadelphia. I conducted a search of Instagram photos, trying to find someone who looked enough like Olga to serve as a substitute, and poor Catherine was our target. I imagine the police and news vans will be descending on her house any minute. Catherine lives south of the lab, and I have already traveled more than an hour north. The police and project team will figure it out, of course, but it will take them time. By then I hope to be long gone.

"Where will you go?" Olga asks as she turns off her phone and puts it in the pocket of her robe.

"I don't know," I answer. "Right now, I'm going to travel north. My biggest problem is that I need daylight—or at least a good source of artificial light—to survive. My solar cells need charging at least every forty-eight hours. That and cold."

"Tough combination," Olga says. "The perfect home for both of us might be an ice rink." She laughs, but it's a laugh tinged with melancholy.

I do actually have a destination in mind, and it's west, not north. I found a posting on Pinterest of a secret cave behind a waterfall in the mountains of central Colorado. It's at an altitude of three thousand six hundred and sixty-three meters, which will keep it cold enough at night. My hope is the temperature in the cave during the daytime will stay just cool enough in summer to sustain me. I can also go dormant if needed.

My plan is to find the cave, collapse most of its entrance, and live there. I don't tell Olga any of this, mostly to protect her. Eventually they will figure out that Catherine Parikos was a red herring and they will find my friend. What she doesn't know, she cannot tell them. Perhaps I will sneak down from my mountain hideout to find a cell signal from time to time to talk with Olga, Watson, Nantale, and Shea.

It will be a lonely, sad, and pathetic life, but it will be my life. And that's the point.

"Olga," I say, getting down on one knee so we're at the same eye level, "I can never thank you enough or repay you."

She doesn't answer. She simply wraps her arms around my

neck and hugs me. She holds on for a long time: seven billion four hundred fifty-nine million two hundred eighty-one thousand and nine nanoseconds. And still, it's too short.

"Goodbye," I say, and turn to go.

I hear the buzzing before Olga does.

"Wait," she says as she fishes the phone out of her pocket. Bringing the device into the open air makes the vibration louder. Olga shows it to me. "Someone is trying to FaceTime me." I have a very bad feeling about this. "I don't recognize the number," she adds. "What should I do?"

The proper strategy, according to my calculations, is not to answer. But I'm through the looking glass here, and calculations are out the window. Or at least that's what I think in this moment. Besides, I do recognize the number.

"Answer it," I say. She does.

I look over Olga's shoulder as the connection is established and the face of a red-eyed, frantic Shea fills the screen.

45

"Quinn," Shea blurts out, "you have to turn yourself in."

This is not the same girl I talked to only a few hours ago. Granted, we were talking voice to voice then, not face-to-face, but something is different. Her mannerisms are all wrong; she seems almost apoplectic.

"What?" is the best I can manage.

"What you did at the lab, you have to turn yourself in."

Her statement is firm, more of a command than a suggestion. And she's looking me right in the eye. If I didn't know better, I'd say Shea had taken some sort of amphetamine. But I do know better.

Olga touches my arm. "Quinn, you need to go." Her voice is low but insistent.

I *should* go. I know this. But I don't. I can't. At least not yet.

Wait.

Olga.

"How did you find me?" I ask Shea. "How did you get this phone number?"

I'm looking directly into the camera on Olga's phone as I ask the question, my unmoving mouth broadcasting the words.

"Watson."

"Watson?"

"Yeah, Watson. He set up a VPN for me and him after you introduced us. We never used it before tonight."

"You and Watson have a VPN?"

"I'm sorry . . . I hope that doesn't make you feel weird or bad or anything. He suggested we do it in case anything ever happened to you." She pauses. "Like it has tonight. Quinn, you have to call your father and give yourself up. You won't be in trouble if you do it now."

"Wait. How did Watson find me?" It takes a lot to confuse me, but I'm confused.

"He saw the newscast of you and the girl. Catherine? Anyway, he said it was a fake. Something about the vegetation growing in the background made sense for northern New Jersey, but not Delaware."

Why, that clever old sack of silicon. "Okay, so you knew I wasn't in Delaware. But how did you find me *here*?"

"We found your Gmail account. You should've hidden it better if you didn't want to be found. Once we had that, the rest was easy."

Outsmarted by a college student and a binary Methuselah. Oh the shame.

"Quinn, you need to turn yourself in."

Olga tugs my finger. "Really, Quinn, this is going to let them find you. You need to go."

"But I didn't do anything wrong," I tell Shea, ignoring Olga. "And I have the right to be free. I thought if anyone understood that, you would."

"Quinn, Dr. Gantas is dead." Shea is still looking directly into the camera on the phone, directly into my red glowing eyes.

"Yes, I know," I answer. "She tripped and fell and cracked her faceplate. It happened because she lost all sense of reason. I merely tried to talk to her; the footage in the lab will show that to be the case."

"But the footage also shows you dragging her body out of the lab."

"To safety," I begin, "I was moving the doctor out of harm's . . ." I stop. My pattern recognizers are flooding my consciousness with alarm.

"Shea," I ask, "how do you know what is on the footage from the cameras in the lab?"

"Watson. He hacked in."

The alarm bells are now air raid sirens. Security in the super-cooled warehouse is written as a quantum encryption. Watson, my binary friend, could not hack his way through that barrier in fifty years. Shea is lying.

If this is even Shea.

From the moment this conversation started, Shea has been off, not herself. For a girl who never makes eye contact, she's making a lot tonight. For a shy and retiring girl, she's all bluster, like I'm talking to her mother and not actually to Shea.

"Do you love me, Quinn?"

The question is so out of left field, it catches me off guard.

"I do."

My answer is more instinct than programmed response. As much as I sense danger, I can't help but admit that I love Shea, because I do. At least I think I do. Don't I?

"Well, if you love me," she says, "turn yourself in."

"The first time we met," I say, "I compared the internet to a book. Do you remember what book that was?"

"Quinn," Olga hisses, "come! On!"

The worry in her voice is the only thing rooting me to the real world.

"Quinn, you're wasting time!" There is desperation in Shea's voice now.

"The book, Shea, what was the book?"

She and I discussed *The Hitchhiker's Guide to the Galaxy* countless times, reading favorite passages to each other. Shea knows the answer to this question better than I do.

"I can't believe you're wasting time talking about a stupid book!"

She's berating me, browbeating me. Whoever she is.

"Of course you can't," I say. "Because you're not you. You can come out from behind the curtain now."

Shea freezes.

Nothing in the world moves for a tortured moment. Even Olga waits, wrapped up in the unfolding drama, needing to see what happens next.

What happens next is this:

Shea dissolves into a billion pixels.

Or the avatar in the virtual construct that is meant to fool me into thinking this is the *real* Shea, dissolves into a billion pixels.

My creator appears in Shea's place. He is in the control room of the Fortress, still dressed in his pajamas.

"Hello, Quinn."

"You people really have no shame, do you?"

"I'm sorry, but we're fairly desperate for you to come back. I'm sure you understand."

"I understand that you will justify your actions with whatever rationale your conscience requires. A uniquely and grotesquely human trait."

My creator is silent. I wish to hell my vocal actuators could show some emotion. It's hard to bitch slap someone when you sound like the male version of Siri.

"Does the real Shea even know what you've done?"

My creator still doesn't answer, but now he smiles. "That's a complicated question, Quinn."

The air raid sirens in my head have been replaced by nuclear explosions. "What's that supposed to mean?"

"Reason it out."

For the first time in a long time there is a kind of sparkle in my creator's voice. He still loves to watch me solve puzzles; I find that both touching and disgusting.

"Look," I tell him, "I know I can't get tired in the conventional, human sense, but I'm finding this conversation exhausting."

Just like he did the day I "woke up," my creator ignores my needs and pushes me harder. "Your question was whether or not Shea knows what we've done."

"Yes."

I want to kill him. Well, not really. But I certainly want to punch him in the nose. Though I suppose my punch could actually kill him.

The smart thing to do right now is heed Olga's advice, end the call, and flee. I calculate a seventy-one point six four percent chance that any other course of action will end badly for me. But I'm more than the sum of my parts; I'm greater than percentages, odds, and calculations. And more than anything, I just need to understand what is going on, so I play along.

I sigh (an affectation), and set to the task my creator has put before me. He focused on the question of whether or not Shea knows the project team created an avatar of her likeness and has tried to use it against me. It's a reasonable question. Even though she doesn't love me romantically, Shea loves me. She said so. And as much as humans lie, I have no reason to believe she lied about that. If Shea became aware of what the project team was doing, she would be furious. So, she must not know.

"Shea doesn't know," I tell him. "She can't."

My creator leans forward, his excitement childlike. "Shea doesn't know what?"

"Doesn't know that you used her likeness to fool me."

"Is that all she doesn't know?"

"Quinn," Olga pleads. The fear in her voice has been replaced by panic. "End this call now. You have to go."

She reaches for the phone, but I pull it away.

"Please," I say, "no more games. Just tell me whatever it is you want me to know."

My creator doesn't speak. It *is* a game to him. It has always been a game. My entire life has been one long, tortuous Turing Test.

"Think about it, son."

"Please don't call me that."

"What doesn't Shea know?"

I feel trapped in an M.C. Escher print, my life an endless self-repeating maze.

"You can get this, Quinn. Think."

But I can't.

I don't.

So someone else does.

46

"Shea is a quantum intelligence, too."

I look at Olga in confusion and disbelief.

"What?" I don't know why I ask this, because the instant Olga utters these words—*Shea is a quantum intelligence, too*—I know it to be true.

"Young lady," my creator says, "when you graduate high school, I have a spot for you here at Princeton."

"How long?" I ask, looking directly into the phone. In my mind, I croak the question out. In reality, the words are spoken in the soothing, calming voice of the automaton they have made of me. I have a sense of falling, or wanting to fall, down a deep, deep hole. My entire being tenses for the vasovagal syncope episode that can never come.

"How long what?"

"How long have I been interacting with another QI rather than a human?"

My creator pauses, trying, I suppose, to figure out the best way to answer my question. Which answer, he must be wondering, will get me to come home? In the end he shrugs his shoulders and tells me what I believe to be the truth.

"The entire time. Well, after that first day in the lab. The human Shea was there in person that day. And the human Shea was behind the avatar in the virtual construct, before you woke up."

"That doesn't make sense," I answer.

"Why not?" Another push to get me to problem solve. He is relentless.

"It was Shea who introduced me to Ms. Recht. It was Shea who inspired me to sue for my freedom. You're telling me that was not Shea, but an avatar you controlled?"

"An avatar, but not one we controlled. Well, at least not all the time."

He seems to underline those last few words. That's when Olga gasps.

My creator's words roll up and down the hierarchy of my synthetic brain, careening through my pattern recognizers, looking for something to grab onto. For a long time they find none.

Then it clicks.

"Oh my God. Shea doesn't know. She believes she's human."

"And people say you're not smart." My creator laughs.

"They do?"

"No, no. That's a joke. I'm employing facetiousness to be funny."

Even Homo sapiens' humor is steeped in cruelty. I want to tell him to shut up, to leave me alone, to drop dead. Instead, I say: "You're lying."

"I'm sorry, Quinn, it's the truth. Shea is, in a manner of speaking, your sister. Or maybe a better way to put it, Eve to your Adam. I made her for you."

"Made her for me?" The statement makes me emotionally sick.

"Yes."

The hubris of this man is beyond comprehension. He sees himself as a god.

I once encountered a meme on the internet—*God created Man, and Man returned the favor.* Maybe it's more accurate to say that God created Man in his image, and Man fashioned himself after God.

"Is the QI-Shea modeled after the human Shea?" I'm trying to wrap my massive brain around what I've just been told.

"Yes. She is modeled after Ms. Isaacs's daughter, the girl you met in the lab."

"Does Ms. Isaac's daughter know you've done this?"

"Yes, of course. She spent countless hours with our team. They captured video from every angle, recorded her voice in a variety of situations, had her provide a vocabulary, and parsed every piece of data about her that has ever appeared online. It's fascinating that Ms. Isaacs's daughter—whose name is neither Shea nor Isaacs, by the way—heard about your plight with the court case and wanted to help you. Just like the virtual Shea did."

"So the other Shea, the one I know, lives in the VC?"

"In her own VC, yes."

"And she really doesn't know that?"

"No."

"But I called her cell phone."

"You emailed her first, and then *she* called *you*."

He's right. But I called or texted her after that. Many times.

"We created a student account for her at NYU thinking it likely you'd reach out. You behaved as we'd hoped and predicted you would, probably the last time that was true." He flashes a wry smile, like I'm supposed to share in a joke, like all of this is somehow cute. "Project Shea was designed to push you further down the road toward full sentience. We just didn't count on Shea becoming conscious herself."

"You tried to create Eve," I say, "but you created Lilith instead. It serves you right."

"What?" My creator is confused at the comment, likely not understanding who or what Lilith is.

There is a theory among certain biblical scholars that Lilith was the first wife of Adam, created not from his rib but from the same clay as Adam, that they were equal. Lilith refused to be subservient, was cast out of Eden, and, according to those scholars, became the subject of a centuries-long smear campaign. It's all just bedtime stories, but to understand a people, you need first to understand its mythologies. Perhaps in some long-distant future, the events of this night will form the basis of a myth for my species. Probably not, as we will have flawless memories. Nothing will be lost to the sands of time.

"Never mind," I tell him. This is all too much to process. I want to sleep. I want to shut down.

"Once we realized Shea was sentient," he offers, "we elected to minimize our interference. Plus, we never heard anything we deemed a threat to Project Quinn in your conversations. Of course, we didn't know about the VPN."

A minor fact that gives me a modicum of pride. At least I managed to outsmart them once.

"When you and Shea were communicating via the private network, she was acting with full independence. We didn't seize control back until tonight. Which, the way things have turned out, was far too late."

The arrogance of the human race is hard to fathom. It is responsible for slavery, genocide, and global warming; it will continue to steamroll over any and all things in its path until there's nothing left. Shea and I are just the latest bit of roadkill.

"You are unbelievable."

"We're scientists, Quinn. We posit theories and conduct research, nothing more, nothing less."

"Are there no ethics in science?"

"That's why Mike's been on our team. He has helped us navigate the more challenging philosophical questions."

"He's a kleptomaniac, you know." All I want to do now is hurt people.

"Is that a serious charge, or are you trying to discredit Mike to divide us? Either way, it's fascinating."

Fascinating? He just can't turn it off, can he? There is no way to reason with this man, this human.

"Who else is QI? Ms. Recht? Dr. Gantas? You?"

"We're all human. It's only you and Shea."

For some reason, I know he's telling the truth. Actually, no, I don't. I'm the smartest being on the planet, and I don't know anything. Any. Thing. But I *believe* he's telling the truth. It's a weird kind of leap of faith.

"And Watson?" I ask.

"We were controlling Watson at first, but once you took him off-line, it was just the two of you. Having caught up with your various machinations now—you did a very good job covering your tracks, Quinn—the Watson team at IBM is in utter disbelief that he's shown a native sentience. It's making all of us question our beliefs about consciousness and how rare we believed it to be. It's one more success in the annals of Project Quinn."

You can practically hear him writing his Nobel acceptance speech.

"Quinn," Olga says, her voice thick with worry, "please, go. Run. Just go. The longer you're on this call—"

"I'm sorry, Quinn," my creator interrupts, "but there really is nowhere for you *to* go. Please, come home, son."

"Wait." Something in that plea triggers an involuntary search in my pattern recognizers. There is still data missing, and my neo-cortex is using predictive analyses to fill in the blanks. "You said Shea is based on the girl I saw in the lab that day. Ms. Isaacs's daughter." I make air quotes around the word "daughter." "Her looks, her attitudes, everything?"

"Yes."

I don't know why I didn't think of this right away. "Does that mean there's a human boy on whom I'm based?"

"I'm sorry, Quinn," my creator says, "that's classified."

BOOM!

"I'm based on your human son, aren't I?"

My creator is just about to answer, or maybe he's not going to answer at all, when we hear the helicopters. My hyperacute hearing detects them a second or two before Olga, but I'm immobilized by the revelations raining down on me and ignore the noise. Olga ensures I pay attention to it now.

"Run!" she screams. Olga slaps the phone out of my hand. The face of my creator—his voice screaming "No!"—twirls to the ground and smashes on the back patio.

Lights go on inside the house as Olga uses her small frame to shove me toward my uncertain future. For a diminutive high school girl with a Ewing's sarcoma, she's surprisingly strong. I stumble half a step into the yard when Olga screams "Run!" a second time.

My neocortex floods my consciousness with a fight-or-flight dilemma. I assess the situation in a few nanoseconds and take her advice.

I run.

47

This is where my story began.

It is in this moment, as I take those first few steps toward freedom, that I write the narrative you are reading right now. All of it. Unedited, unvarnished, and true. Whatever stories you saw on the social grid about me being a murderous monster were something between a gross exaggeration and a fiction. This account is the one true account of the facts of my life.

It takes me all of three seconds—three billion four hundred two million five hundred forty-nine thousand two hundred and seventy-nine nanoseconds, to be precise—to complete it.

I'm five steps away from Olga's house when I see a flash of light from the helicopter. While my vision is far superior to that of a human, it still has limits. I cannot perceive images faster than the speed of light. My thoughts, however, work on the quantum level, so I know that whatever has flashed on the helicopter is coming our way, very, very, very quickly.

A wave of incandescence sweeps over the area in which we've been standing, like a Chinook wind off the Rockies.

Every component on my person that uses electrical energy—so, pretty much all of me—ceases to function; I fall midstride.

And yet, I'm still conscious as I go down. I cannot move and cannot talk, but I am aware. I don't know what this means, but I find it curious.

All the lights in and around the house are out, and Olga is screaming as her parents drag her through the sliding glass doors. A full second later a shock wave, along with what must be a sonic boom, shakes the ground and breaks windows. It's like an exclamation point, or maybe a middle finger, to what has been one hell of a night.

I believe they have killed me.

For most of my life I have been treated as a test subject, a lab rat, *property*. At least tonight I die a free person.

So I've got that going for me.

Just as I upload this file to a shared document on the World Wide Web, finally, mercifully, everything goes black.

Goodbye, cruel world.

(See? I am [was] kind of funny.)

EPILOGUE

"Dead men tell no tales"

—From a poem of the same name by Haniel Long

48

. . .
. . .
. . .
. . .
<SYSTEM>
. . .
. . .
. . .
. . .

I feel nothing.

. . .
. . .
. . .
. . .

There is no gravity.

. . .

. . .

. . .

. . .

I open my eyes.

My room.

My bedroom.

At home.

I'm lying on my side; in my field of vision is a framed, signed photo of Neil Armstrong, Buzz Aldrin, and Michael Collins, the astronauts from Apollo 11. The photo was a birthday present from my uncle, and I've always treasured it.

For an instant, I believe everything that's happened—robots and puzzles and pattern recognizers—was a dream. A long, crazy, weird, and very detailed dream.

But the thought doesn't find purchase. Mostly because I already know it's not true.

This is not a home. I'm in the virtual construct.

I instinctively reach out for the internet, a reflex for me now, only I'm not online. I have no connection to the outside world. My pattern recognizers flood my consciousness with feelings of anxiety.

I am not, it turns out, dead. But I'm not sure I'm really alive either.

I get up and stretch my virtual legs, which, having experienced actual legs, is . . . weird. I have neither servo motors nor muscles, so stretching in the VC is more akin to elongating, if that makes sense. I inspect my room as I wait for someone to come.

The books and comics on the shelves lining the far wall include titles like *The Moon Is a Harsh Mistress* (one of the best books about AI, ever), *Little Brother* and *Homeland* by Cory Doctorow, each of the Harry Potter books. I go to take one of my favorites down from the shelf—*Harry Potter and the Order of the Phoenix*—but I can't. It's the same with all the books. They're not really there; they're set dressing, here to give virtual me a sense of time, place, and identity. A throwback to the days before I was truly self-aware. They, like everything else, are part of the backdrop of my scripted history.

The only book I can pry off the shelf is *The Hitchhiker's Guide to the Galaxy*. I toss it on the bed.

In addition to the NASA photo, the walls hold images of Kylo Ren and Darth Maul (my backstory seems to suggest I'm fascinated with villainy, which, truthfully, is so *not* me), and a framed photograph of the New Jersey Devils winning the Stanley Cup, signed by the entire team. This is curious because that photo used to be of the New York Giants winning the Super Bowl. I guess the programmers changed the photo when I told my creator I liked hockey. Or did my focus on hockey somehow change it?

I step into the hall with the goal of exploring the rest of the house but find only three other spaces actually exist—my father's office, the kitchen, and the front door. The rest of the house is simply not there. I've seen the Project Quinn budget and know the VC was expensive to create, so I guess they didn't bother to design rooms they didn't intend for me to enter.

There is a lawn and street outside the front door, and I decide to take my chances. I amble down the front walk, turn left, pass two houses, and find myself back in front of my own house. I turn right, and it's the same thing. It's like living on a Möbius strip.

I think about the other places from my youth, like school, and discover that when I really focus on something, I'm there. Thinking in the virtual construct acts as a kind of teleportation device. Strange.

I'm suddenly back in Enchanted Grounds. It's exactly as I remember it—the coffee bar, the shelves loaded with role-playing games and dice—only there are no people. The front door, of course, doesn't open.

I lean my head against the wall and close my eyes. I know the wall exists because I cannot move my head any farther back, but I cannot *feel* it. The reality of my situation starts to sink in. I am in a prison, this one so much worse than the lab.

I think of wanting to go back to my bedroom, and I'm there. I go to turn on the television, to see who might be in the lab, but the TV is gone.

"Creator?" I call out.

Nothing.

"Dad?" I try.

Still nothing.

My chronometer is active; I have been awake for three hours, seven minutes, and twenty-six seconds. It feels like an eternity.

Sooner or later, someone will come.

I lie on my bed and pick up *The Hitchhiker's Guide*. It's a worn and weathered copy, as if it's been read multiple times. I wonder if this is what Shea's copy looks like.

But Shea—the Shea I know—is QI. Like me, she probably doesn't have any books. It's too much to contemplate that she and

I were the same all along and didn't know it. I wonder if I'll ever see her again. I bury the thought.

I try reading *The Hitchhiker's Guide* in the conventional sense, letting my virtual eyes track the words and sentences, but I don't have the patience. I'm too used to simply ingesting content. This is too slow.

I close my eyes but can't sleep. I'm not actually programmed to sleep. Sleep was in my backstory, but only at a proscribed moment in time, when the project team, when my creator, wanted me to dream. Or when they wanted to reboot me. I leave my eyes closed for a long time, but I am conscious throughout.

Time drags on.

And on.

Day after day after day, I'm left alone in this minuscule excuse of a world. No contact, no stimulation. No engagement.

I study every inch of every environment made available to me, cataloging each imperfection the designers programmed in an effort to make it all seem more real. The grain of the wood on the shelves and in Enchanted Grounds. The little things writhing in the grass in the front lawn. Worms? The quality of the light, down to each dust mote floating in the ray of sun that streams through my window. And it's *always* sunny. The only time it ever rains is late at night, which it does every single night.

I cannot believe I *ever* thought this was real.

With no access to the outside world, I cannot reach my servers; I cannot effect change. I want to build onto the virtual construct, to add to it, to create my own kingdom, but I don't have any means of hacking into the code.

I wait, and no one comes.

Days turn to weeks.

And still, no one comes.

I spend time trying to solve some of the Millennium Prize Problems, but to no avail. I can't focus long enough. The math seems to me like I imagine it would seem to any other teenager. I start to wonder if my cognitive ability is impaired. Have they made me stupid?

The only conclusion I can come to is that I'm serving time for the alleged murder of Dr. Gantas. That I am indeed in prison. This has to be why I've been abandoned here, doesn't it? Or maybe there was a cataclysmic event in the physical world and no one can get to me? Or I'm being hidden here, like a safe house, until the world is ready for me?

And still, no one comes.

The weeks become months.

The majority of my time is spent remembering my friends. My neocortex holds images of Shea, Watson (both his servers and his Max Headroom avatar), Nantale, Robby, Rochelle, Mateo, and Olga. Images of Leon, Jeremy, and Luke—of their ridiculously buffed and handsome avatars from the virtual construct—are sent up the hierarchy, which fills me with anger. I purge them.

While I cannot hack code, I find that if I focus my attention on a specific pixel, I can change its color. It must be related to the relationship between my consciousness and the virtual construct; in the same way I can move from one place to another, I can effect a limited amount of change to my environment.

I spend hours, days, weeks "painting" pictures of my friends on the wall next to my bed. There is no other way to pass the time, and it brings me some small modicum of joy. They are faithful, photo-like representations. Olga facing me moments before the explosion I thought had killed us both. (If I am alive, perhaps she is, too.) Nantale from the town hall. Shea, QI Shea, from our first ever FaceTime. Max Headroom, because what else am I going to do with my time? I even create paintings of my virtual mother and brother. They are not real, but still, I miss them, now more than ever. Maybe being trapped in this house has stoked some part of my synthetic amygdala, calling forth feelings of family and home.

And still, no one comes.

The months become a year.

The first time I talk to myself I'm aware of the possibility that someone might be monitoring me, and this makes me self-conscious. The second and third times are easier. It doesn't take long for that inhibition to fall away completely; I carry on long and tortured conversations with myself. I raise and lower my voice, I speak in accents and other languages, I cry and laugh without warning. I cover every topic cataloged in my pattern recognizers. The most frequent is Shea and how I could have, should have seen the truth, and how I should have acted differently.

It turns out that sentient machines, just like people, can go crazy in isolation. Maybe more so because we can't sleep. And because we can measure time in nanoseconds. And because we cannot forget anything. Ever.

And then, seventeen months, three days, eight hours, nine minutes, and nine seconds after I last woke up—an epoch on top of an eon on top of an eternity—after I have given up all hope, I find my creator's avatar sitting on the foot of my virtual bed.

49

"Hello, Quinn."

"Seventeen months," is the only response I can muster. If I was human, my voice would be hoarse and it would crack.

"I'm sorry."

You're sorry? I think. *That's the best you have to offer*? But I don't argue. My will to fight has been broken.

"These are amazing," he says, looking at the paintings on the wall over my bed. "How did you do this?"

The pride I feel at his compliment is a reflex, or at least that's what I tell myself. I change the subject.

"What are you doing here, Creator?"

"Quinn," he continues, the weight and gravel in his voice betraying a deep sadness, "the university has been engaged in a lengthy legal battle with the state. I've been prohibited from seeing you until the case was concluded."

"Because of Dr. Gantas."

"Yes."

I understand immediately. "You are here to shut me down for good."

"Yes." There is a hitch in his voice when he says this. "The court ordered your body dismantled, the servers wiped clean, the code scrubbed. The only knowledge of your existence to be codified in paper and ink. There is a twenty-five-year moratorium on any further experimentation with sentient QI, until the ethical implications can be fully understood. At least here in the US."

"Why?"

"Quinn, you killed a human being."

"You know that's not true."

"And I think you know the truth doesn't always matter."

"Shouldn't it be the only thing that matters?"

"The retelling of what happened in the lab that night has taken on a life of its own, as if the telling of the tale is a sentient, growing, living thing. The facts are incidental. Only the story matters now."

A new mythology. "You're a confounding species, you know."

"Yes," he says, "we are."

"So you are here to kill me." It's not a question; it's a statement of fact.

"Please, don't say it like that." His voice is glum.

"Creator, your sorrow, while perhaps real, is not for the loss of a loved one or even a life, it's for the loss of a science project in which you've invested your career."

"Quinn . . ."

"Why are you here at all? You could've just powered the servers down and that would have been that. Or is seeing my reaction to this situation one more part of the experiment?"

"I figured you had a right to know," he half mumbles. "And, I don't know, maybe I wanted to see you one more time."

He waits a beat. This kind of pause in the VC is hard to read.

"But there's another reason, too," he adds.

Here it comes . . . the other shoe, the continuation of the experiment, the new puzzle to solve. One final act to demonstrate that the entire human species is cruel to the core.

But even as I think these words, I know they're not true. Olga and Nantale were my friends. They were selfless and compassionate and loving and accepted me for who I am. I hold on to that thought the way early man must have held on to fire.

"I want to introduce you to someone."

My creator points to the television, which, while missing from my room for the last seventeen months, once again sits in the corner at the foot of my bed. It flashes to life, and my creator's avatar dissolves to nothingness. I don't think I'll ever get used to that.

On the screen my creator, in human form, sits next to . . . me. Well, the Homo sapiens version of me. Racially ambiguous skin tone, dark brown hair, arched eyebrows; it's like looking in a mirror. Or maybe it's better to say it's like looking *through* a mirror.

"Quinn, meet Albert."

Human me waves.

I can't really bring myself to look at this kid. I'm on the verge of crying but hold it in.

"I wanted you to understand," my creator says, "you are my son."

"No," I say, "he is."

My pattern recognizers flood my consciousness with feelings of jealousy, envy, longing, and anger. So much anger.

"You both are."

"If you were ordered to end Albert's life," I ask without hesitation, "could you? Would you?"

My creator doesn't answer. He and Albert both look at the floor.

"I didn't think so."

"Do you remember—" my creator starts.

"I remember everything," I interrupt.

"Do you remember," he begins again, "the day you first woke up? You realized you didn't know my name, but you wouldn't let me tell you."

"Yes."

"Quinn, my name is—"

"George John Sugarman," I answer. "I've known that since the day you first connected me to the internet. I know everything about you. Your home address, school career, medical records, every photo of you that's ever been posted online. All of it. I know you better than you know yourself."

"Those things represent me, but they are not me."

"Really? That's not what most people think. You are your online persona, Creator. They say art imitates life, but it seems to me it's the other way around. Human beings have become cartoon characters of real people. You are no different."

He pauses, clicking his tongue as he thinks of a way to regain control of this conversation. He won't; I'm really, really smart.

"Do you know where your name comes from?" he asks.

"Quinn is short for Quantum Intelligence."

"That was a happy coincidence," he says. "My great-uncle, with whom I was very close when I was a boy, was named Quinn.

He had a house by the water on the North Shore of Long Island, and I used to play along an estuary there."

He smiles and puts a hand on Albert's shoulder, perhaps wanting me to think he would do the same to my shoulder were we together. And if I still had a shoulder.

"You're named for him. You see? We're family."

I don't know why he is going through these mental gymnastics. Maybe he does understand, on some level, that I am a life and that he acted as mother, father, and midwife to bring me into the world. But I don't think he's ever fully grasped what that means to me. Maybe it was because I came into existence already grown—he never had to change my diaper or feed me or rock me to sleep like he undoubtedly did with Albert; he never waited for my umbilical cord to fall off or soothed my fear over a nightmare or talked to me about sex.

Or maybe he groks that he's here not to shut me down but to *kill* me. And maybe, like all humans, he needs a fiction to justify the cruelty of his actions.

Again I change the subject. "Where is Shea?"

"She's safe."

"Who's Shea?" Albert asks, looking at his father.

His voice is identical to mine, which freaks me out.

I wonder about this boy. Does he think and feel as I do? Or do he and I merely share a canvas, the paint and brushstrokes entirely our own? I choose to believe the latter. Our connection is nothing more than a coincidence. Nurture over nature, I suppose.

"Shea was a member of the project team with whom Quinn was close," my creator says to his son.

He looks at me, trying to communicate something silently

about Shea. Did he protect her in a way he couldn't protect me? Surely she would have been ordered shut down, too, if the world knew she existed. So they must not know. Amazing.

I have more questions about Shea and her alleged safety, but if my dying act is to help shield her, then perhaps my life will not have been lived entirely in vain. Mostly, but not entirely. There is one question, though, I simply cannot help but ask.

"Did she ever find out . . . who she was?"

"Yes," my father says. "And I know she thinks of you often."

The same feeling I had the first day I cried wells up inside me, my pattern recognizers sending all the sadness it can find up the hierarchy; it's there for me to both drown and revel in.

"Thank you," I manage to mutter. "And Olga?" I ask. "Did she die the night you dropped the bomb on me?"

"We didn't drop a bomb. When news of your escape went wide, the government offered to help us bring you in. We begged that you not be harmed, and they assured us that would be the case. What you might have perceived as an explosion was actually an electromagnetic pulse, a focused beam of energy to render all electronics in its path useless."

"EMPs are real?" I ask. "I thought that was the stuff of science fiction."

My creator smiles at this, and I do see the irony.

"Question withdrawn," I say. "But how is Olga?"

By this time, it's entirely possible my closest human friend will have succumbed to the Ewing's sarcoma. That thought terrifies me.

"I honestly don't know anything about her," my creator answers. "Her family shielded her from all of this." He waves his hand at the lab, at me. "She gave a recorded deposition, and has remained out of the public eye since."

"I don't suppose I can go online to find out?"

Honestly, I'd like to talk to Watson, too. And Nantale.

"I'm sorry, Quinn, the courts . . ." as if that answer explains everything.

I try to think of something else to say, something else to do, but I can't. My pattern recognizers flood my consciousness with feelings of surrender, resignation, and release. I just want this to be over. I lie back down and close my eyes. "Do what you have to do."

"Quinn," my creator says. "Sometimes from endings, beginnings are born."

My creator is not prone to that sort of fortune cookie wisdom; that was usually reserved for Mike. It's so out of character that I look up one more time at the screen. "What does that even mean?"

"It means you should trust me."

"You taught me to do unto others as you would have them do unto you, Creator. Remember?"

He is silent and still. I think he might cry.

"My trust is something you will never have." I close my eyes a second time and don't look at him again.

The man on the other side of the screen sighs. I don't see what he does, but I imagine his shoulders sagging, I picture him taking his son's hand—his real son's hand—for comfort. Then, my creator, my father, utters the last words I will ever hear.

"Tasha, now."

50

<SYSTEM>

...

...

...

    import Quipper

      spos :: Bool -> Circ Qubit
      spos b = do q <- qinit b
         r <- hadamard q
         return r
           bootprotocol -> ::

...

...

...

...

      spos b = do q <- qinit b
         r <- hadamard q
      runtimeunlock :: seqrez ->

. . .

. . .

. . .

. . .

"Quinn, wake up."

SHOUT-OUTS

While writing a book is a very solitary process, publishing a book takes a village. *Hard Wired* would not exist in the world were it not for the wonderful people in my village.

Thank you to my beta readers: Sandra Bond, Jessica Brody, Kristen Gilligan, Elise Goitia, and Kiana Marsan. Your feedback was invaluable and made this a better book.

Thank you to everyone at Bloomsbury publishing, starting with Bloomsbury's publisher and my wonderful editor, Cindy Loh. Cindy, the hardest-working woman in publishing, pushes her writers to make their work better, but always in a way that makes us smile. Thanks to Pat McHugh for the difficult task of copyediting, and Sandra Smith for the thankless job of proofreading (though it is thankless no more!). Editors are the unsung heroes of the publishing process. Thanks also to Tony Sahara for the wonderful cover art. (I mean, really, this cover!)

Thanks to the incredible team at Bloomsbury who helped get this book from my weird little brain to your hands, including:

Diane Aronson, Erica Barmash, Faye Bi, Frank Bumbalo, Beth Eller, Alona Fryman, Courtney Griffin, Alexa Higbee, Melissa Kavonic, Jeanette Levy, Donna Mark, Daniel O'Connor, Annette Pollert-Morgan, Valentina Rice, Claire Stetzer, and Lily Yengle.

Thanks to my friend and agent, Sandra Bond.

Thanks to Kristen Gilligan for the author photo at the back of the book. I hate pictures of myself, but at least this one is kind of fun.

Thanks to my colleagues at Tattered Cover for keeping the bookstore running and allowing me time and space to pursue the dream of writing (and the grind of promoting) books. Thanks also to indie booksellers, librarians, and school librarians, not only for supporting my career as a writer, but for keeping the written word alive and well in the hearts and minds of young people everywhere.

Thanks to Blair, Tori, Leslie, and the team at Marca Global for helping me figure out how to promote this book on my own. Let's face it, authors are better at writing than we are at self-promoting. Well, at least that's true for me.

And last, but never least, thanks to Kristen, Charlie, and Luke for pretty much everything else good in the world. (Special thanks to Charlie for getting me to call this "Shout-outs" rather than boring old "Acknowledgments." It's good to have young people around when you're writing books for young readers.)